Dear Diary,

The advance from rags to riches has been swift. Thanks to the Indian Negook, we have at last achieved our goal of striking "pay dirt." The strike is wonderfully rich, yielding four or five times as much gold as any ground we have previously worked. At the present rate of recovery, we shall all be very well off by the time autumn forces us to retire to Sitka.

The days now grow rapidly shorter as winter approaches, and Hans, Harky, and Dutch work from daylight until dark, while Michael hunts. Hans speaks of working by torchlight, but the others decline to work any harder, as they already return to the cabin at night, exhausted and bleeding from their palms.

The men's days are strictly scheduled: Breakfast before daylight, work until dark, bathe in the pool (which grows chillier these days, but is still the best part of my day; I have my bath after the men have left in the morning), then the evening meal, after which the take is weighed before we retire to our bunks. Dutch crows and struts like a banty rooster each evening as Hans weighs out the take, but it is easy to forgive him his unseemly exultations, for he has been richly vindicated by Negook's strike.

Michael is proving to be a fine huntsman, adept at bringing fresh meat to the table. The flesh of the goats and sea lions is often stringy and tough, but he has fashioned a mallet from a spruce knot with which I beat the meat tender.

Only Harky seems untouched by our fortune, but he is always such a silent man it is difficult to say whether or not he shares the exuberance of the strike.

I must admit that the gold ignites grand dreams in my own mind, dreams of a fine home and nice things, but it stirs a certain fear as well, an uneasiness I cannot define . . .

Heartbroke Bay

LYNN D'URSO

BERKLEY BOOKS, NEW YORK

A BERKLEY BOOK
Published by the Penguin Group
Penguin Group (USA) Inc.
375 Hudson Street, New York, New York 10014, USA
Penguin Group (Canada), 90 Eglinton Avenue East, Suite 700, Toronto, Ontario M4P 2Y3, Canada
(a division of Pearson Penguin Canada Inc.)
Penguin Books Ltd., 80 Strand, London WC2R 0RL, England
Penguin Group Ireland, 25 St. Stephen's Green, Dublin 2, Ireland
(a division of Penguin Books Ltd.)
Penguin Group (Australia), 250 Camberwell Road, Camberwell, Victoria 3124, Australia
(a division of Pearson Australia Group Pty. Ltd.)
Penguin Books India Pvt. Ltd., 11 Community Centre, Panchsheel Park, New Delhi—110 017, India
Penguin Group (NZ), 67 Apollo Drive, Rosedale, North Shore 0632, New Zealand
(a division of Pearson New Zealand Ltd.)
Penguin Books (South Africa) (Pty.) Ltd., 24 Sturdee Avenue, Rosebank, Johannesburg 2196,
South Africa
Penguin Books Ltd., Registered Offices: 80 Strand, London WC2R 0RL, England

This book is an original publication of the Berkley Publishing Group.

The publisher does not have any control over and does not assume any responsibility for author or
third-party websites or their content.

Copyright © 2010 by Lynn D'Urso
Cover image of misty lake by Georgios Alexandris/Shutterstock
Cover image of branch by jgl247/Shutterstock
Cover design by Andrea Tsurumi
Text design by Tiffany Estreicher

First edition: November 2010

Library of Congress Cataloging-in-Publication Data

D'Urso, Lynn.
    Heartbroke bay / Lynn D'Urso.—1st ed.
        p.   cm.
    ISBN 978-0-425-23680-2 (trade pbk.)
    1. British—Alaska—Fiction.   2. Gold mines and mining—Alaska—Fiction.   3. Alaska—Gold
discoveries—Fiction.   I. Title.
    PS3604.U7575H43 2010
    813'.6—dc22   2010022330

PRINTED IN THE UNITED STATES OF AMERICA

10   9   8   7   6   5   4   3   2   1

ACKNOWLEDGMENTS

I owe a heartfelt thank-you to the staff at the Alaska State Historical Library for their endless patience and help with my many requests for texts, articles, microfilms, and photos over the decade it took to write *Heartbroke Bay*. The efforts of Gladi Kulp, Gayle Goedde, and Jim Simard, among others, were indispensable.

I also owe Jack Poulson, Kristie Swanson, Jonathan Wolfson, Luan Schooler-Wilson, David Hunsaker, the author Stuart Archer, and many others my thanks for their invaluable support through what now, after so many years, I realize have been an imposing number of draft manuscripts and rewrites. Were it not for my agent, Bonnie Nadell, I am not sure Hannah Nelson would have ever found her voice, and the support of my editor, Jackie Cantor, made *Heartbroke Bay* possible. I am grateful to you all.

Lynn

Winter

In autumn the earth tilts away from the sun and winter looms over North America. In the farthest reaches of the North Pacific, where the Bering Sea and the Gulf of Alaska meet, the winds begin to churn, spinning and building into muscular storms that hurry the change of the seasons on.

By November the snow begins to fly. The moon the coastal tribes call *Kokaha-dis*, the "bears-digging-dens" moon, rises, and throughout the sprawl of rugged islands and glacier-filled valleys that make up the territory of the Tlingit Indians the clans begin moving baskets of dried fish and moose meat into the rafters of planked longhouses, measuring and remeasuring their weight against the coming darkness. On a rare windless night in December, the eyes of wolves and ravens carved into the totem poles that keep watch over the villages stare out from under a thick layer of frost.

Now comes *T'ak*, the terrible child-dying time, when ferocious winds tear the trees from the ground and the cold can freeze a man's eyes. *T'ak* passes slowly, slower than the creep of ice crystals up the inside of the longhouse walls. By *Kladashu*, the sixth moon, there is no fat left under the skin of the wild animals and the lamps in the longhouses burn with a dim yellow light. And one by one, as winter rages, even the strong begin to tremble, lose the will to live, and die.

ONE

A locomotive draws a thin stripe of smoke along the horizon. Overhead, the infinite blue dome of a prairie heaven fills the sky. Where the train runs swiftly across level ground, the smoke pales quickly, but on rising grades the engine slows and sketches a series of evenly spaced strokes that hang motionless against the sky. In the middle of the line of railcars rolls an elaborate Pullman car. Within the Pullman car sits a young woman, perched on a severe chair of oak and cane, swaying to the beat of the wheels as she stares out at an unending procession of fields burned to dust by the relentless heat of the Dakota sun. Scattered at random across the fields stand decaying sod shanties, abandoned by their builders as the tariff charged by the railroad for carrying their meager crops to market rose from eleven cents per hundred-weight to thirty, then fifty-five, until finally flood-cresting at more than a dollar.

Four more years, thinks Hannah Butler. *However shall I manage four more years?* Behind her the voice of her employer, Lady Hamilton, drones a chorus of complaints against the chartered Pullman and its crew. At Lady Hamilton's feet sits Victoria, Lady Hamilton's second handmaid, who in the weeks since the entourage's departure from England has become Hannah's good friend, taking notes on a sheet of paper embossed with a crest of rampant unicorns.

"Perhaps a better grade of coal," murmurs Lady Hamilton's personal secretary in response to a demand that something be done about the sulfurous odor of engine smoke permeating the Pullman car. After offering the suggestion, Bernard (who pronounces his name with a purring emphasis on the first syllable) purses his lips and peers over a pair of pince-nez glasses as he waits for Lady Hamilton to agree with him.

The smoke, the smells, a dearth of inspiring scenery—little has pleased Her Ladyship since departing the mouth of the Thames by steamship a month earlier for a tour of the American West. After a voyage of fifteen days to New York harbor, she had turned up her nose at a steady succession of imaginative American inventions, including an electric bread toaster, a confectionary whimsy described by its Italian immigrant inventor as an "ice-cream cone," and a demonstration of one of the new gasoline-powered motor cars. Even the sight of an automatic staircase dubbed the "escalator" had been met with vinegar.

Now, after a week on the rails, with the American prairie unrolling in all directions, Hannah feels trapped, damned to suffer Her Ladyship's endless complaints while boredom nibbles at her like a crab.

Freckled and gap-toothed like the Wife of Bath, she is twenty-three years old and blessed with a prosperous head of shining auburn hair that reaches the small of her back and light gray eyes that look out at the world with the shine of intelligence—a trait considered neither a virtue nor a demerit in English girls of marriageable age. Her nose is straight but perhaps a bit too long. Called comely by some and peculiar by others, she has believed each opinion in its time. Though sidelined from the world of business by her gender, she understands how the usury of railroad corporations grown bloated as show hogs on the sale of worthless stock certificates has brought her to this arid American savanna as surely as it has wrung the sap from the missing farmers, because she had watched, with growing concern, as her father, a once-successful British merchant engaged in the chandlery of supplies to the fleets of English traders, had funneled more and more of her family's fortune into the pyramid schemes of the American tycoons.

A flutter of guilt trickles through her stomach as resentment at her father's profligacy rises; had he not financed his stock purchases through a series of loans from Lady Hamilton's husband, each one secured by a note on the Butler holdings, she would not be here now, subject to the stultifying atmosphere of the clattering carriage, calculating again and again the time it will take for her salary of twenty-three pounds a month to repay the balance that remained on the notes after Lord Hamilton foreclosed on her family's home. Swallowing her resentment, she stifles also the question of what there will be for her after her employment with Lady Hamilton ends; in four years, she will be almost twenty-eight years old, and with the world's economy in rags, and her mother and father reduced to a one-room walk-up on the outskirts of London, it is difficult to imagine anything favorable waiting for a single woman on the verge of middle age—especially one newly released from the thrall of a wasp-tongued tyrant who has been known to strike serving girls during the course of her mottle-faced rages.

Upon Hannah's entrance into Lady Hamilton's service, it had been agreed that draws of up to four pounds a month were to be allowed against her garnished wages for critical expenses such as books and clothing. She is considering how she may do without either when there is a light tapping at the door separating the opulence of the sitting car from the clattering, workaday world of the kitchen car. Victoria rises, cracks the door, and exchanges low words with a scullion maid in a dirty apron, then comes to where Hannah sits and bends low to whisper, "He's here."

Casting a last look at the bleak prospect outside the Pullman's window, Hannah rises, excuses herself, and tries not to hurry as she walks, with the sway of the rail car accentuating the swing of her skirts, through the door of the Pullman into the steam and smells of the kitchen car.

Two days earlier, as the English party had prepared to depart Chicago on Lady Hamilton's tour of the West, she and Victoria had gone to the station by carriage to ensure proper disposition of the numerous trunks of clothes, books, medicines, and delicate foods. Two wagons driven by thick-wristed teamsters followed, piled top-heavy with the equipage of the tour. A youngster perched on the tailgate of each wagon armed with a club of strong, supple ash to deter snatch-and-grab thieves. Hannah hated the city. She felt constricted by the endless threading of pedestrians and wagons through mounds of rubbish awaiting removal and the smell of stables swarming with flies.

A Negro porter threading his way through the throng of passengers and hawkers shouted an offer to bring hand trucks and laborers for their luggage. To Hannah his speech sounded like "Ma'am, Ah'll getcha trucks an de fellahs." Dazed by the hubbub and unsure where to go, Hannah looked puzzled and asked the porter to repeat himself.

"Trucks, ma'am, fo' wheah?" He waved to a gaggle of stringy-limbed black boys in singlets and worn trousers to come forward. Again Hannah was at a loss and turned to the driver, who spit a stream of tobacco juice into the cobbled street and replied to her questioning look with a single word. "Where?"

The Negro laborers swarmed the wagons, hefting trunks and cartons over the side, the light-colored palms of their hands and the soles of bare feet flashing, as they shouted unintelligible instructions back and forth, levering and lashing the freight onto carts and barrows.

Hannah had no idea where the departure platform of the Northern Pacific Railroad was located within the maelstrom of steam whistles and shouting that was Chicago's Union Station. A fistfight broke out between two young boys, and the mother of an immigrant family screeched at her scattering brood in a language bristling with consonants. A blind beggar playing a mouth harp held out a cap to passersby and was ignored. Hannah fought down an impulse to scream for silence and closed her eyes.

When she opened them, a blond man was standing before her. Tall, with wide shoulders and a square, open face that had seen a great deal of sun and a recent close razor, the man stepped forward and tipped a well-kept homburg. The stranger wore a suit of light wool, gray, with thin, vertical blue stripes. His coat, unbuttoned over a pair of matching trousers, accentuated the length of his legs and narrowness of his waist. The legs of the pants were bloused into high-heeled riding boots of the sort Hannah had seen in drawings of American cowboys.

The gray of the suit set off the color of the stranger's eyes, which drifted the length of Hannah's body before finding their way back to her own eyes. Rimmed in deep blue and with centers the shade of undyed flannel, they gave Hannah a moment's pause and a vague sense of recognition, until she realized with a start that they were the exact color and composition of her own. Embarrassed, she looked away when she realized she was staring.

The stranger's blond mustache curled at the corners of his mouth as he grinned at Hannah's discomfiture. Strong white teeth contrasted nicely with the ruddy brown of his face. Removing his hat, he held it to his chest, as if to testify that he was an honest man, and offered his name—"Hans Nelson"—like a title, then after a moment repeated it, appending his geographic origins as validation of his rectitude. "Hans Nelson. Of Blue Lake, Minnesota." Smiling, he stepped closer to Hannah, his eyes roving the details of her face. She, in the manner of a woman who finds herself both unsettled and proud at being so admired, stood more erect and looked away. Victoria crowded closer, eyeing the new acquaintance with the shining eyes and swelling breast of a dove performing a courtship dance. Hannah stammered that they were to board for the West, on the North Pacific Line, "but the dialect of the porters is quite difficult."

Mr. Nelson waved to the sergeant of the bearers, shouted, and directed the delivery of the baggage to the westbound platform.

"I'm bound for the Pacific Coast myself, by way of Butte, Montana, and then west to Tacoma, Washington. From there I go on to the Alaska Territory by steamship." He smiled, waiting for the English girls to be impressed by his adventurism.

Hannah found herself enjoying the forward American fashion, so different from the diffidence of strangers in England. "We have much the same itinerary then, Mr. Nelson," she said, introducing herself, then Victoria, before giving a summary of Her Ladyship's entourage, as the trio followed the cart train of porters through the crowd.

Nelson instructed the luggage handlers in dividing the goods at the cars, saw to a guard for the property going into storage, then escorted Hannah and Victoria to the steps of the Pullman and tipped his hat.

Victoria curtsied; Hannah removed a glove and held out a hand. Hans made a slight bow to Victoria, but his eyes were on the rose-colored blush that spread up Hannah's neck, accentuating the lovely freckles on her nose and cheeks.

———————

Now, two days later, as the steel artery of the Northern Pacific Railroad crosses the Missouri River and rolls toward Montana into a region beyond the worst of the drought, Hans Nelson has come calling and presses a small bouquet of softly pink and blue foxglove blossoms into her hand. As she takes the offering of flowers, Hannah notices how strong Mr. Nelson's hands look, all knob-knuckled and thick, with fingers almost square across the tips and nails scrubbed clean of any sign of work.

After a brief exchange of simple pleasantries freighted with the complex messages of flirtation, Hannah is recalled by the imperious voice of a suspicious Lady Hamilton.

Nelson strides the length of the train back to his car, slowly removing a cigar from an inside pocket—one of the good ones, a fresh Partagás—and slices the tip with a clasp knife before rolling it over a match. As he does, he smiles to himself. Strolling and puffing, he imagines returning to Minnesota with a beautiful, gray-eyed English prize on his arm and a fortune from Alaska in his bags.

Quite refined, he thinks. *Working for that Lady Hamilton.* He reckons a lady as something akin to royalty. And the arch of Hannah's neck and the hourglass shape of her waist and bosom make his groin ache.

"She's perfect," he says aloud. "Just perfect."

Dear Diary,

The attentions of Mr. Nelson grow stronger, and I am greatly flattered. Courtship here in America is apparently done much as they seem to do all of their business—straightforward, and with unrestrained impatience. He is such a handsome man! And vital, as is this great country. The view from the train of all of this space and room makes me shy of returning to England, where all is so stifled by hedgerows. Mr. Nelson has asked to be presented to Lady Hamilton. Dare I believe this is meant as some American substitute for speaking with my father?

———

Maneuvering conspiratorially to Hannah's side, Victoria whispered, "Have Bernard invite him for tea."

Hannah's chin rose at her friend's suggestion, and she glanced sidelong at Hans Nelson, who stood beside her, hat in hand, after being introduced to Bernard.

"Mr. Nelson tells me his family has agricultural holdings in Minnesota," said Hannah.

Hans studied the homburg a moment, then brushed a speck from the rim. "Agriculture, yes. But my own interests are in mining. In Idaho that is. Primarily silver, some gold."

Bernard's eyes swam behind the narrow lenses of his pince-nez, flitting over Hans like a dragonfly, touching briefly and lightly on the new suit, the well-tooled boots, the soft suede belt, before humming, "Silver. Yes, of course."

Hannah spoke up. "Perhaps Mr. Nelson could join us for tea, Bernard?"

The secretary's fingers stroked the spectacle ribbon around his neck as he considered the proposal before inquiring, "Do you have a calling card, Mr. Nelson? To send in to Lady Hamilton?"

"Ah, sorry," apologized Nelson. "I was careless back in Chicago and let a pickpocket relieve me of my wallet. It's embarrassing, but I'm afraid I'm fresh out of cards."

Victoria, eager to participate in any romance, because the search for husbands is the only game allowed women, took the lead and approached Lady Hamilton directly, embroidering considerably on what she knew or imagined of Mr. Nelson's position as one of the new American gentry. In a moment of plebian impulse, Her Ladyship agreed there might be diversion in the tales of an upstart.

———

Now Hans Nelson, with an American sense of open doors and little of class distinctions, has come from the sleeping car he shares with an inebriate drummer of dry goods and two temperate boys of the Mormon faith, passing through the smoking and dining compartments, and past the crowded common seating area where travelers sit on benches of wood, carving at the seats and window frames with penknives. At the entrance to the kitchen car attached to the rear of Lady Hamilton's ensemble he pauses, brushing with a handkerchief at the streaks of boiler ash and cinders that have marked his clothing. To Hannah, who watches through the grit-and-smoke-stained glass of the door, the gesture implies his hope of winning the interview, and her heart tumbles as she imagines herself mistress of one of the wheatland mansions they have seen from the train, of a scroll-trimmed house painted white and blue, with dormer windows and a turreted corner to raise her view above the rolling horizon.

The train lurches, and she staggers. Hans catches her waist in his hands. The swell of her breasts presses briefly between them, and there is a flash bright as magnesium, an instant of heat of the sort that passes between a man and a woman who know without question how their bodies might fit together.

Neither Bernard nor Lady Hamilton rise as Hannah escorts Hans into the Pullman car, tucking a strand of hair into place. Her scent, a pale blend of gardenia and sandalwood, blooms on the risen temperature of her skin, and Her Ladyship, Victorian bird dog of sin and temptation, seems keenly aware of it; her nostrils flare, and the beginning of a scowl splits her face.

Hannah says, "Your Ladyship, may I present Mr. Nelson," and there is an awkward moment as Hans holds out a hand and Lady Hamilton does not take it. He is saved from discomfort by a jolt and the clang of steel couplings. There is a mechanical hiss as the speed of the train slows to a crawl, the engine drained of steam by a split boiler line.

Bernard throws a world-weary smile in Hans's direction and sighs, "So much for one's schedule," as if important plans must now be put in abeyance. To Hannah, his tone implies that such disappointments are naturally to be expected of anything American, and by extension, of Hans Nelson. After a moment, Lady Hamilton murmurs "perhaps Mr. Nelson will entertain us as repairs are made."

Her Ladyship's lack of enthusiasm rolls off Hans without notice; as tea is served with sugar cakes and biscuits, he launches a conversation heavy with forced bonhomie of the sort that serves well in boardinghouses and saloons but draws terse responses in a Pullman sitting car.

Outside, a panorama of white clouds drifts over foothills laced with dry riverbeds. The train creeps into the wasteland of an Indian reservation, and Hans gestures to draw his companions' attention to a cluster of disastrous-looking huts alongside the tracks. Beyond the huts, rye-colored children with arms like sticks prod at cattle that are no more than desiccated hides draped over slow-moving bones.

"Hunkpapa," he says knowledgeably. "Hunkpapa and Miniconjou Sioux. The government gave 'em all the land around here a few years ago to keep 'em off the warpath."

Bernard glances out the window, picks up his cup, and takes a sip. "It doesn't appear as if they have done much with it."

Lady Hamilton sniffs in agreement. "Lord Hamilton's experience in Kabul and Africa was that the primitives are rarely appreciative of largess. It was much the same with the Boers."

"Colonists," sniffs Bernard in near-perfect imitation of Her Ladyship. "In Afghanistan with Chamberlain, was he?"

"No, Lord Hamilton was adviser to Abdur Rahman, after the Khan fled. In Africa, of course, he was with the Suez Enterprise."

Hannah listens as the exchange of chopped and coded references to obscure, bright moments in Britain's affairs excludes Hans from the conversation. She watches, growing increasingly uncomfortable, as Her Ladyship takes a single bite of a biscuit, makes a moue at the taste, and puts it down; picks up a cream pastry and does the same again without offering the plate to Hans. Through the window, sitting hunched in the doorway of a shack, a wretch so poor and miserable that he does not brush aside the insults of insects drinking at the corners of his eyes watches the atrocious privilege within the stalled train, contrasting the plentitude of dishes on the table with the hunger in his children's eyes. When he locks eyes with Hannah, she looks away, unable to hold his gaze.

Leaning forward, Hans helps himself to a slice of cake and pushes into the conversation. "This bunch was brought out here after the battle at Wounded Knee."

Bernard adopts an expression meant to show both boredom and astonishment at the interruption before mumbling, "Wounded Knee? Odd name . . ."

Hans waves the cake, spilling a rain of powdery sugar. "They jumped the reservation and went to Ghost Dancing, trying to pray all the buffalo back to life. When the army caught up with 'em, I guess there was quite a fight."

Mistaking Bernard and Lady Hamilton's stares for interest, he presses on, stringing together bits of information gleaned from distorted, bloodthirsty newspaper accounts to transform the slaughter of nearly three hundred men, women, and children by artillery at close range into a heroic battle. "The Sioux killed a few troopers, but the seventh cavalry gave 'em hell. Chased 'em halfway to Canada and did most of 'em in."

Hannah, in a small voice, says, "How horrible."

Bernard quips bemusedly, "Bit more than a wounded knee, eh?"

Lady Hamilton, her voice tight with revulsion at Hans's unthinking equation of a savage ceremony with proper prayer, murmurs, "This Ghost Dancing. I presume the authorities have put an end to it."

Hans nods, slurps at his tea, and swallows before continuing. "They gave the medal of honor to twenty of the troopers. It pretty much ended the Indian Wars. Of course, what really whipped the Sioux and Cheyenne was General Sheridan coming up with the idea of wiping out the buffalo. No buffalo, no Indians. But some medicine man got 'em all worked up about this Ghost Dance, telling them it would bring back the buffalo and run off the white men.

"There used to be millions," he says, waving a hand at the empty landscape outside the windows to indicate the missing herds. Something inside Hannah churns at the thought of endless slaughter, then eases at the almost wistful tone of her suitor's voice when he says, "It does seems a shame some-how to just wipe 'em all out . . ."

Hannah is not certain whether he means the buffalo or the Indians. Bernard, weary of both buffalos and aboriginals, watches as Hans pops the last of the cake into his mouth. He looks at him over the top of his glasses. "America seems to have no shortage of animals, Mr. Nelson."

Pink light gleams off Bernard's buffed and trimmed fin-gernails as he reaches to pour more tea for Lady Hamilton and himself, ignoring Hans's cup and—to punish her for bringing this blond Visigoth into the Pullman—Hannah's. The subtlety of the jab is lost on Hans, and he is about to con-tinue when Hannah can no longer contain herself and rises, a rush of anger and embarrassment coloring her face.

"My apologies, Mr. Nelson, but I'm sure Bernard has work he must attend to."

Hans, taken aback, looks up at her for a moment before turning his stare on Bernard, as he slowly decodes the insult. Realizing the interview has been a failure, he rises to go.

Putting his hat on to signal a newfound disregard for En-glish gentry and its puffery, he glares down at the secretary. "That may be so, Bernard." The address is insultingly famil-iar, and it galls the Englishman to hear the illiterate Ameri-can accentuate the last syllable.

"But tell me." Hans towers over the slender secretary. "Are men as scarce in England as I think?"

The insult drives home, peaking Lady Hamilton's dud-geon. Bernard turns the color of a plum. Hannah closes her eyes, appalled, yet thrilled by what she has done . . .

Dear Diary,

We approach the Rocky Mountains of the West. This continent seems endless, and I sometimes feel we are bound across a land strange as dark Africa. Mr. Nelson has deeply offended L. H. and her pet—I am forbidden Mr. Nelson's company, but this serves best to add some adventure to our meetings and prevents nothing. Victoria calls me a trollop—in humor, I assure you—and says I have been infected with the same madness that affects the haughty American cowboys in their great hats, which they often fail to doff to L. H. but always tip to Victoria or myself—a further proof to L. H. of their savagery.

Under makeshift repairs, the train pulls into Butte, Montana, where it sits on a siding as a mechanic attempts to weld the split boiler line. With Victoria's assistance, Hannah slips away to a clandestine dinner with Hans, who props one elbow on a table in a rough café and listens, chin in hand, while she describes, in a manner more familiar than she could have imagined possible only a few days earlier, the details of her life. Finding herself at ease, she relates how shortly after her most recent birthday her father had called her in to dinner with a pronouncement that he had "wonderful news."

"John Nightwatch," said Poppa Butler, referring to the second son of a powerful Bristol family, "has asked for your hand."

The Nightwatch fortune had been created during the eighteenth century by the auctioning of Africans from a stable on Blackboy Road. After slavery was outlawed in England, it had been doubled again by the diversion of the family's ships across the Atlantic to the Caribbean, where a triangle of trade involving rum, molasses, and slavery continued to flourish. For years the Nightwatch Corporation had been Poppa Butler's biggest customer for the barrels, cordage, and iron goods that rig a ship, and though the families often socialized, Hannah could count on the fingers of one hand the number of times John Nightwatch had spoken to her directly; he preferred instead to address his remarks to a point in space somewhere beyond her shoulder.

"And your reply?" she had asked Poppa, feeling the breath being pressed from her body.

"He is a fine young man," said Poppa Butler. "And Mr. Nightwatch informs me that he is the recipient of an annual income of three thousand pounds."

He does not mention that the allowance had been settled on John after a series of embarrassments removed him from the family business—not the least of which was a dalliance with a married woman who, Hannah's friends now whisper, has been so reduced in circumstances as a result of the ensuing divorce that she is rumored to be earning her living on the streets of Whitechapel. Apparently Poppa Butler had forgiven John Nightwatch his peccadillo, because three thousand is three thousand, earned or not. When she protested that she felt no particular affection for Mr. Nightwatch, Poppa Butler had glared at her over his rimless spectacles and said, "The match is a fine one, Hannah. I have already assented."

Hers was an England where bells rang on time, grass was trimmed when trimming was due, and the general order of life proceeded as planned. A good English daughter would do as her father thought best; within a week an announcement had been made and plans were laid for an elaborate wedding. Hannah's stomach cramped as she paged through samples of wedding gown silk and invitations.

Hannah does not detail for Hans how a month before the wedding she had invited her father, mother, and John Nightwatch into the parlor, where she fumbled for the words of a speech carefully arranged and rehearsed in the small hours of the night, or how all she could say through her tears and trembling was, "I cannot . . ."

She offers instead only that she and Mr. Nightwatch were incompatible.

"And now you are here," Hans replies, in a tone that indicates he is greatly pleased with this result. Hannah waits for a waiter to refill her glass before explaining how the withdrawal of the outraged Nightwatch family's account from her father's business had guaranteed the downfall of the Butler holdings when the market crashed. She steers wide of Poppa Butler's reluctance to forgive her for losing the income of a Nightwatch wife, but sketches briefly for Hans how his debt to Lord Hamilton rendered her unable to refuse the offer to enter into Lady Hamilton's service.

Hans listens carefully, then waves a hand in a gesture that seems to dismiss the Hamiltons and John Nightwatch simultaneously, saying laconically that a thousand pounds sterling certainly isn't enough to justify indenturing oneself.

"The world is full of money," he adds enigmatically. "All one needs is the courage to go out and pick it up."

Reassured by his open face and attention, Hannah asks, "And you, Mr. Nelson? Have you not considered marriage?"

He pauses, leans back, and folds his arms across his chest.

"I've been rather busy working to make a go of it."

"Of course," says Hannah, feeling on the verge of intrusion. "But you've done well for yourself." An inflection in her voice shades the statement as a question.

Nelson thinks a moment, edges forward in his seat, and lays his hands palms up on the table. "These are working hands, Miss Nelson. Mining is hard work, and sometimes one's success is just a matter of plain luck, up or down." This is as close as he can bring himself to telling her how he once found himself on the seesaw rise to fortune through the discovery of a plum-sized nugget that he sold for several hundred dollars, a windfall he then rolled into an apparently gold-heavy claim pimped by a crooked geologist, only to learn the claim had been salted.

"You and a dozen others," said a sunburned sheriff from behind a desk of whiskey barrels and planks after being informed of the scam. With the scheming geologist long gone, Hans had been forced to descend into the earth as a human mule, working as a slag scaler, breaking waste rock from the walls of a hard rock mine owned by a back-east corporation, where it was every man for himself. Six months later, while Hans was scabbing during a miners' strike, a trio of strong-arm agents employed to quell the strike had mistaken his sharing a boiled pig knuckle with a fellow slagger as the act of a union sympathizer and beaten him.

The memory stills him for a moment, then he shrugs and

gives a tight-lipped smile. "I believe there are even better opportunities waiting in the Alaska Territory. New fields of discovery, not so much competition . . ." His voice trails off; he looks down at his hands and folds them.

Hannah, interpreting his reticence as humility, is tempted to lay her hands on his but restrains herself.

————

After lingering until the café closes, Hannah returns to find Lady Hamilton waiting. That night she pens a short note in her diary:

> *Mr. Nelson, handsome Mr. Nelson, is always kind and a gentleman, but I sense a keener interest. If I speak, he listens without condescension. When informed of my broken engagement to J. Nightwatch and my obligation to Lady Hamilton—Imagine!—he laughed and told me there are women of the West who ride in trousers! I shall be sad to part company with him after our arrival in Washington.*
>
> *L. H. terrifically angry at my defiance of her order to see no more of him.*

————

The next morning there is a summons from Lady Hamilton, brought by a maid in a crisp white apron and dust cap, who gives Hannah's shoulder a sympathetic pat.

"Bernard is with her," she says, lowering her voice. "They are in ill humor."

When Hannah enters the sitting car, Lady Hamilton looks grim, rigid as a wire fence. Neither she nor Bernard smiles.

Lady Hamilton fires without preamble, in a tone usually reserved for discussing scripture. "Hannah, it is time for me to deal with your future."

Dread drives a dull splinter into Hannah's chest. "My future, ma'am?"

"A girl of your age is prey to great perils." She pauses. "It is time you marry."

Hannah's heart skips two beats. In that time a wondering, hopeful thought rises within Hannah that Lady Hamilton is about to suggest that she marry Hans Nelson, then it is dashed as she sees Bernard look away, feigning interest in the workings of horsemen hazing cattle in the distance. When he looks back, there is a fleeting lift at the corners of his mouth, like the smug expression of a whist player who believes he has just played a subtle, brilliant card.

"I have decided it is best if you become betrothed. An unmarried woman of your age is susceptible to sinful urges." Lady Hamilton's words echo the Calvinist cadence of a Scotch parson, and her scowl tightens.

"I have spoken with Bernard. He agrees that you would be a suitable wife for himself."

Bernard nods, smiles, and looks at Hannah over the top of his spectacles before speaking, a prim grimace that reminds Hannah of a toad considering a fly. "It is best, Miss Butler. Being both in Her Ladyship's employ, it is natural for two of our station to agree to this marriage."

Lady Hamilton blows and sips at her tea. "You must marry soon, Hannah. Your thoughts wander, I can tell. In your condition, the wrong man might endanger your soul. And for you to marry and leave my service would be an inconvenience to me. Betrothal to Bernard smooths many wrinkles, don't you agree?"

Hannah struggles to find her voice. When she speaks, the words tremble.

"Beg pardon, ma'am, but such an arrangement does not appeal to me, thank you."

Bernard begins to speak, but Her Ladyship interrupts curtly. "Miss Butler! You entered my employ after the reduction of your family's circumstances."

Her voice grows louder. "One in your situation should be grateful I am willing to use my position to form a proper arrangement for you! I have told Bernard you may wed when we return to England."

At the thought of waking every morning for the rest of her life to the sight of the pallid and sanctimonious Bernard, Hannah feels her blood curdle and shakes her head in an autonomic denial of the unthinkable. The unconscious gesture enrages Her Ladyship further, until Hannah can only stare at the floor, listening to the turbulent rush of her own blood in her ears amid the rising fever of her employer's outraged rant.

Hannah looks up and is met with a stinging slap, then another and another as she ducks her head into her forearms before finally rising to catch and push, sending Lady Hamilton stumbling backward into her silken chair. Stunned and ashen, Hannah turns away, fumbling with trembling hands at her dishevelment. From her chair, Lady Hamilton curses.

There is a sudden quiet, followed by the clink and splinter of a china cup crashing to the floor. Hannah turns to see Her

Ladyship arched and quivering, her dress and bodice dark with spilled tea, her jaw working soundlessly, mute from the shock of blood vessels bursting within her brain.

Bernard gasps, carefully places his own cup in its saucer on the table before rising to his feet, and begins shrieking for a doctor.

TWO

Tears of outrage shine in Hannah's eyes. She stands rigid before Bernard, refusing to look at him, staring instead at the hammered tin ceiling of the Tacoma, Washington, station. Bernard's voice squeaks and trembles as he curses, banishing her from the entourage.

"You," he froths, one finger of a suede-gloved hand thrust at her averted face. "You are . . ." His speech dissolves at the memory of Lady Hamilton lying speechless, the left half of her face drooping in a macabre, stroke-induced grimace.

"Loose, Miss Butler, decidedly a slattern!"

He sputters in frustration, mouthing ridiculous threats of sheriffs and bailiffs. Victoria hides in the Pullman car, knowing she will suffer later for her friendship with Hannah, and worse, for Bernard's impotence. Earlier, she had thrown Hannah's clothes into a case, whispering fiercely that Hannah "*must* accept Mr. Nelson's offer. It is clear he loves you!"

"But . . . ," Hannah had said, unable to marshal the words to say she hardly knows him. "It would be . . . madness!"

When Nelson stepped through the doorway from where he had been listening, smiling the bold, white smile Hannah found so delectable, and said, "Really, Miss Butler, don't you think *not* accepting would be the true madness?" Victoria had slammed the lid on the case, giddy with recklessness, and shoved it into Hannah's arms, whispering, "When shall you ever again have such a chance? It's so *romantic*!"

Now Hans, triumphant at having such a prize as Hannah laid at his feet, laughs and tells Bernard to "get out of the way or you'll wear your ass for a hat," before removing Hannah's portmanteau to a waiting carriage. From the safety of the Pullman car steps, Bernard hurls a promise to Hannah that should she ever return to England, there will be charges laid. "Assault!" he cries, and—absurdly—"Attempted murder!"

Stunned by her sudden, explosive exile, Hannah stares at the wagon, which in turn seems a transport into a giddy freedom or a tumbrel on its way to the guillotine. Leaving on the arm of the handsome blond stranger is certainly a fairy tale, but one that will leave her marooned, eternally deprived of a ticket or welcome home to England.

Her possessions are limited to a trunk of clothing and a small box of books—two journals, one of which is half filled and the other entirely blank, a volume of poems, and a Bible. In addition, she owns two pairs of shoes, an umbrella, and a heavy coat with a fur collar. Hidden between the pages of the unused journal are her life savings: forty pounds sterling, plus one hundred and eighty-three dollars in U.S. currency. The world seems suddenly huge and threatening.

Two blocks from the station, Hans draws on the reins and brings the carriage to a halt. Shifting on the hard plank seat, he removes his hat, stares at it, replaces it on his head, and settles it. Turning to face Hannah, he begins:

"Miss Butler . . ."

He pauses, looks away, and twirls the reins.

Hannah waits for the jaws of some trap she feels yawning beneath her to spring.

Hans eyes a passing horseman, then blurts, "I've some money," before mumbling, "I mean . . . if you'd rather."

The words slip crossways through Hannah's brain, spinning without clear meaning, until assembling themselves into a pattern ripe with a malign offer of prostitution. Voice trembling, she struggles for frost in her reply.

"Surely, Mr. Nelson, you do not propose . . ."

Suddenly awkward as a boy, Hans nods. "Yes. I've some money. And if you'd prefer, instead of this . . ." A loose hand wave encompasses the whole of the bustling street, the patch-work of wood frame buildings to either side, and the gaggle of rough-looking characters who pick their way through random piles of horse dung along the street.

"It's not much, but I've enough to get you back to England. You don't have to stay if it is not your wish."

The whip-snap reversal makes her dizzy, requiring she breathe once, then again, before the notion that Hans is offering her a choice can sink slowly in. Rather than proposi-tioning her, he is offering her the freedom to decide.

One gloved hand reaches out to rest lightly on his forearm. Then in a small and tenuous voice she says, "Please continue, Mr. Nelson. We must see to rooms for the night."

———

A preacher charges a dollar to perform the short ceremony that binds them. Witnesses are included in the price. Then there are papers to sign at a recorder's office, and she receives a document that changes her name to Nelson. After the ceremony, her new husband beams as the preacher shakes his hand, while Hannah feels a knot in her stomach, just below her sternum, as she stares at the man to whom she has been bound.

They rent a room on the third floor of the Empire Hotel. There is a stand with a basin and a carpet patterned with roses. The sounds of the booming streets below come to her through a window that opens outward above a saloon, and she feels as if she is someone else, some other young woman who lies watching as Hans methodically forces his way through her hymen. Afterward, he goes to the hotel kitchen and returns with two plates of kidneys and beans and a spray of yellow honeysuckle, which he drapes across her belly. Once, then again, she lies and watches as the act is repeated. Then on the second day, she awakens to wonder, as her nerves and skin and blood come alive, washing her in new sensations that allow Hans's lips and hands to sweep her over the precipice of a new carnality.

On the third day of their marriage, a sodden and sated Hans gives her a possessive, playful slap on her bare bottom and says, "It is time to head for Alaska, Mrs. Nelson. Time to get rich," after which he shows her a newspaper he has saved in his luggage. A bold headline proclaims, "A Ton of Gold on Board," above an engraving of a crowd of grinning men on the deck of a ship. Earlier in the summer the steamer had returned to Seattle from Alaska with several miners aboard, among whom was George Washington Carmack, an old sourdough who had "dealt himself a royal flush in life" by bending to take a drink from a small tributary of the Klondike River and finding raw gold glittering in every crack of the creek bed. The latest shipment of veterans from the Klondike had disembarked in Seattle carrying satchels stuffed with more than three million dollars' worth of bullion.

"They pitched nuggets of solid gold into the crowd!" Hans said, with something like awe. "Just tossed 'em around like they were nickels."

Gazing at the picture of the ship and its prosperous cargo, he shook his head and said, "I aim to get my piece of that, Mrs. Nelson. I surely do."

Dear Diary,

We are bound north to the Alaska Territory. I am a bit frightened at these grand and sudden changes in my life, but have only to consider my new husband to be reassured. While certainly not the circumstances for marriage of which a young girl dreams, I am sure he will care well for me and our future is assured. As I write this, he is out to send notice of our marriage by telegraph to his family in Minnesota. When next I correspond with Poppa and Mother, it will be as Mrs. Hans Nelson, but I shall wait until we return, triumphant, from the goldfields and I am able to address the debt to Lord Hamilton. It is impossible to know what tale they will have heard of the events with Lady Hamilton, but I pray they will not judge me too harshly. My

husband and I shall have the best reward, however. It will take some
time and effort to realize our acquaintance, but I am sure we shall
be comfortable and happy together.

In a hotel in Seattle, Hannah is bitten by a flea. The hotel, with
its population of layabouts and drunken bellhops, frightens
her; for hours after she discovers the insect, her skin crawls
with the phantom sensation of invisible, many-legged things
scratching and burrowing. She bathes in a pan of lukewarm
water with a cake of hard soap that refuses to lather.

"A bit much, isn't it, Mr. Nelson? Deplorable, really." The
marriage is too young for Hannah to find comfort in addressing her husband by his given name.

Hans, with American familiarity, has no such constraint.
He swishes a razor in a pan of water, forms his mouth into
an *O* to stretch the skin of his upper lip, and carefully draws
the singing blade from top to bottom before answering. "I'm
sorry, Hannah, but my wallet is a bit thin for anything better
at the moment. My money will be better spent on tools and
supplies for the goldfields, now won't it? After all"—and he
pauses to wipe the razor on a towel—"when I was borrowing
the money to head for Alaska, I didn't budget for the cost of
a wife, did I?"

Hannah does not look up from the basin of tepid water,
fearing she is somehow being made responsible for their tenuous finances. With an effort to sound casual, she asks, "Our
money is borrowed?" The water seems suddenly frigid, and a
fatty scum floats on its surface. The idea of more debt chills
her. Debtors lose everything. Margin calls and debt closed her

father's chandlery business. It puts women and children on the streets.

Equally casual, Hans wipes his face with the towel and bends to examine the shine of his smooth skin in the mirror. "Oh, yes. From my brother-in-law."

"Right hard about it he was, too. I had to promise him a three-to-one return before the tight bastard would go along."

A quiver flutters in Hannah's stomach. Three to one? The word *usury* rises to her lips, and she bites it back. "How much have you . . . What is our debt?"

Hans ignores the question and thumbs an imaginary spot from the front of his undershirt, before hoisting his galluses to his shoulders. "It hasn't all been cream, Hannah. They kicked me out when I was sixteen."

Whenever Hans thinks of his mother, Ula Nelson seems to loom, arms akimbo, with a look on her face hard and sharp enough to scratch glass. Widowed at a young age by an over-turned reaping machine, Ula had raised Hans and one sister with the grudging help of her own widower father, a raspy-voiced old-country bastard who never lost his delight in telling Hans that such a stupid lazy boy would never have "a pot to piss in, ner a window to t'row it out of." On his sixteenth birthday Hans had returned from a long, hot day of slitting throats and scalding hogs for a well-to-do neighbor, to find his grandfather sitting on the weathered porch, watching as his mother dropped the last of Hans's possessions onto a meager stack in the yard.

"We can't be feeding you no more," was all she said, but the old man could not resist throwing in his two cents. "You kin come back when you have made somethin' of yourself."

Remembering, Hans bites his lower lip then swallows to clear the bitter taste of bile. "I will, too, by God. Just see if I don't."

There is a tremor in his voice as he mutters, "Always looking down their noses at me, just because my luck has been bad a few times over the years."

Coming behind Hannah, he places his hands on her hips and bends close to her ear. "But now I've a lady for my wife. And we'll show them, won't we?" His nuzzling lips feel alien and intrusive as he whispers promises of the status they will have. While his hands roam, Hannah thinks of how the new homburg and fine wool suit, which had so impressed her at their first meeting, were purchased with borrowed money.

"Ah, God, Hannah. I just want . . . I want so badly to . . ." And because there is no choice but to believe, she holds his head to her breast while he makes promises to care for and cherish her.

> *Dear Diary,*
> *We shall have to work very hard. Poor Hans. He adores me so much—and I him, I am sure—that he sought overly hard to impress me and perhaps exaggerated his situation out of ardor. It is not the bargain I presumed to be making, but still a fine one, to be so loved, isn't it?*

Seattle is an accumulation of weathered gray buildings under a sky of the same drab shade. A rash of cobbled shops line muddy lanes, all selling the same prospectors' things, and with prices for an ever-dwindling supply of shovels, hammers, boots, blankets, packs, and pans doubling daily, the moss-rotted boardwalks are peppered with those too poor to buy a miner's outfit. Hans is frantic. "A few months ago, passage to Alaska cost two hundred dollars. Now the thieves booking for the steamship lines are demanding a thousand!"

The heartless triaging of humans becomes an economic filter, a merciless Carborundum that grinds away the poor and the hobbled, those less able to pay. This is also a great kindness, for those who arrived in the first waves of immigration to Alaska and the Yukon are already dying in great numbers, though the days of summer are benevolent and gentle. They disappear into crevassed glaciers, fall from crumbling precipices, or are murdered by brigands like the infamous Soapy Smith gang of Skagway. They run screaming into the endless forests, where they perish of exhaustion after losing their minds under the torment of a million mosquitoes. An appalling number commit suicide, overcome by a landscape so vast and strong that the burden of their own smallness becomes too great to bear.

———

A derbied huckster sells Hans and Hannah the last available bunk on the *Pegasus*, a seventy-foot harbor tug, converted rudely into service as a passenger liner. After boarding, they discover that Hannah is the only woman on board and that their berth has also been sold to a schoolteacher from California. Hannah negotiates and reasons, but Hans grows impatient and waves a work-knuckled fist until the unfortunate teacher evacuates the bunk to build a nest on the deck.

Hannah leans into Hans at the bulwark, the weight of his

arm pleasant across her shoulders. In the cool, moist air, the steam of her own breath twists and rises, as if her core boils with life, and together they watch the heavy mist obscure the retreating shape of the city.

Pegasus rolls and steams through the green waters of the San Juan Islands at a subtle speed. Proper steamships overtake her, shouting of their superior bulk with insulting whistle blasts, while the captains exchange obscene gestures from their respective wheelhouse windows. Aboard the *Pegasus*, the men smoke and mingle, telling each other briefly of their previous lives and discussing at great length their strategies for obtaining riches. There are many opinions on matters of geology and minerals, and the smoothly planed wood of the galley table is soon covered in penciled designs that a newcomer might take to be engines of war, instruments meant for storming castles or raining a shower of boulders down upon approaching ships, but which instead describe washboards, sluice boxes, and odd, hieroglyphic machines for crushing stones. Hannah observes that among the would-be prospectors it is the most poorly informed who hold forth the loudest and longest, and that all of the raucous, late-night discussions are pervaded with a sense that there may never be another opportunity like this to grab at easy wealth.

Pegasus plows north, shouldering apart the water with her stem. Hannah sits in a canvas deck chair on the bow, watching the world rise before her, staring ahead to where the mountains paralleling the strait converge in a shallow *V*. Hour after hour the hammering beat of the steam engine throbs through the hull, until it seems her heart must begin to beat in time with the whooshing spin of the pistons. She goes once to the stern but the sight of the wake peeling and unfurling away from the ship and a seemingly endless line of islands and peaks dropping slowly below the horizon serves not as a change of view but as a too-graphic reminder of how all that she has ever known or been part of is slipping away, disappearing perhaps irredeemably and forever behind them. Bracing herself against a quickening trepidation, she turns on her heel and returns to the bow, resolving to look only forward.

―――――――

Nights are spent at anchor in small coves where the shores are dark with massed trees. In the cramped and crowded quarters, Hans rigs a curtain of blankets across the face of their bunk to separate them from the other passengers. Behind it, he introduces Hannah to the pleasure of slow, careful coupling, whispers, and the sweetness of two curled into a single pair.

―――――――

The miles and days roll on. Islands and passages are noted in the ship's log and left astern. In a copse of alder trees, the sagging longhouses of an abandoned Indian village, once peopled by proud warriors who outfought, outfoxed, and outbargained all others, only to be decimated by the limitless diseases and alcohol loosed upon them by European traders, fades into moss-covered ruin. For Hannah, coming from England where every meter of land has been deeded, spoken for, and titled since Charlemagne's time, considering the mass and spread of unclaimed land around her creates at first a vertigo and weakness of breath.

Many aboard the *Pegasus* chafe at the length and idleness of the journey, unaware that the passing of time and distance is necessary, not for geographic reasons, but because it requires that they sit and watch for days on end, as a full thousand miles of coast unrolls before them, creating by the end of the journey a sense of proportion and an acceptance of the size and immensity of the land that makes the idea of going still farther, over endless mountain ranges and down great rivers into god-knows-where, acceptable. By churning their impatience into eagerness, it gives them false heart and a belief in themselves that will make it possible to go beyond all that they know or believe, into the wilderness that is the Yukon and Alaska. Outclassed and ignorant, they are as carpenters and sellers of shoes at a county fair, stepping into the ring with a professional boxer, and the length of the journey is the beer that supplies them courage.

The depth of ignorance suffered by the pilgrims is visible in the soft red and yellow pastels decorating the heights under which they pass, for these are the hues of deception. Here in the north, there will be none of the ribald autumn colors they know from the world they left behind, no warning that the alpine blush of August on these mountains is all the admonishment they will have that summer has passed and winter waits impatiently behind the peaks.

THREE

The prospectors arrive in Skagway on the twelfth of September. It is forty-two degrees Fahrenheit at noon, and the first gold the passengers see is painted on the autumn leaves of cottonwood trees scattered across the hillsides. Thousands of men swarm the muddy lanes and boardwalks in a slow, churning riot of shouting, pushing, and rushing that reminds Hannah of a shovel-turned ant hill. Many wear sidearms beneath their coats. The Nelsons have been warned repeatedly of robbery and thievery. Few women walk the muddy streets, and those who do seem evenly divided between those like Hannah, who dress with some severity, and those in brightly colored dresses that accent their bosoms and behinds. Hannah watches in shock as a drunken slattern attempting to climb from the rear window of a crib-sized hut behind a saloon slips and falls.

An unsure, troubled look seizes Hans's eyes, and Hannah searches without success among the features of his face for some sign of the aplomb he has carried since Chicago. Frightened by the deflation she finds there, and the sudden droop in her husband's shoulders, her voice erupts, a decibel too frantic, "Mr. Nelson, what shall we *do*?"

Hans stares at Hannah for a moment from behind a furrowed brow, digging for his confidence. Squaring his shoulders, he eyes the fevered crowd and grumbles, "This lot looks like it would steal us blind. It's best if one of us stays with the gear." Waving a gloved hand at the mound of their belongings, he says, "I'll find a hotel. You keep an eye on the supplies."

By nightfall the sky is growing overcast. A cold rain begins to fall, driven by rolling gusts of wind. Hannah digs an ankle-length oilskin coat from a pack. Hans returns late, wet and hungry. Dropping to a seat on a keg of nails, he blows on his hands to warm them, picks up a stick, and begins carving the mud from his boots.

"There's not a room to be had anywhere, Hannah. Every bed has two or three men in it. They're even sleeping on the floors."

She hugs her arms to her chest to keep warm. "Perhaps we should return to the ship."

Hans's answer is to shrug and begin digging a folded tarp from the stack of supplies. "It's gone. It left for Seattle two hours ago. We'll have to stay here for the night."

"Surely there must be some place we can go," she says, glancing up at the darkening sky to emphasize the rain.

Hans bristles. "I said there isn't anything. Do you think I haven't looked?"

A flush of anger fueled by uncertainty courses through her.

Why isn't he taking better care of her? What of the promises he made in Seattle? She has never slept outdoors in her life.

It is almost as if Hans reads her thoughts, and he softens, saying, "I'm sorry, Hannah. I truly am. But no one was expecting this." He waves a hand to indicate the squalor and the milling crowd. "For now we'll just have to do the best we can."

"And besides," he adds as he begins shifting bags and crates to build an opening in the pile over which to spread the tarp, "there may be more of this sort of thing in the Yukon."

He is right, of course. As she helps anchor the tarp, she imagines more cold, wet nights and must swallow against the throat-swell of tears as she concedes to herself how unrealistic her vision of a romantic tent life has been.

"Take this," says Hans, handing her a rolled blanket. He lifts the edge of the improvised shelter and motions for her to crawl in. "Try to sleep. I'll stand guard."

It grows cold. Huddled beneath the blanket in the mud, she shivers amid fragments of sleep and broken dreams.

Morning arrives adorned in the glittering jewelry of winter. Fresh snow forms a pattern of lace on the broken cliffs above the town.

Again, Hans leaves Hannah with their boxes and bags and goes in search of a room or stable in which they may sort and pack their goods. They dare not leave the gear unattended for a moment. Shovels, cooking utensils, clothing—all are scarce in Skagway, and their supplies would melt into the hands of thieves as fast as the fresh snow is now disappearing into mud. The thin leather of Hannah's boots is soaked through, and her feet are numb. Her skin feels filthy, and hunger and thirst make her dizzy. She gathers snow from the tarp spread over the equipment, compresses it in her fist, and puts it into her mouth. After sucking cold water from the snowball, she crawls under a corner of the tarp, wrestles her undergarments down, and performs an act of public indecency. In the darkness, the smell of her urine rises warm and rank to her nose.

Hans returns near the middle of the day with news of a tent village where others from *Pegasus* have set up camp. There are latrines close by, as well as a number of peddlers selling supplies at pillaging prices. "There's room for us there and a standpipe nearby, so we will at least have water for you to cook with."

"We'll be glad of that," says Hannah. Hans starts to say something then looks away. In the flow of mercenaries there are numerous men of the sort he labored with in the Hobbesian world of the Idaho mines, where bullies and thieves ate from the lunch buckets of weaker men. After a heavy snowfall and a derailed train left the operation short of rations, he had seen a Chinaman kicked and stabbed to death for an apple. After that, he had squirreled food away and eaten alone whenever possible.

Hannah watches as her husband feigns interest in a passing wagon, mystified by the struggle she sees in the flickering glances he throws in her direction.

After a moment he grumbles, "We'll get moved and set up the tent. You can cook something. You must be famished."

"Yes," she agrees. She has had no food since leaving the *Pegasus*.

Hans hesitates, chews at his lip, and swallows, then puts his hands on his hips and straightens as if a decision has been made. "I thought you might be," he says. "So I brought you this."

He reaches under his coat and brings out a small parcel wrapped in newsprint. Folding back the paper, he holds out the remains of a sausage nestled amid a small litter of cold potatoes.

Dear Diary,
Disaster is complete. We have been turned back at the border of Canada for being inadequately supplied. Very distressed in our condition, for winter is upon us with rain, snow, and terrible winds. This canvas tent is our sole shelter and miserable. Many others in the same condition.

The Crown forces of Canada, in the form of a Royal Canadian Mounted Policeman, flips the tarp back over the pile of supplies and speaks bluntly, "Entry refused."

Hans stands up straighter and speaks loudly to make himself heard over the yowling of sled dogs and shouts of men hoisting heavy packs to their shoulders as a string of prospectors prepares to depart for the Canadian interior. "Refused? Why?"

The Mountie folds a fistful of receipts and papers in half and holds the bundle out to Hans. Snowflakes drift through the air like ashes. Hannah feels their cool sting on her cheeks.

"Insufficient supplies," says the officer, flicking his blue-eyed gaze across Hannah's upturned face. Lowering his voice, he looks again to Hans. "Look, man, it's really no place for a woman. Not a woman like her."

Hans stares at Hannah as the Mountie goes on to explain. There have been reports of cannibalism and murder, with one gang of miners raiding another in search of food, and after several parties of ill-prepared prospectors starved to death, the Mounties enacted a requirement that each company carry a year's worth of supplies. Beans, rice, salt, coffee, flour, lard, bacon, dried milk, sugar, and jam are unavailable in the Yukon, and a full ton of staples is required for each and every gold seeker wishing to enter Canada.

Their own mound of supplies, large and cumbersome as it is, is woefully inadequate. Worse, there is little food to be had in Skagway and none at all at a price that will not empty their purse.

After dragging, sledging, and packing their burden back into Skagway, Hans falls into a black mood and walks away, saying over his shoulder, "I'll be back later. Watch our things," before disappearing into the crowd.

―――――――

"Mrs. Nelson? Mrs. Hans Nelson?" The searching call comes to Hannah through the thin canvas wall of the tent. She hesitates as she tries to identify the visitor before throwing back the flap. "Here. In here. I am Mrs. Nelson. Where is Mr. Nelson?"

A small man in a coat sewn from a colorful Hudson's Bay

blanket bends down to peer in, removes a knit cap, and says in a voice with a Midwestern twang, "He's up to the blacksmith's there. Took a pretty good knock, and he's asking fer you. Is that you, then, Mrs. Nelson? You're Mrs. Nelson, are you?"

Hannah rises to her feet and reaches for her hat as she realizes he means Hans has been hurt. Casting a concerned look at the stack of supplies she has been charged with guarding, she hesitates, worried they will be pilfered, then hurries to follow the messenger as he trundles off before her, hurling bites of words over his shoulder as he elbows a passage through the damp-smelling crowd. "It was a nigger boy found him. Gangs all over the dam' town. Behind the horse pens, knocked silly. I'm from Indiana, myself. So he was asking for ya, I come to get ya."

Outside a blacksmith shop that reeks of hot metal and tar, Hans sits on a box, clutching a bloody rag to his head. After stopping in a saloon to ponder his troubles, he had been lured into conversation by a friendly stranger, then offered a drink. Two hours later, he awoke in a puddled alley, his mouth sticky, dry, and plated with the copper taste of the drug the stranger had slipped into the whiskey. Groping through his emptied pockets, he had staggered back into the saloon and confronted the stranger, only to be beaten with a sap.

The blanket-coated Hoosier stands back and chatters as Hannah pulls gingerly at the rag. It sticks to the wound with dried blood. "Ought to do something, but nobody does. They've killed a few fellows, too, for their pokes. Rigging card games and such. Call him Soapy Smith, got a real gang of cutthroats, but nobody does nothing."

Shrugging, he repeats unnecessarily, "And they'll kill ya, too."

Hans leans against Hannah as they stagger back to the tent. "Just about cleaned me out. Got my wallet, all our cash. All we got left is . . ." He stops to feel about in the pocket of his vest with a forefinger and thumb. They emerge pinching a gold piece between a pair of smaller silver coins. "Jesus. Five dollars. Five dollars and fifty cents."

Heavy rains fall that night, soaking the tent and everything in it. In their wet bedroll, Hans curls around Hannah, burning her neck with his stubbled beard.

The next morning a dark, mute beggar stops at the door of the tent. His face is dirt caked, lined with calamity, and as he holds out one filthy hand in silent supplication Hannah looks away, embarrassed by the proximity of such misfortune, and waits for Hans to say, "Scat."

The beggar stands stock-still, hand distended, his unspoken request resonating in the air.

Hans shifts uneasily in his seat. Hannah looks to her husband, who does nothing, then breathes deep to gather her courage. "We've nothing for you," she says, reaching for the flap.

Hans covers her hand with his own. "Wait."

Reaching into his vest pocket, his fingers fish, pause, then fish again. And because in times of calamity people often do the unexpected, or because charity appeals when someone else has it worse, Hans passes into the beggar's soiled paw two small silver coins.

There is no work in Skagway except that of a mule. Hans considers hiring out to bear loads of goods up the precipitous incline of the Chilkoot Pass, but the local strong-backed Indians have established a level of wages for which only the most desperate are willing to labor. Many lie broke and hungry in ragged tents in the mud. Hundreds compete for every job.

The surplus of bodies has spread out from Skagway, guaranteeing unemployment in the nearby settlement of Haines and overflowing into the mines eighty miles away at Juneau. Willing men idle as far away as Petersburg. Prices everywhere are outrageous; an egg brings a dollar, a pound of beans, three. Coffee is a luxury for kings.

Hannah counts and recounts the dollars hidden in her journal; there is not enough for a return passage to Seattle. She calculates, figures, and refigures, then proposes to Hans that selling their outfit will fetch a sufficient sum. He mutters a curse in reply, wipes at a plate of beans with a crust of bread, then grips himself and tries to speak with calm and reason; retreat would be futile. There is no work elsewhere since the collapse of the railroads. Men and their families are going hungry in every state in the Union. Better to stay the course here in the north, find a way to get in on the gold. But first there is the winter to survive.

The next day after a walk, Hans throws himself down on the wet cot. "I hear there's a lumber boat leaving for Sitka."

The old Russian capital lies on the outer coast nearly two hundred miles away to the southwest. Skagway's boomtown hunger for building material and firewood has completely stripped the surrounding countryside of timber-grade trees. The few remaining are small, crooked, and grain-twisted from incessant gales, but Sitka's moderate maritime climate provides trees that are immense and straight.

"I reckon it pays to freight lumber to Skagway. That ought to mean there are sawmill jobs in Sitka," he mutters. "We might as well go find out. Things can't be any worse there than here."

"Perhaps I can work, too. There must be something I can do," says Hannah.

Hans shakes his head, sitting up and reaching for his wife's hand with a mixture of righteousness, pride, and tender concern. "I can't have it, Hannah. No wife of mine is cuttin' fish in a cannery or spooning hash up to a bunch of trashy boomers." He shakes his head emphatically. "It's just not for a lady." Then he drops his brow into his hands. "Don't know how we'll get there, anyhow. Five dollars won't get us on the boat."

Hannah stares at the mud beneath her feet. Her toes have not been warm for days, and she feels like crying. "I have some money," she says. Reaching for her journal, she is enfolded by a regret she cannot name.

Sixty of the one hundred and eighty-three American dollars pressed flat in her journal go to the lumber boat's captain. Hans appropriates the remainder to refill his plundered purse. Hannah does not mention the forty English pounds pressed between unwritten pages in the back of her diary. While he sees to their passage, she carefully rips a seam from her one good whalebone corset, folds the bills lengthwise, and stitches them smoothly along one polished stay.

———

Emptied of its cargo of planks and beams, the lumber ship rides high, lightly ballasted by a cargo of broken humans. A north wind screams in the rigging, driving vapors of black exhaust from a sputtering engine into the forepeak, where a dozen men and one woman squat on wooden benches, huddling together against the gunwale-to-gunwale wallow of a following sea. The smoke stinks and coats Hannah's nose with the gummy flavor of kerosene. One by one the cabin's occupants add the sound and smells of seasickness to the discomfort of the voyage.

There is no heat in the forecastle, and the air is clammy with their breath. Sea air permeates everything, weighting and dampening their clothes with salt. Hannah, like the others, hugs herself in a stupor and dozes, deadened by the slow, pile-driver rhythm of the waves.

A deckhand comes below with a wooden bucket of saltwater and slops the contents across the deck, swirling the rejected contents of outraged stomachs about their feet before it dribbles into the bilge.

"'At's your head and slops pot, too," says the deckhand, setting the bucket on the planked sole and giving it a nudge with his foot. When he grins at Hannah and chuckles, she sees that his teeth are gray.

A muttering man among the huddled passengers wears greasy coveralls and boots of vulcanized rubber. The skin of his hands and face flakes in red patches. A cracked gleam sparks in his glance. Beside him sits a man so large and dark he consumes space the way a cavern absorbs the light of a candle, his face hidden beneath a sprawling salt-and-pepper beard.

The mutterer reaches with one booted foot for the bucket and skids it ringing and empty across the deck to rest before him, then rises. When he stands and reaches for his groin, working his hand into his fly, Hannah realizes he intends to urinate. Looking up to protest, she sees wet, contorted red lips splinter into a grin. The man leers, enjoying the shock on her face. Beside her, she hears Hans shout "not in front of my wife!" and sees him rise to his feet.

From the pocket of the soiled coveralls a knife sings into the air, the blade wavering back and forth in counterpoint to the motion of the ship. Its owner mutters a single word— "Whore"—before taking a step closer to Hans, who steps back until he comes to a halt against Hannah's knees.

The movement of the bearded giant is studied and swift. Without rising from his seat, he grasps the knife wielder by the collar, and with a motion like that of a man pitching a bag of grain, throws him straight up, knocking his head against the unyielding underside of the deck. The sound is surprisingly hollow, like a boot being dropped. The knife clatters, and the giant catches the senseless mutterer as he falls, then eases him to the cabin sole with the gentleness of a mother laying a child to bed.

Leaning over the recumbent figure, the giant probes with a thick finger, delicately surveying the area of skull-to-deck impact. The wide brim of a Western-style hat that has seen a great deal of sweat and sun hides his eyes as he inspects the results of his work. Satisfied, he pats the greasy, disheveled hair of the unconscious man into place with a meaty hand and regards Hannah with eyes startling in their tenderness.

To her own surprise, Hannah ignores Hans's injunction to "keep away" and goes to the wounded man. After righting and setting aside the bucket, she repeats the giant's inspection. The stale smell of a body unused to washing fills her nose, and she breathes through her mouth as she examines her offender. "He seems well enough," she observes. "He is breathing evenly."

Hannah and the giant exchange looks, and he says, in a low voice, as if to explain the incident, "Heartbroke."

"Do you know him, then?"

He pauses and shakes his head. Harky—for that is the man's name—does not know the knifeman by name or face or history, yet knows him as he has known so many of the wounded. Whether by woman or life or God's own cruelty, "heartbroke" is always the same. Nothing else can account for such madness.

Hannah waits for more until she understands nothing more will be forthcoming, then gestures to the man at her feet. "What shall we do with him?"

Harky considers a moment. The question could be one of whether to restrain, nurse, or punish. His shoulders are as wide as an ax handle, and when he shrugs, they move like the withers of a horse. "He'll behave, I reckon."

Hannah nods, accepting the bearded man's guarantee of her safety, and thanks him. Hans, too, is grateful for Harky's intercession and introduces first himself, then Hannah as "Mrs. Nelson, my wife."

Harky shakes hands with Hans, then offers his hand to Hannah, who hesitates briefly before taking it. The paw is so large and powerful she feels as if she is placing her fingers into the mouth of a crocodile. But the thick fingers and broad, hard palm take her hand as briefly and gently as if it were capturing and releasing a small frightened bird.

"We're traveling to Sitka," says Hans, "looking for work. Our plan was for the Yukon, but we've been excluded for want of supplies."

Harky nods. When he answers, it is with the hesitance and cadence of a man for whom speech is infrequent. "Me, too. Partner run off, took the supplies."

"Do you mean to say you were robbed by your own partner?" asks Hannah.

Harky knits his brow before answering. "We only had half enough. Guess he figured that was enough for one." The partner skedaddled in the night, crossing the border beyond pursuit. Nothing in his tone indicates he is angry or feels cheated.

"You've nothing left?" asks Hannah.

"I've got a kit." Harky tilts his head toward a bundle under a bench beyond the unconscious madman—a few clothes and the bedroll he slept in as the partner robbed him.

Hannah places a hand on his forearm in sympathy and invitation. "Will you join us? Perhaps it is time for tea."

Harky is about to decline when a meaningful look from Hannah spurs Hans to add, "My wife is English, so I'm afraid tea means dry biscuits and hard cheese. But we've plenty, so do join us. Bring your gear."

Harky's gait as he crosses the cabin to fetch his pack is awkward. He walks with a slight forward roll, feet splayed, and oddly balanced. He steps across the prostrate mad-man and bends to lift his pack, but the lunatic's eyes spring open, and he screams. Swift as a trap, the knife sweeps up from the deck, slices across Harky's stomach and stabs down hard into his boot.

Harky pins the knife with one meaty paw and draws back the other, then pauses a moment as if thinking things over before striking. The lunatic's yell is cut off in midshriek.

The attack is over before Hannah can move. She watches, stunned, as Harky works the knife free of his foot, flips it away, and grasps the madman's head in both hands.

"Don't look, ma'am," is all he says. From the vise of his hands and the bunching of his shoulders she realizes he intends to break the madman's neck.

"Stop!" she cries, thrusting one hand forward. And again she is struck by the tender regard in Harky's eyes, a deep brimming within the irises that speaks of long suffering as he looks up at her.

"Don't kill him, Mr. Harky," she pleads. "If you kill him . . ." She starts to say, "You shall regret it," then says instead, "I must ask you not to do this."

Harky stares at her a moment, then slowly relaxes his grip and eases the unconscious man's head to the deck, kneels a moment, then rises.

"Guess we can tie him up or something." His tone is doubt-ful, and he looks more doubtful yet, as Hans and the other passengers burst into action, calling for the ship's crew to bring ropes and take the man away. He does nothing as the knifeman's arms and legs are lashed, nor does he assist dur-ing the melee as the captive is hoisted up the companionway and dragged away to confinement. He watches with what to Hannah seems great sadness.

Harky sighs, "He won't live long anyway." Meaning that in a land as rough as the territories, one so unhinged as the madman cannot escape a bullet indefinitely. Only reluctantly does he yield to her request that he open his knife-sliced shirt for inspection.

"We must see to your wounds," she insists, then gasps, not at the miracle that has seen Harky's wool shirt laid open with only a small, bloodless line across his stomach to show how close the blade passed, but at a welter of puckered scars criss-crossing his chest and belly.

Harky looks away, embarrassed, and mumbles, "The war." By fits and starts he reveals how at the age of fifteen, having already grown large on a diet of Texas beef and endless stacks of his mother's thick potato pancakes, he had run away to join the army of the Confederacy and fight for the South in the Civil War. During the fighting, no matter what tree or stone he had sought shelter behind, some part of his large body had protruded. Over four years of war, the slapping sting and burning irons of passing bullets had gouged a multitude of red furrows and grooves across his shoulders, neck, arms, breast, back, stomach, and buttocks. By the time he was nineteen, he had been wounded twenty times.

When Hannah kneels to draw the raveled gray sock from his foot, she is further shocked; there are toes missing and divots of flesh gone from ball to heel. Harky cannot bring himself to describe to a lady how an exploding canon shell at Gettysburg had blown him out of his boots and concussed his spine to such a degree that for the rest of the day, the night, and all of the next day he had lain deaf and paralyzed, unable to resist, as battlefield rats gnawed his feet. All he can do is finger the hole in his boot to show where the lunatic's blade pierced the gap where his toes had once been.

Harky breaks the awkward silence that follows by digging in his pack and saying, "I've got dried apples." When Hannah looks perplexed, he adds, "For tea?"

———————

By the end of the day when the ship comes to anchor, an affiliation has formed among the trio, with Hans and Hannah doing the bulk of the talking. Harky's answers are slow, and he offers little of himself, though it is clear from the way his gaze lingers on Hannah when he thinks she is not looking that he is much taken by her good manners and decorum. He seems content to sit in her company without speaking.

———————

That night in muted conversation in their bunk, Hans teases Hannah that she has a new admirer. She nestles under his arm and denies it, smiling. "He is . . . ," she says, feeling for a proper word, "my protector."

"But does he seem a bit sad to you?" she asks.

Hans fingers a knot in a deck beam above their bunk and thinks a moment before answering. "Yes, I suppose he does. But I've known others like him, old graybeards who fought in the war and have difficulty enjoying themselves. When I was a boy, an acquaintance of my grandfather grew so melancholy he killed himself by drinking lye."

Hannah thinks of the gun she glimpsed in Harky's pack

while he was digging out a replacement shirt and struggles for a moment to resolve the kindness in his eyes with his readiness to break a man's neck. It was a large gun, of the sort she has heard called a horse pistol, and it gleamed with the sheen of steel that has seen much handling. She wonders if Harky has ever contemplated suicide.

———————

Harky, wedged in his bedroll on deck between the mast and a locker holding fenders and mooring lines, is not thinking of suicide, though he has many times in the past. He thinks instead of the only woman he has ever lived with, puzzling over what it is in Hannah's manner that brings Marta Gutiérrez to mind. Like all of her people down in Mexico, Marta's eyes were brown, not gray like Hannah's, nor did she have Hannah's fine figure. Marta was built low and wide, more, as Harky liked to tease her, for holding her ground than for being admired. Marta would laugh and wrap herself around him at his teasing, claiming to be his *gordita*; he in turn was *popo*, for Popocatépetl, the largest volcano in her district, for both his size and a tendency toward sudden anger that had dogged him for years after the war.

Harky sighs to think of the day Marta asked him to leave. All her brother Alvaro had done was throw a stone at a dog, but the sound of its yelping was enough to send Harky into one of his red-eyed angers, and he had dislocated Alvaro's shoulder. Marta had not screamed or yelled or grown angry herself, but only placed a hand on his arm and told him that living with a volcano was no longer possible.

Harky groans and pulls the bedroll tighter. If he is not grateful that the wild angers have abated over the years, he is at least relieved, even if all that has been left in their place is an intermittent gray hollow. He is almost asleep when it comes to him that Hannah's hand on his arm had felt like Marta's.

———————

An improvement in the weather allows the passengers to emerge into the brisk air on deck. At fifty-eight degrees north, the days of early winter are short, and the captain of the lumber boat finds good anchorage during the dark hours in small bights and bays along the way. By the harsh light of a gas pressure lantern shining through a galley porthole, Hannah sits sideways on the bulwark every evening, writing in blue ink on the pages of her diary:

Voyaging seems endless, dear diary. So many miles by ship, trains, and boats have passed since England. I never imagined the world to be so large and I have a great deal of leisure to make my entries here, for time and miles pass slowly "under our keel," as the sailors say. Already the weather is less inclement as we make west toward the benign influence of the open sea, or so it has been explained to me. The captain spoke of a current that runs along this sea coast as far as the islands of Japan and brings with it warmer airs and waters from distant California. What a remarkable thought! I presume it is my English blood that contents me so to be aboard ships, which mode of transport I find particularly enriching in my current surrounds. Always there are beautiful peaks, cliffs, and islands as far as the eye can see in all directions along these waterways, which carry the most frightening names—Peril Straits, Murder Cove, and such. We have passed beyond the zone of icebergs and glaciers, which apparently approach the sea only from the fjords of the mainland. There are numerous whales and dolphins in these waters, and a crewman fishing a hand-line from the stern brought aboard a flatfish so immense that its delicate white flesh fed all aboard to bursting, and there remained yet half the carcass. Hans estimates the weight of the fish to be better than 200 pounds! There is something in this Alaska territory that makes one feel rich, for want of a better word, as if one has already struck gold or inevitably will, in spite of our troubles. Perhaps it is the sheer abundance of life—the whales, the great flocks of seabirds, the immense and copious fish—or the distances involved. Perhaps it is but a Romantic illusion inspired by the abundance of rugged and natural beauty, but I cannot help but be hopeful that my husband and I shall do well here.

On a wager, Harky pulls the anchor without assistance on the last morning before reaching Sitka, a task usually reserved for three crewmen. As Hannah and Hans watch, the Texan's coat stretches tight across the muscles of his back and shoulders as he swings the dripping iron flukes aboard. When Hannah claps and hurrahs, an unreserved grin splits his face, exposing stubbed teeth, spaced like fence posts across shrunken gums, and she is taken by the innocence of his delight in pleasing her. Harky holds the anchor out to her by the stock, as if presenting her with a steel flower, and makes a small, embarrassed bow.

Sitka presents a fine contrast to the gangster-led riot of the gold rush in Skagway. Neatly painted vessels, lined two and three abreast, fill the small harbor; and the finely shaped onion dome of an Orthodox church, rising white above the town, reminds Hannah of paintings she has seen of trim Baltic ports. There is a bustle along the waterfront as the lumber ship comes alongside the quay, with mooring lines being thrown to waiting hands, but none of the threatening disorder that introduced their arrival at Skagway. Hannah breathes deeply, feeling a relaxation of the concerns that bind her. There is hope and reassurance in the orderly discharge of the ship. The stevedores and longshoremen are roughly polite, and there is little cursing or spitting.

The promise of ease proves true. A room is available in a hotel near the harbor, with a bed, sheets, and space for their goods in a storeroom off the back. Harky offers to lend a hand as a porter before going off to find his own lodging. When Hans questions the security of the unlocked storeroom, the hotel clerk, looking serious as an owl in a large bow tie and thick glasses, stammers that "thieving ain't allowed in this hotel."

After settling in, Hans insists on treating Harky to dinner and drinks as thanks for his intervention with the knife-wielding lunatic. A café nearby offers a dinner of venison, clams from a tide flat south of town, and peas grown in the loamy garden of a local family. The café's flatware looks absurdly small in Harky's paw, as he makes slow, clumsy attempts to imitate Hannah's English style of holding her cutlery. Hans laughs and exaggerates the American style of attack, chewing and exclaiming simultaneously. Fearing he will starve, Hannah encourages Harky to abandon his attempt at decorum and resort to a more effective shoveling.

"I'm sure it requires efficient stoking to feed such a great boiler, Mr. Harky," she says. She laughs and mimics him by spooning a mound of peas into her mouth.

The Texan gives a small, unwieldy smile, embarrassed at his clumsiness, and says, "Harky, ma'am. Just Harky. I'd ruther you don't call me mister."

He has found lodging in a jury-rigged bunkhouse, where after a season of processing salmon along the waterfront, the manager of a cannery has laid off the factory's crew of Chinamen and foreigners and hired a bull-cook and housekeeper to convert the workers' quarters into a hostel to accommodate the town's swelling crowd of single men.

Hannah and Hans make love slowly that night, leery of squeaking springs and thin walls. For the first time since leaving Seattle, they sleep deeply and long.

FOUR

4 OCTOBER 1897

Our fortune has changed since arriving in Sitka. Thanks to Mr. Harky, Hans has found work as machinist in a mill sawing timber. My husband returns each night smelling of the pungent resin of spruce and cedar trees, and the wages paid are fine, too, enough to keep us in bed and board as well as contribute a bit to our "grubstake." Now it is mine to find employment as well, and I search each day. Hans objects, but not strenuously, as it is apparent it will require the efforts of both of us to finance another try for the goldfields.

This is a most pleasant settlement, with friendly inhabitants (Americans in general are more open to the inquiries and demands of strangers), and shows considerable influence of architecture and culture by its Russian founders. The Indians are greatly swayed by the advanced culture of whites, and many worship under the dominion of the Orthodox priests, who are much in evidence about the community in their long skirts and fierce beards.

———————

After the snow and iron-hard winds of Skagway, the climate of Sitka feels soft. Day after day, rain drizzles in from the south, obliterating the view of the sea. In such weather, everything seems somehow more private, and as Hannah wanders the muddy streets inquiring after work, she notes the curtains of the settlement are often drawn. Newcomers to the rainforest community distinguish themselves by pulling hats and hoods low across their eyes and navigating by landmarks at their feet, chins bent to their chests, while locals have the ability to ignore the rain and raise their faces as Hannah passes.

As she walks, groups of idling men watch her with the intensity of those who have not touched anyone they love for many years. Among the population of Sitka there are twenty men for every woman, and a number are prostitutes. She finds occasional company among mothers and wives, but for the most part she is alone, surrounded by men. After being propositioned by a drunk, she becomes reluctant to move about unaccompanied, particularly along the waterfront, where there are saloons and sad, painted hussies who wear too much perfume.

The winter-bound miners gather around these painted women the way cattle gather at a salt lick, drawn by urges and cravings that must substitute for the faraway arms and homes of those they have left behind. At night, transformed by the magic of alcohol into objects of affection, the tarts cause inebriated men to fight over the attentions of women whose names they do not know. Others brawl from frustration, with the bitter worms of jealousy that crawl through their skulls whispering that they, the forgotten and the luckless, are "sucking hind teat," while those already in the goldfields grow fabulously wealthy . . .

On the first of November, Hannah meets a Jewish shopkeeper who offers her employment. Uliah Witt is an elderly, bookish man, who came to Alaska with the intention of teaching music. He has little patience for the requirements of a merchant's ledgers and inventories, but is good at selling dry goods directly to Sitka's residents, all of whom had previously been accustomed to ordering from catalogs. He first sold his goods—wool shirts, heavy boots, tools, and cordage—from a tent erected on a platform of raw planks, but in an insight of genius, Uliah understood the rough Alaskans hungered as much for the fine things they had left behind as for practical metal and cloth. Business boomed when he began stocking and selling yard goods for window curtains, magazines and novels, sheet music, fine shoes, and furniture decorated with inlays and carvings. Soon he owned a large shed with shelves, which in time became a proper, painted store decorated with a false front, storerooms, a bay window peopled with mannequins, and a sign hanging from the eaves. His bookkeeping, however, remained a hodgepodge of scribblings on various tablets, unruly boxes of bills, and receipts pigeonholed into a rolltop desk. Instead of spending the time needed for proper accounting, Uliah Witt preferred teaching a handful of Indian children the intricacies of the violin.

"I write in a fine hand," Hannah tells him, "and know enough of accounts from my father to assist you. Selling ship's goods in England is surely not so different than dry goods in Alaska, is it?"

Uliah hires her more for her clear way of speaking and the elegant way she removes her gloves—which reminds him of his own wife, dead under the saber of a pogrom-mad Cossack in Poland when his name was still Wittgenstein—than from any desire to see order in his books.

Hannah draws a new ledger from Uliah's inventory, sharpens a group of pencils with Hans's shaving razor, and sets herself to the task of bringing order into Uliah's life. She enjoys aligning figures in neat rows down the cream-colored columns of the ledger, ordering the history of Mr. Witt's business into chronological files, and building a system to record the future. Soon Hannah starts adjusting the shelves of merchandise, rearranging stemware and bolts of fine cloth into a household department, separating the sewing needles from the saddles and shaving supplies.

Now, customers often greet Mrs. Nelson before addressing Uliah as they enter the store. The women of Sitka come by for bobbins of thread and squares of baking chocolate, for which they have no immediate need. A man sporting ten years' worth of whiskers purchases a razor. Uliah cleans out a storeroom, installs a bed and stove, and encourages the Nelsons to make it their home.

Hannah is reassured by the schedule of work—seven each morning until four in the afternoon, Monday through Saturday—and gives little consideration to the future. Although Hans speaks often of prospecting and gold, Hannah sings as she works, and the cold, hungry misery of Skagway fades until it is no more than a past entry in her journal. Winter comes down from the north, pushing all thoughts of spring back into the purple shadows, and jeweled feathers of snow drift quietly down from the pearly skies.

Each morning Hans and Harky walk by lantern light to a cobbled beach north of town, where a small launch gathers the sawmill crew for a short run across the water to a camp established on one of the humpbacked islands that guard Sitka Sound from the sea. They carry their lunches in lidded tin buckets and make coffee in a pot hung over a fire of cedar scraps. Some days Harky jokes quietly with Hans as they linger over hand-rolled cigarettes while waiting for the launch to return them to town. Other times he is sullen and stares at the ground. On those silent days, the Texan works harder than any three men, hefting and poling the heavy logs and cants of lumber about with a furious energy. At the end of every day their hands are as black and rough from hardened sap as those of Negro field hands, until an Indian woman explains to Hannah how a bit of butter used as soap will cut the resin from the men's hands. When Harky sees how well this works, he exclaims, "I'll be damned!"—then turns red and stutters his regret at cursing in front of a lady.

Hannah is tempted to attend church services on occasion, but the lingering tenets of the Church of England leave her uncomfortable among Lutherans and Baptists. Hans declines to join her, preferring instead to stop by a bar for a discussion of the future with other idling gold hounds, in an endless exchange of opinions on the virtues of placer versus hard rock mining. Harky sometimes joins him but says little as he attends to his beer.

By January it has become the Sabbath habit of the Nelsons to part company after luncheon, with Hans setting course for the saloons and Hannah joining Mr. Witt for an evening of music. Uliah owns a cello, a violin, and a piano and plays all three. For him, music takes the place of religion. Early in life, he had studied the different musics of the world to see what they might have to say about the riddle of humanity's purpose, but before solving the riddle, he had seen God take away some, but not all, of his hearing, sealing off just enough of the high notes and finer tones to prevent him from reaching a level of ability sufficient to satisfy his teachers. They encouraged him to take up the Talmud instead. Declining, he continues to play out of avocation and habit.

By frontier standards, his playing is virtuoso, and it thrills Hannah to sit by the stove in his apartment, listening as the crackle and pop of burning wood add counterpoint to his rhythms. He plays sparely, saving notes like bright dimes until he has a dollar to spend, then paying them out in delicate silver streams.

For Hannah, who plays no musical instruments, to hear the cry and sob of strings under Mr. Witt's fingers here on the ragged border of the wilderness seems a miracle. Afterward, she sometimes walks along the shore in the last, soft light of evening, then returns to the cabin, where under the spell of the evening and the music, she finds herself overwhelmed with contentment, which she persuades herself is a symptom of love for Hans, who wonders at the ardor with which she mingles herself into his warmth, under the covers, throughout the night.

Dear Diary,

The newspaper carries word of a terrible avalanche of snow on the Chilkoot Pass above Skagway that has killed more than sixty men, with many others missing in the chaos. Thank you, God, that my husband and I are not in that terrible place. Boats come weekly bearing men defeated by the winter of the interior. Often they are missing fingers or ears and wear the black marks of frost on their faces. There are natural baths of hot springs near Sitka, which Mr. Witt says are heated by volcanic action deep within the earth. These hot springs are very popular in the treatment of the miners' chilblains and rheumatisms.

Wintering in Sitka is delightful, and I sometimes think to stay here, but Hans's stubborn Norwegian blood will never allow him to willingly abandon the dream of growing rich on gold. There may be little choice, however: Our savings grow slowly, even as the cost of the goods necessary to enter the Klondike continue to rise. A small keg of common nails now costs eighty dollars!

"You keep a diary, Mrs. Nelson?"

Hannah sits in a chair by the store window for the better light, writing between customers. She looks up at Uliah as he speaks and raises her voice in answer.

"I do, Mr. Witt."

Uliah smiles and begins to poke at the order of goods on a shelf. "And what do you write? Stories of love, eh? Your adventures?"

Hannah blushes. She often feels the urge to write of those things, but always imagines others reading her words someday and edits for good effect, avoiding passages she fears to be too revelatory. Mr. Witt's question unsteadies her in a pleasant way; she has never heard a man mention love so easily. She knows Hans, if pressed for some slight reassurance of his love, would look out the nearest window and say, "ah," in a distracted fashion.

"Just observations, Mr. Witt. A record of my thoughts, events, that sort of thing."

"Ah, well. Surely love is the only thing truly worth writing about, don't you think, Mrs. Nelson?"

Hannah, unsure of his meaning or how to respond, toys with the place-marking ribbon that hangs from the spine of her journal, then looks up questioningly.

Uliah continues. "Love is certainly the rarest thing, yes? Everyone has experience with friends, emotions, work, what you call 'that sort of thing.' So one diary is much the same as the next. But a record of love, that's an important thing to leave the world, do you see?"

Hannah thinks then answers. "But surely love is a common subject of diaries all over the world? After all, everyone falls in love sometime, and most marry sooner or later."

"Yes, yes. I was married myself once, a long time ago. And women all over the world write pages and pages of love in their diaries, I'm sure. But do they really know what is love? Or do they write simply hoping for love?" Uliah shakes his head, then adds, "How many of us ever really know what love is?"

Something in the question discomfits Hannah, and she answers to dispel her own doubts. "Well, we marry out of love. It comes naturally, doesn't it, when you meet and join with the right person?"

"Marriage is common, certainly. But I'm afraid that is more often motivated by business, or simple biology. No, to see one person truly loving another, that is the rarest of things."

"Whatever do you mean, Mr. Witt?" Hannah is not sure she wants this conversation.

Uliah raises his hands, palms out in a calming gesture. "Please don't misunderstand me, Mrs. Nelson. When I say business and biology, I mean nothing so harsh as that sounds. After all, that is the way God made us. Women need security. They want to have homes, have children." He cups his hands together as if holding something delicate. "They build nests and hope to fill them with love."

"And men? Surely men hope for love as well."

"Yes, yes, but we are more . . ." He swirls his hands about and gropes for the right phrase. "Men are more driven, somehow. They build the nest to get the girl, not for want of a nest. That's what all this chasing after gold is about, running crazy to get rich.

"You see the rich man, the man with money, a nice home, nice things. He has a beautiful wife. You think, 'Aha! I will get rich and have a beautiful wife, make some children.' So a man goes insane, runs away to the Yukon or something, all because he believes, without thinking properly, that if he is good at some business, his biology will win and his lineage will continue. Do you see?"

"I believe I understand your meaning. I understand, but do not completely agree. Surely you loved your wife, Mr. Witt?"

Uliah lifts his shoulders. "Oh, there was great affection between us. A wonderful woman. And I am sure we could have come to love each other truly if . . ." He shrugs again and clasps his hands together, sighing. "But she died before we had time to learn how. Pity, because we had the wonderful example of her parents to follow, a love like I have never seen."

Hannah closes her journal, looks up at Uliah, and leans forward in her chair.

"They were old when we married. Her mother was a gross creature, fat and with marks on her face. I almost did not marry her, because they say you have only to look at the mother to see your future wife. But I couldn't believe the beautiful girl I was marrying could ever become old or ugly." He laughs, indicating his own stooped, aging body. "Nor did I believe that I could become as I am now. So we married."

Hannah asks, "And her parents?"

A winsome smile curls the corners of his mouth. "Ah, it was something to see. Two old people, she so thick and indelicate, he all spots and wrinkles. In the fifth year of our marriage, my wife's mother became ill. Sick in her mind, addled, and daft. Never knew her own family anymore, just sat and mumbled all day in a chair. And do you know, my wife's father brought her flowers every day and sat with her, holding her hand and reminding her of all that they had shared, their children, how they used to dance when they were young.

"And that, Mrs. Nelson, is love. Because there was nothing in it for him and never would be again. She didn't even know he was there, and there was no chance she would ever offer him solace as he grew old, because her spirit was already gone. But he gave himself every day to whatever slim opportunity there might be that he could offer her one more moment of comfort and love."

Hannah feels her eyes grow damp and a knot form in her

breath. When she relays the story to Hans over dinner that night, he looks puzzled for a moment, then asks if there is more stew.

———————

Harky comes from the bars one February night and knocks at the door to the Nelsons' room. There is drink on his breath, and after removing his hat when Hannah answers, he asks for Hans. The men hold a mumbled conversation in the darkness outside the door, after which Hans comes back inside for his coat.

"I'll be out for a while," he says. He has the air of a conspirator and leaves without looking at Hannah. She listens, wondering, to the crunch of their boots in the snow diminishing in the direction of the waterfront.

Outside the saloon, a sign on the door disabuses Indians and Chinamen of welcome. When Harky and Hans enter, the air is thick with the smell of men smoking and drinking. The Texan holds two fingers aloft to signal a barman with the huge, tattooed arms of a blacksmith. As the bartender taps beer into two mugs Harky's eyes roam beneath the brim of his hat. Hans, too, inspects the crowd of darkly clad customers before taking a gulp of beer. The customers, all male, are uniformly engaged in the tasks of a frontier saloon; card games are being played out on green felt tables; knots of men smoke and kibitz over billiards; others nod, stuporous with drink.

"Do you see him?" asks Hans. Harky nods toward a table in the back, where a slim, hatless man waves a hand in their direction. The stranger has wide-set eyes that goggle high atop his face, occasionally looking in separate directions, giving him the appearance of a bird constantly wary of attack from above.

Harky leads the way through the crowd, parting the throng like a ship. Hans follows close behind.

The stranger does not rise, but says to Harky, while holding out a hand to Hans, "I wasn't sure you was coming back." Then to Nelson, "The name's Dutch."

Hans shakes the proffered hand, introduces himself before sitting. There is a long silence that is more comfortable for Harky and Hans than for the Dutchman, who is voluble by nature and twitches with impatience as they both size him up.

"Harky tell you about me, did he, Mr. Nelson?" asks Dutch, leaning forward on his elbows, toying with an empty mug.

Hans takes a drink of beer and swallows before replying. "He said you're looking for partners. That you might know something could do us all some good."

Dutch gives a vigorous nod. "Yea. Yea, I guess we're all in the same boat, huh? Damn Mounties won't let a fellow into their goddamn precious country unless he's already rich, huh? Fuck 'em, I says. Fuck 'em."

Harky curls his hands around his mug, covering it, and says, "Tell Hans what you told me."

Dutch tilts his head back, then wipes his nose between two fingers as if to signal a decision made. His chair chalks against the floor as he pushes it back, reaching into his coat. Each gesture is freighted with drama. Removing a spent twelve-bore shotgun shell stoppered with a whittle of wood and wrapped in a soiled handkerchief, he opens it with a flourish, spreads the rag out flat, and holds the shell above the table, tapping at the lip with a nicotine-colored finger. Not lead shot, but flakes and speckles of flat, dull sand spill out, the color of gold.

"That's what I mean," says the Dutchman, indicating the spoonful of gold dust with a thrust of his chin. "Don't have to go to some damn foreign country, not when there's good American gold to be had." He leans back in his chair, triumphant.

Hans sits openmouthed. Harky looks over his shoulder at the crowd, then reaches out and flips the edge of the handkerchief over the gold to hide it.

Hans downs the remains of his beer and raises the empty glass, waving it at the bartender and holding up three fingers. Dutch twists the handkerchief into a knot around the gold and stuffs it into his breast pocket. His head wobbles on his neck, and he makes a snorting noise, like a pig attempting to giggle. No one says anything as the bartender rattles three fresh mugs down, scoops up the empties, and palms the silver coin Hans lays in his hand.

After they are alone again Hans says, "Well, it looks like you've done all right for yourself. What do you want with us?"

Dutch bobs his head, agreeing, then holds a finger up in front of his face. "That's placer gold. Takes a lot of shoveling and digging to sort out placer. Now, I ain't got the money just yet for an outfit and need partners to help with the work. My friend Harky here"—he gestures at the Texan—"he tells me you and him are outfitted, but the damn Mounties give you the boot anyhow, just like they done me. Well, I say Canada can go to hell. I don't need to go all the way up and down the Yukon, scratching after everybody else's leftovers. There's gold right here in Alaska, too."

"And you've got it found? Is that what you're telling me?" asked Hans.

"Yep. Just need the partners and outfit to go get it. It's

way-the-hell-and-gone off up the country. I don't want to go off alone and get killed by some Indian or something. And besides, just look at him"—he indicates Harky, who has sat quietly through it all. "Does that man look like he can work? I'll say! We'll run a ton of sand a day, maybe two, and us'll have a dozen fruit jars full of color apiece by next fall. My claim, you fellows' outfit, and we split even all around. How's that sound?"

Hans appraises the slipshod character before him, then considers the slender condition of his own badly whittled grub-stake. He has seen lynx trappers flutter a feather on a string over a trap to bring the curious, wary cats within range of the steel jaws, and he feels the golden gleam luring him in much the same fashion—unavoidably, but slowly and with great suspicion.

"I've a wife," he says. ———

"All the better. Can she cook and keep care of a camp? That'd free men up for working, if laundering and such is done for 'em."

Hans nods proudly. "She's a good wife."

The three lean closer together, heads nearly touching, and switch to whiskey to signify the advance from just talking to partnership. Dutch is cagey at first, but drink loosens his tongue, and he cannot hold secrets long. Two hundred miles to the north, the sands of Lituya Bay sparkle and flash with gold. It lies in buttery ribbons wherever there is bedrock under the beach, and all a fellow has to do is remove the overburden of sand and gravel and sluice the gold into a bucket.

When pressed for details on his discovery—how long was he there? How much gold did he recover? Has he filed a claim in his name?—Dutch grows vague, closing his eyes and waving a hand in front of his face, saying only, "That's where it's at, all we need do is go get it."

A deal is struck. Hans, Hannah, and Harky will contribute tools, supplies, money, and labor. Dutch will lead the way. A boat must be hired to ferry them and their gear the considerable distance to Lituya Bay, which lies north of Cape Spencer and is exposed to the full fury of the gulf. In a month, the grip of winter will begin to ease and the cycle of storms and gales that rip the cold, angry seas abate. The prospectors agree; departure is set for the Ides of March, or as soon thereafter as the weather will allow.

27 February 1898

Thus far we have been unable to employ a ship to transport us north to Lituya Bay when spring arrives. The seamen are nervous about the Gulf of Alaska for its reputed terrible seas and weather, with many particularly superstitious of Lituya Bay. Those willing to make the journey at all offer prices for charter that are outlandish. Hans is beside himself, caught as we are in this cycle of rising costs, and becomes difficult when I suggest any alternative to prospecting.

I must admit to "gold fever" myself, after seeing Dutch's display of nuggets; there is an allure in that shining metal that is somehow beyond the regard for wealth. Little but gold itself would tempt anyone into a business venture with one of character so odd as that of the Dutchman.

Hans sits slumped, twirling his hat listlessly on the upraised fingers of one hand, fired from the saw job for failing to grease the bearings in the mill. Things overheated and seized tight, shutting the entire operation down. The loss of wages has alienated the other workers from Hans, with the exception of Harky, who for reasons understood by no one, laughs out loud as the crew boards the launch back to town. After landing, Harky and Hans set course for an afternoon at the saloon.

"Ma always said the boldest fighting cock was still just a chicken, Hans."

Harky's meaning escapes Hans, who is intent on his brooding. Harky is as intently good-hearted and for one usually so truculent, quite wordy.

"What do you really think of Dutch, anyway? That was nice of your missus to put up dinner for us all last night. I ain't had fried chicken in a long time. Just get venison every night at the bunkhouse."

Hans examines the muddy toe of one boot. "Gas and feathers, mostly. But the gold is real enough. Problem's just getting up there to get it."

Dutch had barked and chatted without ceasing all through the meal, spinning yarns of sailing the South Seas and the Sandwich Islands, talking about a wife and kids back home waiting for him to "bring home the bacon." At various times he claimed to be from Ohio, California, and Oregon, with careers as a painter, a cowboy, and the owner of a race horse.

Harky shook his shaggy head slowly and smiled, as if considering the humor in Dutch's folly. "Closest he ever come to the South Sea is that ugly whore from Owyhee what works at the Bucket-o'-Blood."

"Let him rustle us up a boat. Then he can show us what a sailor he is," says Hans.

Three nights later, Harky bangs on their door with the news that Dutch has done exactly that.

FIVE

The next morning Dutch lopes ahead of Hans and Harky as they walk along the shore searching among the masts and hulls of the crowded harbor for a particular rig, much as a man scans a crowd for a face he knows only by description. A fine breeze scatters the sun's reflection into diamond dust across the water and there is the warm, salty smell of seaweed in the air.

Dutch walks with a peculiar bent-kneed stride, pausing often to point excitedly at one boat, then another, looking back over his shoulder at the men following behind. Harky steps carefully from stone to stone, balancing awkwardly on his scarred, odd-numbered toes.

"He said it was a white hull, cutter rigged. Maybe that's it there, that handsome one," says Dutch. Unclear as to the details of a cutter's design, he knows only that the word sounds fast, and points to a well-kept sloop with the slim lines and graceful shear of an ocean dancer.

Hans shakes his head and points beyond the sloop to a

plug-shaped hull with a cobbled rig. Bits of canvas tacked to the cabin top tell of humdrum efforts to stop random leaks. The only neat thing about the vessel is the lettering across the stern, which gives the name of the boat as the *Tara Keane*.

"There's your cutter. That's a sloop you're pointing at," and under his breath mutters, "If it wasn't for the gold . . ."

Harky shrugs, says, "Someone's aboard," then points at a dinghy bobbing astern of the cutter on a rope. Dutch cups his hands to his mouth and shouts a long, "Hello, the cutter!" as if he were the admiral of a fleet signaling a man-o'-war. After a moment the cutter rocks slightly and a sliding hatch is thrown back.

The face that emerges is bleary-eyed and tousled. Michael Severts had been three sheets to the wind the night before when he met Dutch in a saloon and the two had bragged and told yarns deep into a bottle of whiskey. By the time a second bottle was breached, Dutch was playing rich man with his shotshell of gold and offering Severts a full share in the partnership in exchange for the contribution of his boat, which Severts described as the "slickest kind of cutter, built of Port Orford cedar and stout live oak." This morning, his memory of the arrangement is vague.

Severts gives a brief wave and disappears below deck for a moment, then emerges clad in wrinkled denim pants and a sweater blown out at the elbows. He looks around at the day, which is unseasonably warm and seductively bright, before climbing into the dinghy without hat, coat, or gloves. As he rows, the oars dip and shine in unison. When he comes alongshore, he pulls and backs expertly, turning the tender sideways to nudge lightly against the bank.

In spite of the hangover that throbs between his eyes, Severts balances neatly against the rocking of the dinghy, reaches for the bow line, and steps over the side. He is twenty-seven years old, athletically slender and wide across the shoulders, with curly, blue black hair that needs cutting. The sun glints on a peppering of fine gray at his temples. He is clean-shaven, but his face and chin are darkly shadowed for want of a recent razor.

Hans feels a worm of doubt as Michael steps toward the waiting trio, a slight, unnamed hostility of which he is only vaguely aware. If asked to explain the source of his distrust, Hans would claim to be a natural judge of character. But the true cause of his unease is this: Michael Severts is beautiful.

Blue eyes paled from staring into fires of Irish peat look out from an open and friendly face. Michael's nose is straight, finely proportioned, and his features perfectly balanced. His lips are full and red as a girl's, and there is a slight, smiling lift to one corner of his mouth that implies a scoundrel's charming willingness to laugh at himself. The only imperfection in his appearance is a tendency to hold one shoulder a bit higher than the other and a slight cock to his head, the result of a back injury that has plagued him since an accident with a jumpy cart horse during his early years. Rather than detract from his looks, the imperfect stance serves only to give him a slight air of vulnerability, which makes women want to draw him to their breast.

The sum of his looks and movements is such that he draws the attention of women wherever he goes, and men find themselves buying him drinks. Hans, having the experience of his own good looks, has some understanding of humanity's

ever-willingness to impute unlikely virtues to the attractive.
And it is this that imparts a small cock of suspicion to his
eyebrows as he looks the mariner over.

Michael is equally cautious. He celebrated Dutch's possession of gold because he has none of his own and nights are for
fun and whiskey. The drunken idea of partnering with the
odd Dutchman was simply bar talk, a way to keep the drinks
flowing. Now the uneven fellow is here shouting, accompanied by a glowering giant and a man giving Michael the skep-
tical up-and-down appraisal of a policeman.

Dutch launches in, oblivious to the awkward silence,
pumping furiously at Severts's hand, saying, "Hiya there,
Captain," and "Meet yer new partners." Turning to the others, he pulls them forward by their sleeves. "Harky, Hans, this
here's Michael, fellow I was tellin' you about."

Hans shakes hands briefly, then stands with his arms
crossed, unspeaking.

Dutch points at Michael's boat. "There she is, there's the
boat," inaccurately parroting what he remembers of Michael's
description. "She's the slickest kind o' cutter, all orchard cedar."

Harky squints at the anchored cutter with the uneasy eyes
of a landsman, rubs his nose, and says with succinct doubt,
"Sorta small."

Like any good sailor, Michael bristles to the defense of his
ship, forgetting for a moment his intention to scuttle any
partnership agreement. "Forty-two feet. Plenty of boat. Got
me here all the way from Oregon, didn't she? In good hands,
she'll do whatever is needed."

"And you're the good hands, are you?" asks Hans. "Think
that boat'll get us and all our gear up the coast?"

"She'll do anything I ask her," replies Michael, forgetting in the senseless allegiance all boat owners feel for the imagined, feminine qualities of indifferent canvas and wood how a dozen nights of storm-inspired terror and exhaustion can make any vessel seem wildly inadequate.

"And you?" asks Hans, lifting one eyebrow. "What is it makes you such a sailor?"

Michael pauses at the question, considering if he wants to justify himself to this stranger, then shrugs, too hungover for the work of taking offense. "Learned the trade young on packets between Ireland and Scotland. Always figured if a man can follow the stars in the North Sea, he can sail anywhere. It's not so different here."

"How's about we take a look aboard?" asks Dutch, eager to pose with his hand on the tiller.

Michael stalls. He is not eager to have this gang see the firm young woman—perhaps a tad too young—whose name he cannot remember, and who sleeps this morning beneath his blankets.

"Well, it's a bit of a mess now. I've got the head off the engine. The valves, you know."

Michael looks pointedly from Harky to the small dinghy, as if measuring his great bulk against the freeboard of the punt.

"Maybe it'd be better if I get her cleaned up and move in to the dock. Save ferrying back and forth in the small boat."

Harky nods, imagining the wet rush of the delicate rowboat overturning. He has not swum since the Yankees turned General Hammond's flank at Franklin's Ford, and his tattered company was forced to swim for their lives, with the whip-crack and whine of bullets about their heads and the salt taste of blood in the water.

"Tomorrow then?" asks Hans.

There is agreement all around.

———————

Michael Severts sits alone in the cockpit of the *Tara Keane* over early morning tea and resolves firmly to decline incorporation into the company of miners. He is unafraid of hard work and enjoys well enough the fantasy of gold, but the prospect of summering far up the coast in some back bay, without the conviviality of women or whiskey is not attractive. He takes a last decisive swig at his mug and goes forward to haul the anchor. As Harky and Dutch lead the way to the dock, seaweed scattered along the edge of the tide glows in the morning sun. Hans and Hannah come behind, her arm linked through his on the dew-slicked stones. Everything is hazed in radiant amber light, coloring their faces warm and ruddy. Along the horizon, anvil-shaped clouds billow and swell like anemones on the ocean bottom. The air is cool in the shadows, warm in the light, and the long, buzzing trill of a varied thrush calls heed to the imminence of spring.

Hannah wears a waist-length jacket over a white blouse of ribbed cotton and a skirt of light wool. Her hair, gleaming from the hundred brush strokes it receives every morning, catches Michael's eye as he coasts the *Tara Keane* into the pier under jib alone. When close by the pier, he eases a sheet and throws the tiller hard over, and the cutter spins slowly round, backing the jib to take all way off the boat. The dinghy on its tow rope bumps against the broad transom as *Tara* stalls, stops, and begins to move broadside, slowly nudging into the pier as the tide sweeping along the beach eases her into place. His neat exhibition of seamanship brings a smile to Hannah's face, but passes without remark from the others.

Michael steps from deck to dock and passes a breast line round a cleat, securing the boat to the pier. Something stirs through Hannah's veins at the lithe motion with which he bends to the line. She holds out a gloved hand as Hans introduces her. "Mrs. Nelson, my wife," Hans says.

"Pleased, Mrs. Nelson." Michael takes her hand briefly, squeezing lightly without shaking. There is a flutter under Hannah's breastbone at the Irishman's full, dark eyelashes. Michael's decision to beg out of the deal wavers as he takes in the slope of Hannah's bosom, her creamy skin and shining eyes.

Michael invites them aboard, reaching out to Hannah, who gathers her skirt in one hand before taking his offer with the other. The deck tilts and heels under Harky's weight as he clambers across, and he has to grab at a shroud for balance. Surprised at the motion, Dutch, too, is awkward, and teeters on the pier like a reluctant hound.

Once aboard, the miners stand stiffly, as if attending a party where they are unsure of their welcome. But Hannah shields her eyes and looks about at the details of *Tara Keane*'s rigging. The child of a chandler, she has an understanding of the qualities that make a ship and takes note of its strengths and shortcomings.

She notes a stretch of the bulwarks has been recently replaced, in a neat, workmanlike job that is in conflict with the general air of patch-and-promise that dominates the boat. The standing rigging is done up neatly, with splices and eyes well served with tarred twine, but the deck seams show crawled caulking that has been touched up rudely with pitch.

Michael watches as Hannah takes inventory. He sees the approval in her eyes as she fingers a line properly coiled and hung from a belaying pin and bends down to give the bulwark repair an approving pat. The curve of her waist enthralls him.

Hans paces the deck as if measuring it for cargo. Dutch peers about with what he assumes to be a sea dog's squint. Harky perches gently on the low cabin top and looks concerned.

Hannah turns to Michael. "Who is she named for? Tara Keane is an Irish name, isn't it?"

Michael is pleased by Hannah's use of the feminine. The others—landsmen, obviously—are untouched by the rhythm of the oceans and refer to his boat as it.

"Aye. It's my mother's name, Tara. She was Keane before she married Francis Severts. We're from Inishbofin, a bit of rock off the west coast of Ireland."

"A salute to your mother, hey Michael?" asks Dutch. He looks to Hannah as he continues. "The Irish always love their mothers, don't they, Mrs. Nelson?"

"I'm sure they do, Dutch."

Severts holds Hannah's gaze for a long pause, breathes a bit deeper, and his brogue grows thicker as he continues. "It's an Irish name, but me mother is half English. Her own mother being from Coventry, that is." His head cocks a degree to the left, and he stares at Hannah without blinking, as if waiting for a response to this miscegenation. Receiving none, he adds, "And that gives me own blood a pint of English, doesn't it?"

He cocks a crooked grin. "I wrote her that I'd named a boat for her. Thought that might please her." Then he kicks with his toe at a shaving on the deck. "Might've exaggerated some of this tub's qualities a bit, I guess." He leaves out that he writes her often, long letters full of fantastic promises to return home rich and pry his mother from the grip of his father, a violent, illiterate man who suffers a permanent hunch upon his back.

The residents of Inishboffin had been used to seeing the faces of Tara Keane and her children decorated with welts and bruises, and it had been as much to escape the ravaging of their father as it was to earn their own way in the world that Michael and his brother had run for America. But Liam soon grew pale with homesickness and returned, while Michael stayed on, working his way across the country as far as Oregon, where he found himself tending bar when news of the gold rush broke loose. And when word came to Michael that an outraged husband had been seen buying a fresh box of shotgun shells, he briefly regretted entertaining the saloon's patrons with the quip, "What's another slice off a cut loaf?" That had so deeply bruised the cuckolded fellow, that Michael quickly allowed the threat of buckshot and the promise of gold to propel him out of Portland in search of a way north. Two days later, at the mouth of the Columbia River, a few dollars and a dollop of charm had won him possession of the long-neglected cutter upon whose deck they now stand.

He goes on to explain, "She was wasting away with moss on her topsides when I found her. I fix a bit here and there as we go, but it's a long race to the finish."

Harky thinks for a moment that Michael means his mother was growing mossy and old, then realizes his error and marvels at the foreign language of sailors.

"Could we see below, Mr. Severts?" asks Hannah.

Michael leads the way, sliding back a hatch over the companionway. "Watch the ladder. There's a hand grip to port here, if you need it."

Belowdecks, *Tara* is spartan and neat, with settees that double as berths to port and starboard in a main salon. There is another, wider berth forward over lockers and chests. A stove squats in the middle of the cabin, bolted to a sole of unpainted pine. Dishcloths and socks hang drying from a line above the stovepipe, which runs sideways beneath the overhead to exit through a portlight. Hans must duck to clear the roof beams as he looks into the forepeak, and Harky stands immobilized, afraid to move. Everything smells of cooking, kerosene, and dampness. When Hannah opens a cupboard, the odor of mildew leaps out.

Michael pulls aside a tarp, revealing a cast-iron engine. "A two-cylinder, twelve-horsepower Hundsted," he says proudly. "Feeds on petrol or oil."

Picking up a crank, he demonstrates the starting procedure, which is to fiddle with a gas pressure torch until it is burning well, then apply the flame to a glow-plug in the cylinder head until it glows cherry red. The heavy flywheel is turned over with a bar and screw until a piston is at its apogee, after which a fuel valve is opened, the flywheel kicked over, and the hopeful operator leaps back out of harm's way—a process repeated over and over until with luck and the proper combination of mass, motion, heat, and compression, the Hundsted roars into action. A grooved wheel on the engine rotates a belt pulleyed to the inboard end of the propeller shaft.

"And she has the advantage of being able to reverse

her propulsion," says Michael, demonstrating how this is achieved by removing the drive belt, twisting it into a figure eight, and reinstalling it. "It can be done with the engine running, but you best be a regular pickpocket with your fingers, or you might come up short one or two."

There is a long discussion of equipment and stowage, stores and supplies, and the details involved in mining. Dutch again draws the gold from his pocket, passing it from hand to hand for all to marvel at its density. Michael and Hannah do not look at one another, yet each is keenly aware of the other's presence. It is Hans that brings the talk back to business.

"Even shares all around, then?" he asks Michael. "Your boat, our gear, Dutch's gold, and Harky's back?"

Michael hesitates before answering; there is the long journey to consider, then a summer of work and isolation. On the other hand, there is Hannah, who stands with her arms crossed as she waits for him to answer, running one hand from her shoulder to her forearm in a gesture so unconsciously sensuous and feminine that he imagines an intimate invitation in her voice when she entreats him, "Please join us, Mr. Severts. We will be partners."

And he answers, "Yes, I'll do it."

There are handshakes all around to seal the company's bargain. Michael and Hans lay out modest plans to remodel the cabin's interior to maximize storage space and allow the heavier goods—chains, nails, tools, and canned goods—to be stored low in the hull, thus increasing the stability of the boat when fully loaded. Hannah and Harky stay with their jobs, adding what cash they can to the kitty.

———————

Hannah slips from beneath the blankets in the dark, leaving the warmth of her sleeping husband behind, rising early in pursuit of the quiet moments she has come to value for writing in her journal. Slipping her feet into felt boot liners that double as slippers, she feeds a bolt of wood to the stove, muffling the noise as best she can, then opens the flue and damper. Holding her hands to the warmth, she moves a kettle from its trivet to the iron stove top when the fire begins to crackle. While she waits for the water to boil, she watches a full, late-rising moon clear the peaks above town, changing from orange to silver as it goes. The tea is a rough leaf from China and comes pressed hard in the shape of a book. It is bitter, full of stems, and much preferred by the Asian cannery workers over the loose Ceylon or Indian tea with which Hannah was familiar in England. That heady, delicious brew is unavailable in Sitka, as what little arrives in Alaska is quickly shipped off to the Yukon, where Canadian prospectors are willing to pay half its weight in gold.

After steeping and sweetening the tea, Hannah glances out the window, takes a sip, then sits to write in her journal. She writes slowly, as if considering carefully what she wants to say, and pauses often to watch the first new white light of morning rise along the half ring of mountains that guard Sitka's eastern flank. With the sun's rising, the bright tenor of a bell calls faintly but clearly to worshippers making their way to services beneath the onion-domed spire of the Orthodox church.

Good Friday

We leave in two days. Much of our cargo has now been packed and stowed aboard, with the exception of our clothes, dishes, a few mechanical items for which Hans still searches, and what fresh meats we will take. All have been quite busy shopping and stowing, striking out endless items on endless lists. I feel a good deal of trepidation, but at the same time, what excitement! I shall miss Mr. Witt, who has been most invaluable in our preparations. If not for him, I would have forgotten the need for a Dutch oven and garden seeds! The men think only of mining and tools, thus, obtaining a thorough supply of all other goods is left to me.

Mr. Witt makes much of the date of our departure, speaking of Passover and Easter as a time of transition, the coming of light and rebirth, and so on. I pray our departure date is as auspicious as Mr. Witt claims. The weather seems much gentler now, and daylight extends itself rapidly. We gain seven minutes of sun each day, three-quarters of an hour every week! Everything in these northern latitudes seems expansive or extreme. There is little subtlety in nature here.

Our new captain seems a splendid choice! He seems quite a physical man.

———

Late in the afternoon, after the turn of the tide on Easter Sunday, the mainsail rumbles aloft on its halyard. The billowing canvas runs rampant, slapping at the wind with a sound like tumbling boulders, and Michael hauls on the mainsheet. The sail fills, forming a perfect, arching belly, and *Tara* immediately heels, surging forward until Michael tugs at the helm to turn downwind. As the boat gains speed, Hannah's heart lifts at the rush and gurgle of water building around the bow, and she sees Michael smiling, a great, broad grin that seems to infect all the crew. They point, laugh, and shout as Michael instructs Hans and Harky in setting the jib. Dutch assists with random yells of "Ahoy!" and "Heave away!"

Michael eases the sails, paying out jib and main sheets with both hands as he steers with one foot, controlling the power of the thundering sails with the casual delight of a teamster reining a span of spirited, well-trained horses. Sitka Sound is nearly flat, with only a low swell running in from the southwest; perfect conditions for sailing. *Tara* roars along with a bone in her teeth, foam hissing from her bow.

Michael works at a chart with parallel rules and dividers, plotting a course that will clear a scattering of rocks and small islands. The torn edge of the tree line above Sitka recedes quickly, becoming a smooth line. As *Tara* pulls away, the high peaks along the spine of Baranof Island climb into view and a full deluge of rare, high-latitude sunlight breaks over the sea in a variety of precious colors and shades.

Day passes into evening, and the hue of the water grows deeper and stronger. Gulls maneuver, rising and falling in *Tara*'s wake. Hannah's chestnut hair is loose in the wind, lifting in waves that curl about her face, and each of the men aboard is, in his moment, stricken by her beauty.

Michael looks around at the others, then asks Hannah to take the helm while he goes below to rummage for a cap. Pausing in the companionway, he watches her eyes grow large at the feel of the tiller, which trembles from the flow of the rudder through the water. She cries out, laughing, "It's like holding the wind in your hands."

Tara runs perfectly west into the evening sun, pushed along by the wind and the tide. Hannah goes below to build sandwiches of salt ham and cheese for the crew, and listens, swaying and slicing in time with the roll of the boat, to the chuckle of passing water as she works.

The sandwiches are passed around. The wind holds steady. On a low sandy island to starboard a distant cloud of gulls flowers tentatively aloft at the passing of a young eagle and settles again to form a line of white that could be a late-spring snowdrift or a dune of fine sand.

In the distance stands a mountain as symmetrical as if it had been turned on a potter's wheel, with volcanic shoulders that are even in all directions and a smooth crown. Beyond it lie a number of lower broken peaks.

"Mount Edgecombe," Michael murmurs, making an adjustment to the ship's heading to swing the bow to bear on the inactive volcano. Pointing to an abrupt-sided island rising from the sea at the base of the mountain, he says, "Saint Lazaria Island. Chart says there's a cove on the east side. That'll be our anchorage for tonight."

As *Tara* ghosts into the shadow of the island, passing between columns of rock carved from the island by millennia of hammering winter storms, Michael instructs Harky in preparing the anchor.

A thick gyre of seabirds whirls from the cliffs, alarmed at the rumble of the anchor chain and the slow flap of the jib. Thousands of beating wings stir a sound that comes and goes like surf as the cyclone of birds passes overhead. Puffins, guillemots, cormorants, petrels, and kittiwakes crowd the sky, diving into the air and spiraling in frightened coils before attempting to resettle on narrow cliff-side perches, only to startle at the panic of their neighbors and launch again, fluttering and piping into the flocking throng. The mirrored water is a litter of broken feathers and down. Slowly the storm of birds eases and the shrill calling and whistling settles into an arrhythmic discord like the tuning of an orchestra.

Belowdecks there is the sound of objects being shifted about and muttered conversation. Lockers and cupboards open and close, and Hannah hears Hans chuckle at something Michael says. The lid to the stove clangs, and the smell of wood smoke drifts in the air. It grows dark, and stars begin to twitch overhead. Alone in the night, Hannah relives the drive of the sails, the sounds and the light, and the bubbling life that filled the sky and the sea, trying to carve the sensory impressions into her memory.

Harky comes on deck carrying a blanket roll and looks about for a space large enough for his bed. Hans and Hannah will share the large berth forward, Dutch and Michael the single bunks of the salon.

The cabin is crowded. As bedding and gear are shifted in preparation for the night, Hannah and Michael pass each other within the close space of the passageway between forepeak and salon, and his hand in the small of her back sends a rush of heat through her veins. Later that night, as the spirit-cries of night birds wheel overhead, she learns of a special form of dream, of lifting and rising with an unlimited sense of freedom, that comes only to those who travel under sail, by the wind, on the sea.

SIX

Sunrise unfolds, and it is as if a dam has burst, inundating the world with silver light. The cove is windless and still, and the snarled thickets of brush covering the island glow emerald amid patches of burning gold. When Hannah goes on deck to brush her hair, she laughs aloud at the antics of a seabird splashing about with webbed feet as red and outsized as a clown's.

The anchor rises muddy and dripping from the sea floor and is stowed in its roller. The Hundsted fires at first try, and Hans and Dutch maneuver *Tara* out of the cove while Michael teaches Hannah to light a kerosene stove that swings from a gimbal on the bulkhead, raising his voice to be heard above the *pok-pok-pok* of the engine. The burner smokes and stinks while he fiddles with a lever, pumping at the pressure tank until the flame is blue. The coffee beans that Harky grinds in a small hand mill smell warm and wonderful.

As *Tara* clears the entrance, a black cormorant squatting goggle-eyed on a rock peers like a simpleminded dowager over its hooked yellow bill at the passing boat. Hans remarks that the bird resembles Dutch in appearance and intelligence. No one laughs. Dutch stares away in the distance. Harky rumbles, and Hannah feels shame at her husband's unthinking cruelty.

Michael blows at his coffee. "Damn fine bird, the cormorant. Swims as well as it flies."

Dutch, more easily reassured than he is offended, spins into a tale that no one believes, of seeing cormorants "in the land o' the heathen Chinese," tethered by the neck to long cords, diving into the water to fetch fish for their Butler.

"They fishes 'em at night. There's a torch what attracts the fish to the light and ever' man's got a half-dozen birds. They just choke 'em by the neck and shake the fish right out into a basket."

Hans makes a Pinocchio motion with his fingers to his nose and rolls his eyes.

A light breeze ruffles the surface of the sea. Harky and Dutch haul at the sails as *Tara* settles on a heading that will pass them well clear of a reef. Hannah fries eggs and bread on the stove as *Tara* moves west at a slow, steady pace, all sails set and drawing.

Michael drills all hands in the operation of the vessel, defining sheets and halyards, sail trim, and the finer points of following a compass. He demonstrates tacking and reefing, passes on tips for avoiding oversteering in a following sea, and provides a minimal education on balancing the helm "so the rudder doesn't fight you or you fight the boat. Nothing will wear a man faster, and the sea never tires.

"There'll be times when I need you, especially after we clear Cape Spencer. After that, there will be no more shelters until we fetch Lituya Bay. We'll shorten sail at night, but keep going, and I'll need a wink or two of sleep now and then."

Saint Lazaria falls behind, growing smaller as the lessons proceed. Hannah proves an apt pupil, but plays herself down. After Hans tries the helm and sends the boom crashing from port to starboard in an accidental jibe, she takes the blame, claiming to have been too slow on the sheet.

The Sound widens, the islands draw apart, and the horizon expands as *Tara* rounds Cape Edgecombe. Dutch scans the immense distance with darting eyes, peering left and right in search of some dire symptom of doom: a squall line—though he has no idea what one looks like, but supposes to be something dark and furious in the distance—or an angry sea spout, a rogue wave; surely something in all of that space must lurk evil and hungry for men's bones.

Harky is silent and stares into the distance before asking, "How deep would the water be here? Below us right now?" He thinks of how little it is that separates them from the might of the ocean and the impenetrable darkness of deep water.

Michael's answer is to sing. Throwing back his head, he hails the great ocean's spirit in a fine, ringing tenor, wailing out a song of Inishbofin, where he and his brother fished tub trawls for cod out of a two-man dory, rowing for hours across the gray, heaving waters and running home under a leg-o'-mutton sail only after the dory had settled low under the weight of a dozen hauls of fish. The words are in Gaelic, alien and magic, and Hannah wonders at their spell when she sees Harky's foot begin to pat in time with their ancient rhythms.

Beyond the cape, the wind strikes up a tune and the sea becomes a willing dancer. A swell rising from the southwest builds until the cutter must dip and bow to each passing wave. Michael orders the sails sheeted in until the leach of the main flutters like a bird's wing at the top of each surge. The ship heels. Small gear left loose in the cabin shifts and crashes to the sole. Hannah smiles at the exuberance on Michael's face.

———————

The crew settles into a routine, hopscotching from harbor to harbor up the coast. On the afternoon of the third day, which has been nearly windless and seen little distance marked off on the chart since noon, Michael starts up the Hundsted and uses precious fuel to motor into an islet-studded bay. He manhandles the dinghy over the side, touching his nose and says, "The lot of us are stinking. It's time we did something about it."

Ferrying back and forth to the shore, he carries first Dutch, then Harky, who sits upright, clutching at the gunwales, trying not to make any sudden motions. Hannah and Hans go in last together, then they wait as Michael returns to *Tara* a final time before returning with a shotgun and pack.

Leading the group up a faint trail, he grins, bursting with barely controlled eagerness. At the end of the track, above a rocky beach sheltered between slabs of dark stone, there is a split in the bedrock from which steaming, sulfurous-smelling water flows.

"A fisherman told me about this hot spring. It's the only bath for a hundred miles." He opens the pack and passes out towels, soap, and a change of clothing for each of them. Hannah feels her cheeks burn at the thought of his hands sorting through her things.

"Ladies first, hey, gentlemen?" says Michael, leading Harky and Dutch away. Hans stands guard while the heat of the water turns Hannah's skin pink. When she is done, her muscles feel relaxed, her skin smooth and elastic. She dries herself languidly before dressing. Hans's face turns ruddy and fierce from the bath, and he wishes aloud for a razor.

There is a *haloo* from the bush, and Hannah shouts back that the coast is clear. The three men emerge from the trees, grinning and waving. Harky and Dutch each hold a brace of grouse in their hands.

"Our captain's a crack shot," whoops Dutch, waving a bird overhead. "Six birds out of the flock with only two shots!"

Hans and Hannah walk back down the path to give the others their privacy, then sit on a log, plucking at the birds. The soft, warm feathers drift at their feet.

"This is all fine," grumbles Hans, "but I wish we could get on to the goldfield."

Hannah is about to chide her husband for his impatience but swallows the admonishment when Michael comes along looking fresh and invigorated. The others are close behind him.

Harky drops to his haunches beside Hannah, measuring out shreds of tobacco into a straw-colored paper. Licking and twisting the makings into a cigarette, he inspects it closely, then uses it to gesture at a stand of tall, straight trees.

"Good timber around here," he rumbles.

"That's true," says Hans. "But we're after gold, not trees."

Harky does not reply, but considers the pile of plucked grouse a moment, cocks his head to listen to the rustling silence around them, then looks again at the trees. They are not so large that he could not lift and heft them into place in the shape of a cabin by himself, much as he had done for Marta more than twenty years ago down in Mexico.

Popping a match with a horny thumbnail, he draws at the smoke and blows it out, muttering, "Gold ain't everything."

Only Hannah hears the longing in his voice.

The first day of April, 1898

It is difficult to find privacy or quiet to make my entries in this journal, but I must try, as the experience of this voyage is so wonderful. Hans chafes at the confinement, but other than the difficulty of private functions, I mind it little. Harky and Dutch clearly wish it over, but I sometimes feel I could go on forever. Mr. Severts enjoys it, laughing and joking from morning till night. His spirit adds much to the character of our party.

There is a wonderful, orderly progression to life at sea in a small boat, though every hour of each day offers something different. It sometimes feels as if the rest of the world has disappeared, leaving only what we see around us. The problems of life are reduced to those of the ship: whether the sails are properly set and trimmed, what cooking can be allowed by the condition of the sea, what is safe, and the most efficient way to be propelled in the right direction. There are clear rules of seamanship and physical laws that govern every action. The simplicity soothes the mind.

The prospectors dawdle over breakfast. Michael has decided to wait for high water to depart. From their present position behind a small island, they will stand nearly due west after leaving, reaching far out to sea before tacking north on a course designed to bring them landfall one hundred miles up the coast, near Lituya Bay. Icy Strait empties into Cross

Sound, and the rushing outflow of this water will flush them well out to sea, where Michael hopes to avoid the rip and boil of currents running close to shore.

He is less cheerful this morning and lingers over the chart, measuring and remeasuring the course and distance. If the sea is kind, they might arrive within two days, but the furious Gulf of Alaska is not known for its benevolence. Storms, tide rips, fog, and contrary seas have much to say about when, or if, they will make their destination.

He reads aloud from the *Sailing Directions for the Coast of Alaska*, a booklet printed by the government that details the findings of a recent survey of the Alexander Archipelago and Gulf of Alaska by the U.S. Navy. His Irish accent curls softly around the words of the entry for Lituya Bay: "The entrance to the bay is extremely dangerous and must be attempted only at high slack water due to the strength of the current, which is reported to exceed twelve knots. During the outgoing ebb, southwest swells break with great force across the width of the entrance."

He clears his throat and continues. "Lituya Bay was first discovered and explored by the French explorer LaPerouse, who suffered the loss of twenty-three crewmen in a single tragic event after surf overturned two boats at the entrance. Extreme caution is advised."

Dutch's throat works up and down before he mutters, "Jesus Christ," and licks at his lips.

Hans and Michael exchange wondering glances at Dutch's oath, and Hans asks, "How was it when you were up there, Dutch?"

Dutch scratches at a plate of fried potatoes with a fork. "Well, uh, I ain't had no problem there."

The fork trembles lightly in his hand. They press him for more information, but he stammers and says, "I forget. It won't be no problem, that's all."

For reasons of its own, the cast-iron engine is reluctant to start, and the day is well advanced by the time it pops, chokes, and roars to life. Harky mashes a finger as he muscles the anchor aboard. Hans grumbles that the porridge is like glue; Michael's banter sounds forced; Dutch goes forward to sit alone, staring at the mountains.

The airs are light, and it is the hand of the tide that pushes *Tara* offshore. Steep, briefly spaced swells come charging from out of the southwest, the spoor of a storm somewhere over the horizon. A vessel built for sailing does not power well, and throughout the day *Tara* slats and slams out of rhythm with the ocean. Sails slack and engine pounding, the cutter corkscrews and twists through the waves. Harky wedges himself into a corner, and his face grows dark. An unexpected pitch and roll slams Hannah across the galley, bruising her shin, and she breaks a dish.

The wind comes just as the purple hands of night begin to reach into the eastern sky, a contrary force that buffets *Tara* hard on the nose. As it strikes, the soft, slack sails become suddenly rigid as wood and bedlam breaks upon the cutter with a terrible banging of blocks and groaning lines. The trailing gulls rise screaming, and the rails run awash in green foam.

Harky steers as Michael and Hans crawl forward to bring in the jib. Leaving the staysail to its work, they move aft to fight a reef into the main. The sails struggle against them, wild as terrified horses, and there are skinned knuckles and streaks of blood on the canvas before they are done. Hannah helps where she can, paying out sheets and coiling them in again with the aid of the Texan, whose grip on the tiller turns white with strain. A moan issues from belowdecks where Dutch squats, huddled in fear.

After the sails are shortened, *Tara* heels, steadies to her course, and shoulders into the waves. Cold showers of seawater burst over the rail, flying the length of the cabin to rain down on all of them.

Across the horizon, the wind-vexed waters tumble and fall in endless waves, their peaks rising thin and sharp between *Tara* and the sun before crumbling into foam, and for that moment of suspension between heaven and sea, the light piercing the rim of each wave turns the water clear and green as an emerald. Gusts of spume cast into the air form a smoking mist that gleams like amber in the clean light.

Michael takes the tiller from Harky, exalting in the trumpets of spray. "It's better than that god-awful pitching and rolling," he says, then pointing west into the setting sun, he shouts, "Look!"

Tara drops between swells and rises, and at the top of each wave Hannah stares to windward. The sky is streaked with angry red fingers of cloud, and the sea boils in a scene of such cold, violent beauty that she watches without wincing as pellets of flung water sting her face.

Michael jiggles the mainsheet and plays with the staysail, bracing himself with one foot against the cockpit coaming as he adjusts the balance of the helm. A piece of light cord run from tiller to cleat holds the rudder just so, and he soon has *Tara* sailing herself to windward.

Behind them the coastline grows distant and the winter-clad peaks are white and rose-colored with alpenglow. In the north, to starboard, two stern peaks rise above a line of lesser mountains. Mount Fairweather is sharp and hard against the sky, Mount Saint Elias shouldered and muscled; both are improbably massive, rising so high that they glow with soft pink light long after the sun has disappeared and the sea writhes in darkness.

Belowdecks the cabin is turvied, a funhouse of angles and pitches, where passage is had by walking on wind-heeled walls and clutching at handholds. The night is long; sleep comes riddled with shallow dreams.

Michael stays on deck, huddled in sweaters, feeling the lift and run of the sea beneath him. The others take turns lying curled behind lee-clothes, broad panels of canvas fastened along the length of a tilting bunk's edge and lashed to eyes in the cabin top, designed to keep a sleeper from tumbling to the deck. Harky chooses to lie clutching at the floor, fearful that the cloth will give under his weight. Dutch lies unmoving, his eyes cramped shut, hands gripping his blankets, and by candlelight Hannah sees his lips moving—whether from fear or in search of the desperate solace of silent prayer, she cannot tell.

As the numberless waves pass under *Tara*'s keel the hull thunders, drumming louder and louder. The wind continues to build, and by that interval of night when darkness is total and time no longer passes, Michael decides to shorten sail. There is a flurry of effort, with much cursing and flapping of loose canvas as he wrestles in a reef alone.

With the coming of dawn, the weather eases quickly.

Hannah lies listening to the rattle of blocks and lines mingle with the snores of her husband. When the hatch slides back and Michael's face appears, it is tousled, red-eyed, and smiling. His chin is shadowed with a dark growth of beard, and he rubs it, saying, "Beautiful morning. Any chance of getting a hot cup of tea?"

The air is crisp and damp, and Hannah shivers in clothes moist with salt, the smell of kerosene from the burning stove coming with her as she brings up the tea, moving quietly to avoid waking the sleepers. Michael takes a deep drink, smiles, and holds out the mug to her in offering. Taking it, Hannah feels something intimate and forbidden in the quiet sharing. The cup feels alive and warm in her hands.

"Might as well get moving," says Michael. He gives the helm over to Hannah before climbing onto the cabin top to shake out the reef. The cutter shudders and stands upright; the headsail flaps, rising as it sweeps the foredeck and bellies full of air. *Tara* heels, lunges as if spurred, under way again.

At noon Michael opens a varnished cherrywood box and removes a sextant, a watch, and a tablet. After giving the timepiece and tablet to Hannah, he hands her a pen, stands, wraps an arm around a shroud, and raises the instrument to his eye. Calling out "mark" as he captures the sun on the sextant's mirrored horizon, he instructs her to note the time, then the declination of the sun as he reads its measurement from a scale engraved in brass. This is repeated until an average can be distilled from the numbers to place them accurately on the globe.

The cutter is still one hundred miles from their goal, but now stands at such an angle to the wind that a single tack should carry them straight downwind into Lituya Bay.

3 April 1898
58 degrees, 12 minutes N.
137 degrees, 15 minutes W.

Dear Diary,
Note how I now write in the language of the sailor, in latitude and longitude, and minutes of arc. I have learned my sheets from my halyards, port from starboard, and can steer without leaving what Mr. Severts calls a "snakey wake"—for which, I must admit, I feel quite proud of myself! There is such wonder and elation in the act of sailing that were I a man, I am sure I would be satisfied with a life at sea.

My sense of time has become elastic as we bore on through the stormy night and into this day without pause. It is remarkable to consider that we departed our last anchorage only twenty-four hours ago, when it seems to have been any number of days or even none at all, like something experienced in another place or time. It feels as if that particular method of measurement—breaking days into twenty-four hours, a light and a dark—is useful only in that it allows the mathematical magic of navigation, in which Mr. Severts has been wonderfully patient in instructing me. All in all, between my newfound skills and his companionship, I am finding this voyage quite thrilling.

SEVEN

The evening wind clocks round to the west and eases to a zephyr, stroking the fabric of the sea into dark ripples. The swell dies away. *Tara* moves slowly under a slack curve of sails, accompanied by the languorous rattle of blocks and lines.

Hannah and Michael prepare a hot, thick stew, boiling barley, carrots, and potatoes together with meat from a can before spooning the mixture into blue metal bowls. Hans and Harky take turns steering and eating, holding the bowls in their laps.

"Feels good," rumbles Harky, wrapping his hands around the heat of the bowl. Dutch stirs under a bundle of blankets, grunting a disinterest in food.

The last limb of the sun drops out of sight, and Hans points to a first star shining low in the east, a bright sparkle of blue near the edge of the horizon. The temperature drops rapidly. Slowly at first, then with increasing frequency, random stars begin to pepper the sky, filling in the dark spaces. Michael sorts a certain star from the constellations and points.

"That's Polaris, the North Star," he says, going on to explain that this is the pole star, fixed in position directly above the axis of the Earth. All other constellations—Ursa Major, Orion, Cassiopeia—travel in ceaseless arcs around it, each accompanied by its own confederacy of attendant stars.

"Follow it. Keep it dead on the bow, and it will pull us due north, straight into Lituya Bay." Hannah stares, holding her breath in wonder at the feel of the world spinning above and beneath her, and a sea that stretches beyond the horizon to the stars.

———

The night passes, midwatch and dogwatch, with Polaris dancing before them. *Tara* nods to a low swell from astern. In the darkness, Hannah hears the high-pitched keening and pipings of night-hunting seabirds in the void beyond the reach of the binnacle light and sees the sharp, angular shadow of an albatross, asleep on the wing, blot out the stars.

———

The swell rises with the dawn, and *Tara* sails into fog. The sun becomes a silver pearl that comes and goes. The air is thick with moisture, and the crew peers into emptiness until Michael digs in a locker, emerges with a brass trumpet and blows, pausing between notes to listen for replies.

The wind steadies into something tangible, a body with being and intentions. The sails grow potbellied and full, dragging the boat behind them until the speed of their passage wets everything with beads of cold water that drip down their necks and wet their faces.

Michael's trumpet wails, and everyone listens, hushed and straining, for any response that may promise they are not alone in the void. Only kittiwakes scream back in surprise. The ocean swells, drops, and rises beneath them; above, a patch of blue sky comes and goes. But around is only a blanket of gray wool that leaves them blind.

Sightless, they imagine the sound of breaking surf up ahead; Michael checks and rechecks the chart for dangers. Estimating their position from the sum of time, speed, and direction, he marks a small, tentative circle on a line representing the cutter's travel, then points and says, "We are here."

The world remains unseen. The minutes pass like hours, and the hours without change, until suddenly the wind gusts, curls, and gusts harder again before lying down with a somnolent murmur.

The seas continue to rise.

"There's more wind coming," says Michael. "I can feel it in this swell."

His jaw works in concentration. Plow lines mark his forehead. The fog whispers through the rigging in tattered streams.

"Wind'll clear this out," he says hopefully, pointing at the invisible horizon with his chin. "If it doesn't, we'll have to lower the sails and drift. Can't risk running ashore." He is leery of the habits of fog: The mist has its whims and a penchant for pranks that can draw unwary sailors to their doom.

Turning up his collar, he tells of being lost as a boy with his father, who was drunk and left the compass behind; of how they drifted for days, eating raw cod and licking dew from the sleeves of their oilskins while the currents shuttled them aimlessly to and fro through blind shoals and reefs, the surf breaking all the while around them; and of how on the fifth night the moon rose and drove away the fog, revealing the silhouette of their home island lying dark against the stars less than three miles away, the tide's aimless urging having deposited them only a short row from where their voyage had begun.

"And there was my mother, in the middle of the night, with a lantern on the beach to guide us in and a pot of oats waiting on the stove." What he does not tell is how his father shifted the blame for the forgotten compass onto his son's small shoulders and beat his slender legs with a knotted rope until the welts broke and ran with blood. Or of how his mother had cried out in protest and Francis Severts called her an English whore, then split her lip for good measure. Neither does he speak of how later, after the fog closed down again, his mother had called him to the cowshed, and helped him out of his pants to daub liniment on his wounds, while muttering against the damned hunchbacked Irish pullet, against whom they must ally if they were to survive.

True to Michael's prediction, by midafternoon the wind rises and tears at the fog, bending it into long shapes that rise and fall around the cutter. A patch of sky appears overhead, and in a blink the fogbank is torn and blown completely away, expanding their world from purblind and limited to unboundaried blue skies and the sparkle of light on tumbling seas.

Before them, Mount Fairweather rises, beckoning, shining with such dazzling brilliance and purity that it becomes a color beyond white. For a heartbeat of time, the sight of it takes away all of their self-absorption, allowing happiness to break free in their hearts.

From offshore, the scope and mass of the geology before them is such that they seem in immediate danger of being swept by the waves and the wind into the stony grasp of the coast. In the pure, cold air the details of the land come to them with such clarity that it is only by measuring on the chart the distance from their position to the mountain that they can believe they still have far to go.

Michael measures and calculates, scribbling at a piece of paper, estimating the state of the tide. As he works, the tip of his tongue probes unconsciously at the corner of his mouth, and he occasionally raises his gaze to ponder and figure before rendering a final verdict: It is too late to make landfall today. They must tack back and forth under shortened sail until dawn, cruising slowly on station until morning.

The swell, which has grown slowly from the west all day, continues to rise, and *Tara* rolls uncomfortably through the night. Dutch staggers to the rail with increasing frequency, clutching at his stomach and moaning. By first light, he no longer bothers to return to his bunk but curls into a fetal shape in the cockpit.

As they stand in toward the coast, the glow of the advancing morning begins to spread pink across the sky, growing until the first burning thumbnail of sun springs abruptly into view and immediately becomes too bright to look at directly. A long shadow springs from the mast and falls across the deck, dividing Hannah's face into light and darkness. Reveling in the simultaneous feel of the warmth of the sun and the cool of the shade spilling at an angle across her skin, she shivers not from cold, but from the delicious sensation of being divided.

Michael's navigation has been impeccable; just ahead, converging rivers of ice come together behind a high ridgeline that is gapped to the water line just at the place where they imagine Lituya Bay must be. *Tara* sails closer, all hands scanning the foaming coast for a break in the line of white surf, and then pounds ashore with a baritone rumble. The beach appears to be burning; salt mist flung from the backs of the breakers hangs like smoke in the morning light, drifting and rising in amber-colored clouds of spray. Beyond lies a strand of beach studded with black boulders; behind that lies a bench of dark forest, a tangle of black and green trees that spreads to the crown of steep hills guarding the feet of the mountains, which in turn shelter rivers and plains of blue ice. The scene is a palette of cold colors; blues and greens lie in great swaths below the stone and snow of the mountains, underscored by a band of pale sand along the shore. The curve and decline of dragon-scaled ridges implies the hidden shape of a fjord.

It is Harky who spots the entrance, pointing at a cloud of seabirds that rises and hovers over a point where the line of the sand dips out of sight behind the arching breakers.

"There!" he shouts, waving a forefinger. The gulls, plumaged in various combinations of gray, black, and white, appear to be taking turns folding their wings and dropping headfirst out of sight behind the wall of green surf, wheeling and plunging into the water in pursuit of small fish being flushed from the bay by the tide.

Michael and Hans leap to the rail, shading their eyes against the sun. Beneath the birds, a spreading plume of sediment forms an undulating, milky green fan.

"He's right," says Michael. "The birds are feeding in a current. That light color is silt flowing out of the bay."

"Damn," mutters Hans. The mouth is narrow, pitched at an oblique angle to the sea. No more than a stone's throw across, it is anchored on the south by a jumble of bedrock that rises into a steep wall; a shoulder of cobblestones and boulders bullied by storms of unimaginable ferocity guards the north. Across the width of the channel, wild, tumbling surf staggers against the outflowing current, exploding into spray.

Hans yells above the surf, "We can't make it through that." Everyone looks to Michael, who shakes his head in agreement, pulls at the tiller, and rounds *Tara* up to tack away offshore. Looking away to the west, toward the horizon from which powerful gray humps of water advance with increasing speed, he says, "Tide's still ebbing. And this swell is growing. I'm afraid we're in for another blow soon, worse than the last.

"When the tide turns, maybe this entrance will open up. The surf might lie down a bit when the current reverses and starts running back in. If it doesn't, and the weather gets rough, we'll be caught on a lee shore." His tone implies it is every sailor's nightmare to be trapped between the hammer of the wind and a surf-pummeled shore, struggling to claw off under sail. If driven into the surf and broken on the rocks, their bones will litter the sand.

Hans yells at the Dutchman, who sits yellow and wretched in the cockpit. "Is that what's going to happen? Will the surf ease on the flood?"

Dutch's wild eye roams between Hans and the sky, the other stares hopelessly at nothing. As he struggles for an answer, his mouth opens and closes, slack as a dying carp's. His shoulders lift and squeeze, contracting in a motion Hannah recognizes as a full-bodied shrug born of fear and ignorance.

Hannah grasps the implications of Dutch's confused silence immediately. Dutch does not know. He knows nothing of Lituya Bay or the dangers they face. The instigator of the expedition has no knowledge at all of this place.

Tara pitches to an oncoming sea, and Hans's roar is matched by a detonation of spray being flung across the deck into the cockpit. Hannah tastes salt in her mouth and wipes her eyes. When she opens them again, she sees Hans grabbing Dutch by the arm, angry alarm rising in his voice.

"You've never been here before, have you, you bastard?" Hans is livid. A purple vein writhes beneath his forehead. "You've led us here with lies!"

A wail breaks from the Dutchman's mouth, a weak sobbing whine cut short by the slap of Hans's palm. Harky rises from his perch atop the cabin and pulls himself aft.

Michael stands openmouthed, staring at Dutch. The bow of the cutter swings in the wind. "What's this?"

Hans grips the sagging Dutchman by the collar and glares at Severts. "He's never been here before, never at all. He doesn't know shit about this entrance, he can't tell us . . . shit . . . anything about this place." His words stumble over his outrage. Dutch claws weakly at his hands.

Hans spits. "All lies, isn't it? The gold, everything."

Dutch finds his voice and whines, "No. The gold, it's here. I swear it."

Harky pushes aft, breaks Nelson's grip with an easy twist, and shoves Dutch to a sitting position. His voice is low and steady as he holds Hans back with one hand.

"You never was here, Dutch? Is that true?"

Dutch shakes his head once, then again.

"How come?" asks Harky. "Ain't there no gold here?"

Hans snorts, "Of course there's no gold here," then screams, "Lying bastard!" and lunges.

Harky shoulders Hans away again, looking stunned. Dutch begins to babble, frightened by the murder in Nelson's face.

"I never did say I was here. I just say there's gold to be had here. And there is."

Harky, looking puzzled, cocks his head in question.

"The gold in my pocket, it's from Lituya Bay, I swear. I know it for a fact."

Michael steers *Tara* back to her course, shakes his head, and asks, "What the hell, Dutch? You mean you've really never been here? Never run placer anywhere around here? Where's the gold from, then? And why are we here?" He looks in unbelieving wonder at the surf barricading them from the shelter of the bay.

Hannah, like everyone, is stunned. All of the work, the voyage, the money spent on supplies and tools. All for a lie? For a fantasy?

"I'm tellin' ya. There's gold here, alright. I got that poke from the miner that dug it, a fellow that prospected up here last year and tol' me of it." Dutch hunches into his coat, his head sagging toward his knees.

A look of repugnance breaks across Michael's face as he understands what Dutch is saying. "Mother of God, idiot, you think the man would tell you where he found gold? He could have found it anywhere! He could have won it in a card game, or stolen it, like you did, you bastard."

"I didn't steal it!" shouts Dutch, indignant. "He left it there, he was that drunk. I just took it so's it wouldn't be stole by someone else. I was gonna give it back, but never seen 'im again."

"Sweet mother of God." Michael leans to the rail and stares at the oncoming seas, eyes growing dark, as if in dire contemplation of a message written on the heaving gray faces.

When he looks again to the shoddy Dutchman, the transformation of his countenance is frightening. Anger contorts the muscles of his face, straining the cords of his neck, and his lips are drawn tight and bloodless. When he glances at Hannah, she has the sickening impression it is someone else behind his eyes, someone she has never seen before and who does not know her.

Looking wildly around the cockpit as if seeking a weapon with which to brain Dutch, Michael turns aft to stare openmouthed at the shore, then ahead again at the seas that continue to grow steeper and grayer with every passing minute.

"It's a pretty goddamn mess you've put us in, you lying shit." There is flint in Michael's voice. He stares at Dutch without blinking.

"If we don't get into that harbor, I promise you this," he says, pointing. "I'll wrap you in chain before we're driven ashore. I'll make damn sure you drown, cause there won't be any way we'll ever get off when that weather hits."

Hannah feels her stomach coil into a knot at the horrible image of such an execution. Dutch breaks into a sobbing moan, tears stream from his eyes, and he begins to snot and blubber.

Harky sits down beside him, lays a hand on his neck, and sighs, "I ought to break your damn neck, Dutch. Just pitch you over." There is no real threat in the words. His grip on the miserable Dutchman's neck is somehow both protective and punishing, his hulking proximity a shield against attack.

The Texan looks around at Hans and Michael and makes a sound like a groaning bull. He glances at Hannah, who has neither spoken nor moved.

Harky wipes a meaty hand across his mouth and blows out his lips. "Ain't nothing else for it. We're here now. Might as well get on with it."

He squeezes the back of Dutch's neck until the miscreant gasps in pain.

"I reckon gold's as liable to be in this place as anywhere, and we're already here."

Hannah hears her own voice concurring with Harky's fatalism, but it sounds far away. "We've nowhere else to go. And perhaps Dutch—or rather the miner whose gold he took—was not lying." She looks from Michael to Hans, then for a moment at the gravity of the mountains.

"If we return, we will still be denied entry to Canada. All of us will. But we are victualed and ready to prospect."

Nodding to Harky, she continues. "As you say, we are here. Let us get on with it. If it happens that there is no gold here, we will be no worse for having sought it than if we return to Sitka before having even begun to search."

There is a long silence, broken only by the sound of the surf and birds, as each member of the party inventories the options and comes to the only available conclusion: The oncoming weather has decided for them.

Michael trims a sail and scans the horizon. Hans glares in turn at each of his companions, chews at his cheek, and shakes his head. Harky slouches into place beside Dutch as if sharing a bench with a friend.

The silence is broken when Michael speaks softly, as if to himself. "It's all we can do anyway. There's a gale coming. We have to get inside that bay. We can't ride it out. There's no time to get sea room for that." He nods to the west, where the conjunction of sea and sky has grown dark. "Couple of hours, no more. Then it's going to blow like hell."

Asking Hans to take the helm, he starts below to coax the engine to life. "We'll need it for this. Slack water won't last long, and going in under sail would be too chancy."

As Hans steps to the tiller, he lashes out with a booted foot. Dutch screams in pain and grabs at his shin. Harky scowls, squirming in his seat, but says nothing. Hannah closes her eyes, appalled by her husband's violence.

The engine hisses and *pok-pok-pok*s to life. The thrust of the propeller changes the rhythm of the hull through the waves to an unkindly wallow, a surge and spiral that sets Dutch moaning. His lips are caked in dried, gummy flakes, his eyes rheumy in a countenance of utter dejection and misery. Hannah sees his hand steal into the pocket of his coat, the cloth squirming as he fondles the shotgun shell of gold.

Eyes closed, his lips move as if mouthing a litany of excuses for his fabrications.

For an hour *Tara Keane* jogs back and forth within sight of the entrance. The wind begins to tear at the waves. The surf across the narrow mouth seems at first to be the same, until Michael points and says, "It's dropping," waving at the plume of silt, which appears to be diminishing perceptibly as the tide approaches its lowest point. The seas rolling in from the west no longer break with such ardent ferocity across the small section of the mouth, but surge forward, crumbling into sloughs of foam as they go, rippling into the channel as bands of smaller waves that pulse helter-skelter into the bay. The wind bites at the back of Hannah's neck and worms its cold fingers beneath her collar.

When Michael spots a seagull sitting placidly among the tumbling water of the channel, he watches carefully. The gull's head jerks and bobs with the effort of paddling forward, but it is being pulled backward into the bay; the tide has turned, the current is flowing inland. If they are going, it is now or never.

He pushes the tiller hard over, and *Tara* comes round in a surge, idling slowly ahead as he aligns the bow with the narrow entrance, counting the seconds between the crests of the successive swells.

"It's dead low tide," he calls out. "I have no idea how much water we'll have under our keel in the channel. We may strike bottom between surges, so keep a firm grip. If we broach in that surf, we may be swept over."

Dutch crawls forward, intent on sheltering inside the cabin. Michael shoves him roughly back into his seat. Hans puts his hand on Hannah's shoulder and says, "Go below. Get into a bunk and brace yourself."

"No," says Michael, "stay topside, Mrs. Nelson. If *Tara* is swept and rolled, better to be washed clear than trapped below."

Hans looks as if he intends to argue, then nods for Hannah to keep her seat.

Michael instructs Hans and Harky to loosen the lines that hold the skiff in its chocks and place floats close at hand. Should *Tara* be capsized, these will serve as life supports on which some of them might survive the surf and be washed ashore. He orders all loose lines coiled and tied to avoid entangling unwilling swimmers.

Harky moves slowly and carefully, focusing with great deliberation on each task. Hans rushes about, securing lines and lashing loose objects on the rolling deck.

When Hannah looks at Michael, his long curly hair covers and uncovers his face in the wind, and a small smile tugs at his lips. His rage now evaporated and his grip firm upon the haft of the tiller, it is as if the murderous, reptilian spirit that had so vehemently expressed itself in his promise to drown Dutch has been swept away. In its place is character Hannah finds enticing but even more mysterious: That of a man exultant in danger. Wondering to herself at his fierce intensity, she takes a firmer grip on her seat.

As the vessel closes with the entrance, the color of the waves seems to darken and the spray becomes colder. Hannah gazes around at the absolute, shining beauty of the mountains, the sharp, clear light that heaves in gray and green patches on the water, the utter white of the surf that runs away as far as she can see in both directions, and she is struck by how strange, unpredictable, and wonderful life is, that she could find herself so far from home, on the edge of death, surrounded by such beauty. She has never felt so intensely alive, and she understands in a flash why Michael is smiling. Laughing out loud, she draws a worried look from Hans and shakes her head to reassure him she is not hysterical.

A series of higher and longer swells rolls beneath the cutter. First one, then another and another, until a final giant wave runs roaring ahead, blocking all sight of the beach with its broad, smooth back. Behind the mountain of water runs a sweeping hollow that seems to suck the boat backward. Michael throws a quick look astern; the coming swells are small, as if the rush of the passing giant has absorbed all energy from the train of waves. The engine stalls, pops, and roars as he leans on the throttle; *Tara* seems to shudder, vibrating as the spinning propeller chews its way through the water and surges ahead.

Gradually the cutter builds speed, climbing onto the back of a small swell and clinging there, riding forward in the grip of the tide. The stern slews, Michael strains at the tiller, yelling, "Hang on!" and there is a moment of weightlessness as *Tara* drops. There is a dreadful noise, like the sound of a large bone being crushed as the keel strikes bottom.

The shock drops Harky to his knees. Dutch shrieks and claws at the air. Hannah is thrown to the side, Hans stumbles, grabbing at the rail. Before she can right herself, a wall of water breaks over Hannah from astern, and she is submerged in a welter of foam so cold she gasps and breathes in, swallowing a mouthful of salty grit.

The world dissolves in an icy green roar. Pummeled and tumbled, she coughs, gagging at the saltwater in her lungs, and realizes she is once again in the air. As *Tara* rolls and swings, Hannah sees Harky grab on to Dutch, who was swept out of the cockpit by the wave, then feels a hand twisted into the collar of her coat drag her upright to a sitting position. Michael has saved her from being swept away.

Hans alone remains on his feet, standing upright with both arms twined about the mast. Michael staggers to his feet, still gripping the tiller and Hannah's coat, and lets out a wordless yell of triumph as the stern lifts into the next breaking wave. *Tara* heaves forward on the swell and begins moving, the inrushing tide shoving them urgently forward.

There is a choking *pop* like a gunshot followed by a sizzling sound from below. A gout of steam rises from the companionway. The onslaught of water has driven away the hatch and poured below onto the engine, which now revolts against the frigid flood by quitting. As the engine dies, the cutter swerves, drives, and twists in the current, and the lack of its roar inserts a quietness into the mad rumble of the water.

Michael shoves the tiller into Hannah's hands with a single command—"Steer!"—and leaps forward, whipping a knife from his belt and slicing at the lines that bind the jib into a bundle. As the shore rushes toward them, Hannah jerks the helm hard over, and *Tara* swerves broadside to the current, which grabs the cutter and shoves it toward the boiling center of the channel.

Michael clears the jib halyard from its pin and throws it to Harky. "Pull! Haul for all you're worth!" he shouts, and yells to Hans to lend a hand as he leaps back across the cabin to the cockpit.

The jib rattles aloft, cracking like gunfire, snapping in the wind. Before Harky and Hans finish raising the sail, Michael is snatching in the sheet hand over hand. Together they imprison the wind in the canvas, and Hannah feels the rudder come alive. The sail billows, lifts, and hauls; *Tara* follows, swinging from imminent collision with the shore.

With an almost casual grace, the ship emerges from the boiling inrush of current and is thrust smoothly into the placid shelter of the bay, where the emancipation from danger and noise is as complete and stunning as if a battling host had suddenly laid down its arms.

Tara glides into the calm. The surf murmurs at their escape.

EIGHT

Tara's passengers—bedraggled, sodden, and bruised—stand and sit in various limp poses, dizzy with rebirth, torn between an impulse to celebrate their survival and mourn the prospect of isolation before them.

Lituya Bay lies broad and flat as a meadow. Gusts of wind embroider the gray green water with dark twisting lines. To port and starboard, the land rises steadily eastward until folding abruptly into steep hills.

Ahead, the hump of a single small island sits squarely in the middle of the fjord, which reaches inland several miles before splitting into north and south arms. The top of the *T* is a massive back wall of scaled granite, veined with vertical, debris-choked ravines that lead down to fans of dirty snow.

The grip of winter still clings to this place, with snow lying hip-deep to the edge of the water except along the beach immediately behind them; the mountains towering above the back wall are laced with frozen waterfalls, their summits strung with cornices of windblown snow. To Hannah, it seems a world impossibly removed from the temperate light and blooming spring forests of Sitka, and she places one slender hand wordlessly across the other atop her belly as if protecting herself from a blow.

"Jesus," whispers Hans. The sibilant exclamation speaks for each of the prospectors, who face a scene of such grand isolation that their death or survival is rendered inconsequential. For a moment, the power of the prospect strips the group of all worldly concerns: Dutch's perfidy, the hunger for gold, all ego and alliance—each and every impulse or appetite is forgotten as they stare at the future before them.

Tara chortles through the water, without course and under only the most tenuous control. Slowly Hannah becomes aware of an ache knotting itself into her body; her muscles are shivering, and her skin is growing numb. Wind knifes through her sodden clothes. Hans and Michael, too, are shivering. Dutch, hunched into a dripping ball, quakes so badly he appears to be convulsing. Only Harky seems unfazed. Miraculously, his greasy felt hat still sits on his head, limp and shapeless from its recent soaking. The cold wakes each in turn from the dreamscape around them.

Michael speaks first, his voice low and even. "Hans, would you take the helm? I've got to inspect below for damage. That blow when we struck bottom may have sprung something.

"Mrs. Nelson, as soon as I've looked things over, you'd best get into some dry clothes. We all need to do the same, but ladies first, hey?"

Hannah marvels at the swing in his mood. An hour past,

he was threatening Dutch with murder. Now he is all charm and concern.

A quick inspection proves the integrity of *Tara*'s construction. The blow from the grounding has started a few small leaks weeping along her keel, and several frames beneath the engine are cracked, but she remains sound and is in no danger of sinking. The condition of the propeller and shaft cannot be ascertained until the engine is repaired and started. Michael builds a roaring fire in the stove, and soon all hands are warming themselves in dry clothes, waiting for a pot of tea to boil.

All of the men except Dutch, who remains flaccid with defeat and shame, show the resilience of soldiers pressed into action. There are vital tasks to take in hand, a situation to control. There is seawater to pump from the bilges, tangled sails and lines to sort out, gear thrown from lockers to secure. The engine must be doctored, the source of its seizure diagnosed and repaired. A hammer and saw must be found to repair the stove-in hatch. Hannah finds herself relegated to mopping and drying, auditing the foodstuffs for water damage.

Michael steers for a bight along the southern shore as the others work to clear the chaos. When satisfied with their position, he rounds into the wind, luffing the jib to take all way off the cutter. Harky wrestles the anchor on deck and lowers away. The fjord is deep, and the entire length of the anchor line slips through his hands before he signals to Michael that it has reached bottom.

There is no rejoicing among the gold seekers, no enthusiasm

or excited making of plans to establish a base camp or begin exploration. Hannah cannot bring herself to address Dutch directly. Michael ignores his presence, a contortionist's task within the confines of the cutter. Hans shoulders Dutch roughly aside whenever they pass. When Dutch attempts to help with the engine, Hans raises a backhand as if to slap him away, and Dutch retreats to the deck. Only Harky acts as before, asking Dutch to lend a hand as he makes repairs to the hatch.

The strain aboard *Tara* is matched by the atmosphere outside the cabin, where wrinkled gray clouds move across the sky, devouring the blue in great bites. By the time order has been restored to the ship, dark weather slicing in from the western horizon has soured the heavens to the color of a corpse, permeating everything with a flat yellow light that leaves no shadows.

The voice of the wind rises from a whisper to a dirge, then an octave higher to a grieving wail. *Tara* tugs at her anchor, shrouds moaning. The stays hum a lament. On shore, trees bend in the gale.

The first rain rattles in with a sound like a handful of gravel being slung across the deck. Within moments, the full force of the front has moved in as a downpour that hisses as it falls, reducing the world to a cacophony of wind and darkness.

Hannah places an open pan on the deck, gathering enough rain in a few minutes to wash the dishes. After the lamps are extinguished, she tries to curl against Hans beneath their damp blankets, but he tosses wildly in his sleep. She tries to pray, but words of supplication will not form in her exhausted mind. Her pillow grows wet with silent tears.

Despair, dear diary, despair.

The hunt for gold has placed us in dreadful circumstances. Lituya Bay presents a stern and awful appearance. It is rugged, dark, and fearsome. Harky's description of the madman on the voyage from Skagway to Sitka seems applicable, as it does seem a most "heartbroke" bay. Harky also calls this "hungry country," and I fear he is correct. This place may consume us.

I try to forgive Dutch for the lies which have brought us to this place. He maintains desperately that he did not lie, that he never said straight out that he had found the gold in his possession. I replied that he avoids being a liar by only the most slender of definitions, that he is, nonetheless, a deceiver. Damn him, damn him, damn him, and I do not regret my cursing!

I have, however, begun to regret what error of my own has taken me so far from my home in Bristol. I feel so low and frightened. Hans is distant, and much depressed by our misfortune. We have not been as husband and wife for some time, as there is no privacy in such close quarters. He takes less notice than I.

How I miss my dear friend Victoria and the comfort of our "girl talks," and Mr. Witt and his music.

It has rained without cease since our arrival two days past. A brief glimpse of the fjord on our arrival has been our only chance to survey the stark terrain, as the downpour obscures the scene at all times. The men row ashore at intervals through the day, but return quickly, soaked to the bone and freezing. Sodden clothing hangs in every space aboard the boat and wets everything about it. If the

storm does not abate soon, I am afraid the confinement will infect
us all with the malady the miners call "cabin fever." Mr. Severts
says the rain is in our favor, as it will melt a great deal of the snow
that covers everything and allow prospecting to begin sooner—an
observation which seems most optimistic.

———————

A single shovelful of sand changes everything.

While Hans and Michael mutter of returning to Sitka, shooting Dutch, or both, Harky subdues his dislike of the water, drops a shovel and pan into the skiff, and rows awkwardly for the beach. Dutch, eager to breathe air untainted by animosity, accompanies him.

The day has dawned without storm. The water is flat as a table and the color of tarnished silver. Shreds of mist still hang among the hills, and the farther reaches of the fjord remain hidden behind a veil of rain, but in the west the sun struggles to break through beneath a streak of gold.

In Harky's hands the oars chop at the water without rhythm or grace, and he steals wary, sidelong glances from beneath the brim of his hat toward the mouth of the bay half a mile away. Dutch, too, is chary of the current, which they both fear may suck them into the terrible surf. Seals, bug-eyed with curiosity, follow the wandering course of the skiff in its advance toward shore.

Once ashore, Harky tilts the skiff to its side, shoulders its considerable weight by the gunwale, and carries it well up the beach. Michael has given him stern warning of the tide's ability to rise with speed and stealth behind the unwary, and of its eagerness to steal anything left within reach. Harky accepts the Irishman's admonition as more proof of the sea's treachery and urges Dutch to hurry.

Tools in hand, the unlikely duo wanders among a Stonehenge of tall boulders spaced along the concave bight of the shore. Michael's prediction to Hannah—that the rain would chew at the drifts of snow, exposing the earth to the prospectors' shovels—has proven only partially correct. Near the mouth of the bay, the snow has grown rotten and crumbling, with portions of open ground visible at the mouths of small creeks, but farther into the bay, where the glaciers chill the atmosphere, the moisture falls as wet snow and the intermittent mutter of distant avalanches can be heard.

The baritone rumble of the earth falling in on itself and the thunderous quaking of the glaciers dropping icebergs into the bay puts Harky much in mind of cannon fire. He grows nervous at the memory and struggles against the melancholia that rubs against the walls around his heart.

The sand is dark chestnut and littered along the water's edge with bits of shell. A wandering line of tracks describes the explorations of a cloven-hoofed animal, perhaps a deer or a mountain goat nosing along the interstice of forest and beach before veering inland. Behind a small point of land scattered with broken stones they find the ambling, plantigrade tracks of a grizzly—deep, platter-sized depressions marked across the top with the indentations of non-retractable claws. Harky stops beside a boulder the size of a washtub that has been flipped aside by the bear as it sniffed and dug at some intertidal delicacy. He stamps his boot track over a track and sees that the grizzly's foot is fully as long and a good deal wider than his own. Dutch peers ahead and behind, then into the woods, wondering aloud if they should return to the cutter for the shotgun. Harky shrugs. He carries his pistol in his coat, but knows the caliber would be woefully inadequate against an animal with a head the size of a keg of nails.

"We best just stay out of the brush. See him on the beach, we'll head the other way." He is not eager to return to the confines of the boat or the tippling skiff.

At the mouth of a green, mossy creek that trickles across a fan of pea-sized gravel, Harky punches at the ground with the shovel. The metal blade rings without penetrating the stony surface.

Moving over a pace or two, stepping carefully to keep his balance among the water-slicked stones, he slices into a soft deposit of sand. Garbed in black oilskins that droop on his dissolute frame, Dutch stands like a priest at communion, holding the pan out level to receive the offering from Harky's shovel. Bending at the waist, he lowers the metal lip of his chalice into the stream at a shallow angle, scoops a few spoonfuls of water into the mixture of sand and gravel, and begins washing.

At first the score remains nothing to nothing. Dutch is poised to tip the contents out on the ground, when Harky reaches out with sausage-fat fingers and tweezes a bright pebble from the pan. The small stone glows green and wet, and Harky briefly considers taking it as a gift for Hannah before dismissing the idea and thumbing the bead back into the pan.

Dipping and rocking, Dutch continues sluicing the lighter

elements of the slurry into the stream, working the muck down to a few spoonfuls of sand.

"Wait a minute, Dutch."

Dutch pauses before pitching out the concentrate. Harky bends down to look, bends closer, then drops the shovel and takes the pan.

Holding it in one hand, he tilts it this way and that, trying the light from different angles, shifting it softly side to side in a subdued panning motion, then probing at the finest black and green bits that linger in the curve of the pan. Among them is a speckle of yellow dust as faint as the scales of a butterfly's wing. It is gold, fine as flour, but still dense and heavy enough to be segregated from its sister elements by the rocking of a pan.

Harky says, "Guess that's it."

And it is.

NINE

Dear Diary,

It has been two weeks since our departure from Sitka, and construction on our home for the summer has begun. Mr. Severts is a wizard with the broadax and saw! He carves wood into thick planks for a table, benches, and a door, while Harky and Dutch work at bringing logs to the beach, where Hans takes them in tow behind the skiff to deliver them to our site. It will be a shanty of wood and mud, but seems palatial after the close quarters of the boat. There will be no fine finish, as the men are eager to begin recovering gold.

Throughout the day, first one, then another of the men—and sometimes all at once—drops all he is doing and wanders off to shovel at the sands. So far our "poke" is only a small glass jar in which a few flakes and grains of gold reside. Hans filled the jar with clear water, which magnifies the appearance of the tiny bits of gold. Everyone enjoys shaking the jar and watching our wealth swirl about, as if it were one of the crystal-and-water snow scenes Poppa used to bring Mama from Paris.

We are eating well, as we must consume all of our eggs, fresh
meats, and vegetables before they spoil. Soon it will be flapjacks or
bannock bread for breakfast, bannock bread and beans for "lunch"
as Americans call it, and beans and bannock bread for supper. I am
becoming adept at baking the bread, which is simply flour, water,
salt, and baking powder, in the Dutch oven.

———————

The discovery of gold has seen Dutch somewhat forgiven,
but he remains much subdued. The cutter lies at anchor, the
pendulousness of its mast drawing arcs against the sky, as
the miners pack the remaining goods and cargo ashore. The
smell of mildew clings to everything, even wood and metal,
and seems particularly strong on the pages of Hannah's
journal. On the first clear, bright day she drapes the green
branches of spruce trees near the camp with blankets and
clothing, hoping the odor will dissipate in the crisp air.

Logs of wrung-out silver driftwood are notched to lie neck
to ankle across each other in the rude shape of a cabin. Moss
gathered from the forest floor is used to chink the uneven
spaces between the logs. Squirrels chitter in indignation
from the trees.

The carpenters have no patience, nor is glass available, for
such niceties as windows. The interior of the cabin would be
dark and dreary were it not for the roof, formed by stretch-
ing the cutter's canvas jib over a low framework of poles and
weighting it in place with boards and stones. Hans wants to
cover the roof with sod as well, but Michael argues that this
will rot his sail. Sunlight through the sailcloth bathes the

interior in dim yellow light. Harky must hunch his neck to pass through the door.

The dirt floor of the cabin measures twelve by sixteen feet. Michael drives four short poles into the ground with the flat of an ax, fastens horizontal planks to the posts with wooden pegs, and uses a brace and bit to bore a line of holes through each plank. With a coil of small-diameter line, he weaves an open netting between the planks by passing the rope from hole to hole across the frame and covers this with a layer of resinous spruce branches to form a bed for Hans and Hannah. Michael, Harky, and Dutch will continue to bunk on *Tara*, but the woodstove is moved into the cabin for Hannah to cook on. Only Dutch complains of the cold.

He is also the one to discover the shattered wreckage of a boat strewn among the debris of the shore and all hands fall-to with saws and crowbars to salvage what they can of the weathered planks. From the size of the planks, Michael estimates the craft to have been larger than the cutter. There is no evidence of the cause of the ship's end or the fate of its crew, but its planks go to good use as shelves and a food locker in the new cabin. Hans sets aside the longest and best to build a sluice box and shaker, saving many hours of hewing and sawing that would otherwise be required to produce lumber from logs. The silvered bones of the ruined vessel remain a stark reminder of their isolation from the outside world.

———

After a night of heavy rain the tracks of a grizzly are found close by, crisp and sharp in the sand. Hans and Harky decipher the animal's path, tracing where the grizzly pawed at a shovel left out in the rain, approached the wall beyond which Hans and Hannah slept, circled the cabin as far as the door, then departed the way it came.

The tracks are well defined, unsoftened by the rain—clear evidence the visit occurred only a short time before Hans opened the door at first light. The prospectors marvel that the Nelsons heard nothing.

Michael brings his shotgun ashore and leaves it with a carton of shells.

It is Dutch who suggests that the bulk of the food be returned to the cutter. "No sense baiting a bear into bed with you, is there Mrs. Nelson?" says Dutch. "Old Elijah smells that bacon, he's liable to come in without knocking."

Most of Dutch's suggestions are brushed aside without consideration, but this one makes sense to all, and the potatoes, meat, cases of canned goods, and sacks of beans and flour are taken back to the boat for safekeeping.

In the time it takes to build the cabin, the earth tilts a bit more toward the sun and the days grow longer and brighter. Dawn comes before four, the sun falls into the western sea each evening after nine o'clock, and its tenure in the sky extends daily.

Michael discovers a small creek that flows in the shape of a fan across a flat slope of exposed bedrock before entering a pool. The new long days of sun heat the smooth, black bedrock, which in its turn warms the shallow water trickling across its face to a temperature suitable for bathing. After a long day of labor, the sensation of emerging from the warm water into the cool, crisp air delights Hannah's skin in a fashion she experiences as exceedingly carnal.

One evening, Hannah sees a blue-backed swallow darting and skimming above the straw-colored grass, which has been exposed by the melted snow. She points it out to the men, who are busy sharpening axes and saws. The next day, Harky and Michael surprise her by trimming a small opening into an empty tin can, nailing it to a tall pole, and erecting the makeshift birdhouse beside the cabin. By evening a swallow has begun inspecting the offering. The next day it returns, accompanied by a mate. With this sure sign of spring, the prospectors begin to chafe with an eagerness to take the land by the scruff of the neck and shake the gold from its pockets.

Making a careful survey of the topography along the coast, they probe with pick and shovel wherever bedrock runs near the surface or a streambed forms natural riffles. "Scientific prospecting," Hans insists, pouring over the resultant crudely drawn map, "is our only route to riches."

Their hands grow dirty, then crack, splitting across the calloused pads like ground that is too hard and dry to grow crops. They shovel with simpleminded intensity, stooping endlessly over the sluice box, until their backs and shoulders ache. Dutch whines that they forgot an item of great importance, namely liniment for their muscles and bones.

Hope rises and falls like a tattered sail, as one carefully worked pan of sand reveals a cluster of small nuggets and the next five hundred shovels yield nothing. They scatter farther afield, prospecting alone into the openings of the forest and along the hills deeper into the fjord, but the fear of bears, whose tracks are seen often, confines them to the water's edge. Hans damns their lack of rifles; only Harky is armed, and his pistol is too small. By general agreement the shotgun is left within Hannah's reach at the cabin, a decision in which she takes no part, having no experience with firearms and a greater caution for their use than for the threat of marauding bears.

While the men dig and wander, Hannah works to make their lives more tolerable. She cooks, cleans, launders, and mends. There are socks to darn and oilskins to treat with paraffin. Finding an outcrop of shale that shears away in flat pieces, she undertakes to pave the cabin's muddy floor.

When she sees a newborn mountain goat tottering behind its mother on a bluff across from the camp, she acknowledges the fullness of spring by carrying buckets of kelp up from the beach and mixing it into windrows of soil for a garden. There are soon potatoes, carrots, and cabbages pushing up thick rows of sprouts.

Buttercups or something like them begin to pop up in patches of ground warmed by the sun—and once, in the middle of the day, when the others are out of sight, Hannah looks up from the stove where she is preparing a large pot of beans and salt pork to see Michael in the doorway, a fistful of the yellow flowers in his hand.

"Just to say thank you, Mrs. Nelson. This work'd be much harder without such a fine woman to care for us." He holds out his offering.

Hannah stammers, "Thank you." When she reaches to take the flowers, there is a precarious mingling of their fingers, and she feels the heat of a blush cross her face.

June 21, the Summer Solstice

The summer is passing so quickly, dear diary, and I rarely have time to address you, as the work is endless. Our fortunes improve bit by bit. A swale of ground a mile or so to the north seems willing to yield its golden fruit at a tolerable rate. After three weeks of prospecting, the site has been chosen for erection of a "Long Tom" sluice box. My largest towel was appropriated to carpet the bed of the box—the action of the sluice settles the finest particles of gold into the weave, where it clings as the lighter soils wash away. Hans says invention and ingenuity are the hallmarks of the successful miner!

He also has improvised a scale from two of my spoons suspended from opposite ends of an arm by a bit of wire. It uses lead shot from one of Mr. Severts's shotgun shells as measuring weights. Every evening we gather around to measure out the day's "take," which varies from a small spoonful to several ounces. My image of gold has always been glittering jewelry or shining nuggets like walnuts, but here it is of the smallest sort, dull, and fine grained. Only in the aggregate is it impressive looking at all. Were it not for the weight—it is very heavy in the hand—it would be possible to mistake our gold for something base and of little value.

Nonetheless, our little poke-jar will soon be full! Mr. Severts has donated a piece of canvas from which I am to sew small bags in which to place the rest of the season's riches. Mr. Severts is ever the charming optimist; it is quite a large piece of canvas and will yield numerous bags. I joke with Hans that a few such bags should see our debts cleared, but he grows quite serious and says it will require at least a dozen.

Mining gold is not glamorous work. The men wear through their clothing at a fantastic rate. Every day I repair shirts, pants, or coats tattered at the elbows and knees. Our footwear shows considerable deterioration, and the tall rubber boots the men wear when working in the streams are already all but ruined. Harky suffers considerably from the cold water on his feet, but he does not complain. The men cut cards to determine who shall have first access to the bathing pool every evening. I prefer the solitude of mornings, when I may linger.

Yesterday a canoe of Indians entered the bay at high tide, but passed our camp without acknowledging us. As they entered, it appeared that they made some pagan ceremony, with one of the men rising to his feet in the bow of the canoe and assuming an attitude of prayer, holding his arms wide as he looked up and chanted to the sky in heathen language.

The vessel was quite remarkable, being easily as long as the cutter and paddled by more than a dozen men. It appeared to be highly decorated with carvings and painting. We speculate that they are a hunting party after the numerous seals that inhabit the ice at the head of the bay, for they proceeded in that direction and disappeared behind the small island, but whence they have come is a mystery. Hans showed consternation at the appearance of the Indians and was reluctant to leave me alone. Which concern was greater—that the Indians might molest me or that they should take the gold— I cannot say, for Hans is obsessed and talks of nothing else but gold. I promised to fire the shotgun as a signal if the Indians appear again.

TEN

A yellow buttercup lies pressed between the pages of Hannah's diary. Beside it, from a second bouquet Michael presented her along with a tiny, pink-rimmed seashell, are a number of small blue forget-me-nots with pale violet centers. He comes regularly bearing small gifts and warm words. Hannah, telling herself he has no motive beyond kindness, ignores the coincidence of his visits with Hans's absence, but she must admit to herself that at day's end she looks forward to the Irishman's return from the diggings rather more than her husband's. No matter how tired he is, Michael asks after the small details of her day; Hans cares only for his dinner and the bed.

Hannah places the seashell on a shelf Harky installed for her on the front of the cabin. During good weather, she prefers to sit outside with a stump of wood for her chair while she darns and sews, peels potatoes, or writes in her journal. The shelf is handy for holding materials and cutlery. It also holds an arrangement of special bits of driftwood, brilliant blue feathers from the Steller's jay that is constantly trying to steal shiny objects or bits of food, and stones or seashells of particular color or form. The pink shell nestles perfectly into the pearly cup of a lustrous, blue black mussel.

She is sitting on her stump, enjoying the feeling of sun on her back, sharpening a knife, and thinking of nothing but the rough, crisp feel of blade on stone, when she starts at a shadow passing over her hands, then jerks upright at the alarming rushing-water sound of a raven's wing close overhead.

The ebony bird circles and rattles to a halt on the end of a roof pole, cocks its head from side to side—turning the obsidian blink of first one glittering eye and then the other on her—and lets out a rusty *KA-HAW* so unnaturally loud and piercing it brings Hannah to her feet with the knife and sharpening stone thrust out before her in a dramatic defensive posture.

This seems to amuse the raven greatly. It leaps up and down in a side-to-side trot, throws up its bill—which is black, heavy, and thick as a cigar—and shouts at her posturing.

A shake of her apron and a timid "shoo" serve only to further amuse the raven. It rears back, flexing and re-flexing its wings, as if in imitation of her impotent flapping.

Another flap, another "shoo," and the raven pulls itself upright, regarding her over the chisel of its beak, as black and haughty as an Ethiopian king. The bird's confidence is total, its attitude imperial, and of all the truths the bird knows, this one is certain: Kings do not "shoo."

"What do you want?" asks Hannah. The raven does not reply.

There is a staring contest for a moment that ends with a blink of the bird's black-diamond gaze. It tilts its head to the side, as if to look at something beyond Hannah, before leaping bodily down onto the shelf in a rustle of feathers.

Hannah has time to yell only, "Hey! That's mine!" as the raven snatches up the pink shell from its blue mussel cradle and flaps into the air. She feels the wind from its wing lift her hair and ducks, yelping.

Hannah stumbles and rights herself, recovering first her balance and then her indignation, after which she begins to defame the bird in shrill language not usually learned from pastors or mothers. Anyone watching—and there are several someones, all of them black-eyed and amused—would have noticed the cock of her throwing arm as she spun about, prepared to hurl whetstone and invective alike. They would have heard her shriek as she stumbled for a second time and sat—with a cry oddly like the *KAWK!* of the raven—hard upon the ground.

The source of her new alarm is a creature garbed in a contrivance of furs, feathers, shell, and bones. The shaman stands stock-still, observing and abiding, as if waiting for the odd seizure that possesses this woman to fade.

She squawks again, this time like a frightened duck, then demands, with a touch of ire, "Who are *you*?"

Over the shaman's shoulder, the raven struts along the branch of a spruce tree and tosses the pink shell into the air, then ignores it as it falls to the ground. A second raven whoops from a lookout in the crown of the tree.

The man's face is wrinkled and dark as a nut. Fading tattoos mark his face from lip to chin, and his forehead is crossed with blurry lines. Nostrums befitting a wizard are hung or stowed about his person in bags and pouches sewn of animal parts, and he wears a conical hat of carved cedar. He remains unmoving, his visage neither comforting nor disturbing to look upon. Hannah suffers the odd sensation that he is not really there, that he is a cipher, incorporeal and ethereal.

The impression is enhanced by the lack of color in his eyes, which are black as his feathered familiar across the full orb and, having no irises or whites, give no indication of where he is looking. Hannah, discomfited, feels his gaze as one feels the stare of a blind man, the fix of an eye that sees nothing, or perhaps everything, through senses keen to the unknown and unknowable.

"Who are you?" she asks again, placing her hand on her heart, though there is nothing frightening or threatening in his presence.

The shaman makes a noise like that of his raven, a call that sounds to Hannah's ear like "ne-GOOK."

"What?" she asks, startled. Already used to the shaman's silence, to hear him speak is astonishing.

The shaman's eyes open a hair, and he says again, "Ne-GOOK, ne-GOOK."

Hannah climbs to her feet, her breath returning, and says, "Ah, well, of course you do not speak English. I may as well be asking the raven."

She speaks more to herself than to the apparition before her, and his reply sets her aback.

"You already been talking to the raven. Didn't unnerstand a dam' thing he said, either."

She stares, openmouthed. Both ravens imitate her, opening their mouths wide, exposing red throats and spreading their wings.

"What? I mean." Her mouth works at the words. "I beg your pardon?"

Negook—for that is his name—says, simply and clearly, "You asked him what he wanted. He told you, but you don't unnerstand." Then he waits a moment, hoping to avoid further insult to Hannah. Among the Tlingit people, even children have the courtesy to ignore stupid questions, because to acknowledge the ignorance of the one asking might embarrass that person. Answering an obvious question is rude and condescending. But Negook has some experience with white people and knows they do not understand much, least of all their own ignorance.

"He showed you he wanted the shell. Then you got mad."

Both ravens whoop, raising and lowering small feathered horns at their temples. Negook shakes his head and mutters in the Tlingit language, whether to himself or the ravens, Hannah is not sure. What he says is, "White people are crazy."

Negook has walked the long trail from his village to Lituya Bay many times since this bunch arrived, following the line of blazed trees from the canoe haul-out up through the twin hills that are shaped like a young woman's breasts, along the ankle of the bluff that rises parallel to the shore, and down into the fjord, where he stands observing and unseen. When his old bones do not want to make the trip, he sends the ravens to watch in his place. The whites have neither gathered a single egg from the gull colonies on the cliffs at the head of the bay nor killed a single seal. He thinks they must be eating dirt.

He has seen their strange inventions; he once went to Sitka with a band of young men hoping to trade mink and otter furs for bullets for their rifles and had marveled at a machine with a place to sit and two wheels going round and round. The bicycle went by as fast as a man could trot, the rider's legs pushing up and down. When a white man asked Negook what he thought of the contraption, the shaman had not said that only white people would think of a way to sit down and walk like hell at the same time.

Hannah briefly considers firing the shotgun to attract the miners but decides not to, fearing that to do so would somehow validate the shaman's dubious opinion of her sanity. And above all, her English blood considers it critical to be seen as calm and sane, even by a wrinkled old wood spirit dressed in puzzle-twined garb. It is also her English blood that speaks for her next words, which she immediately fears will sound more addled yet. "Would you like some tea?"

Negook is silent a long time before responding. When he does, the answer is so ordinary and so unlikely it takes Hannah the space of a long breath to understand.

"Got coffee?"

Negook sits on a drift log dragged into camp to be sawn into firewood and becomes still as a stone. A breeze curls through the camp, circling about the cabin and playing with Hannah's hair as she grinds the beans and boils water. The feathers arrayed from Negook's cloak and hair hang motionless, as do the wisps of beard about his face, as if the wind passes through the shaman without encountering his substance. Hannah's natural urge is to polite conversation, but she can think of nothing to say. Negook is still and quiet, pondering, as he has pondered for days, how best to get to the business at hand.

He eyes the crude cabin, the slant of its walls and the loose arrangement of stones and boards that hold down the canvas roof.

"You will not stay here a long time." He wants to believe this and sees the evidence he needs in the shoddy construction. When the Tlingit build a house, they use wooden wedges and mauls to split long, straight planks from large trees carefully selected for their perfectly smooth grain. The planks are assembled around corner posts and pegged into four strong walls and a roof to protect all the members of a clan, then carved and painted with symbols and figures that remind them who they are. The cabin looks like something children would build for the pleasure of tearing down.

Hannah considers how to best answer what question there is in the statement and replies, "We plan to depart in the fall. Until then we will be mining our claim."

Negook feels a twist of anger in his belly at the proprietary words. The Lituya-kwan band of the Tlingit people has been hunting and trapping the seals, birds, and fish of this fjord long enough to learn lessons as old as the mountains and the ice. The white people have been here for fewer days than it takes for meat to rot or the moon to grow fat and already they call it theirs. He pushes the anger down, back out of sight. There is something much more important to be dealt with.

"This is not a good place for you."

Hannah pauses, a cup in her hand. "Whatever do you mean?"

Her speech patterns stir an inkling of memory from Negook's distant past. He is so old his mind remembers things that he sometimes cannot find the words for, and he gropes now among the loose bits stirred by the rhythms and tones of Hannah's speech. In particular, the way she says "Whatever do you mean?"

When it comes, it comes clearly: The Boston men, the traders that came hard on the heels of the Russian bastards, they used those words. And before the Boston men and Russians there came a few ships with men who spoke the same way and said they were sent by a great king on an island far away, a place they called England. The head Englishman called himself George Van-Koo-Ver and told the Tlingit that everything now belonged to the English king.

White people were always showing up and telling the People that this was not the People's land anymore. Sometimes it was necessary to kill a few of them, but that always seemed to make things worse, because whites did not seem to have any laws.

Negook digs around and finds an American word he enjoys using and mutters it to himself. "Horseshit."

This land belongs to the One whose name is not spoken aloud. The Lituya-kwan are the keepers and users of the land and waters, but it is the great Bear God Kah-Lituya that owns this place. Even the Tlingit come here only on his sufferance, for he is easy to enrage and his anger is dreadful.

Many years ago, Kah-Lituya was kind to the People for a

long time and let them take plenty of seals and mountain goats back to their longhouses from this place. But the People became arrogant, forgot the ways of appeasement, and even worse, grew lazy.

Over the objections of the shamans, a band of sixty-five people built permanent longhouses here instead of the temporary hunting and fishing camps tolerated by the Bear God. Incensed at the trespass, Great Kah-Lituya came down from his ice cave in the glacier, took the mountains into his wicked jaws, and shook the world. The earthquake generated a tidal wave that killed every man, woman, and child in the presumptuous band, tore away their longhouses, and for good measure scalped every bush and tree and blade of grass from the hills. Even the barnacles and chitons that cling to the rocks at low tide were obliterated. Over an area of several square miles, every living thing died.

Since that last fury Kah-Lituya has been kind to the Tlingit. Now and then he will swallow a few if they forget to pray to him as they come and go through the currents at the mouth of the bay, but he has not shaken the land so badly again. But the presence of strangers has always irritated Kah-Lituya. After the Englishmen came white men from a place called France. Kah-Lituya drowned twenty-three of them at once, swallowing their boat at the entrance to the bay, after which they were smart enough to leave forever. So that is the danger now. If the Bear God comes down from the glacier, he will not discriminate between smiting the whites for their offense or smiting the Tlingit for allowing it.

Negook accepts the coffee Hannah holds out to him and takes a sip. It is not possible to mention Kah-Lituya's name to these people, for that would surely enrage him, but they must somehow be made to understand and agree to leave. He raises the cup and passes it before him in a broad gesture that takes in the forested hills and fjord.

"These trees. They are all the same size." After the last tidal wave, the devastated area regenerated itself as an even-aged woodland of uniformly sized timber, whereas the forest that was out of reach of the tsunami is made up of trees of all ages, from saplings to ancient giants. He waits for Hannah to understand.

She looks in the direction of Negook's gesticulation, as if she is seeing the forest for the first time. The evenness of the second growth is apparent and appears as a distinct division, through the forest that is a mixture of greens and blacks on the ancient side and a paler, brighter green on the new. But this is meaningless to her. She is used to the carefully manicured, homogenous woods of England.

Negook tries again. "Everything was gone. Now there are no old trees or young trees. Everything came back at the same time."

The shaman sees the flicker of doubt across Hannah's face; she is starting to think he is just a crazy old man. He swigs down the entire cup of coffee, oblivious to the scalding heat, and holds out the cup to Hannah, who hesitates before taking it gingerly. Obviously, the only approach is direct, so he repeats his earlier warning.

"This is not a good place for you. You will not stay here long." Surely these fools will not ignore straight words.

Hannah stands straighter and pulls back her shoulders. "Mr. Negook," she says, for she does want to address this elderly man with respect, even though he is decidedly strange. "Mr. Negook, we will leave Lituya Bay when the mining season is over. We have come for the summer and cannot alter our plan. I assure you, we will do nothing to interfere with you and your people." Then, as an afterthought, she asks, "And where are your people? Your village? How did you get here?"

Negook's only reply is a vague gesture to the north. There is no need to tell the whites how to find the village. That could only lead to trouble.

"Will you leave when you have enough gold?" When the People have enough salmon drying on the racks or seal skins scraped and stretched or berries in the buckets, they quit taking.

"Enough? Well, I suppose we shall. When we have enough."

Negook stares at the sea where the smooth, slender shape of a sea lion is briefly silhouetted at the peak of a swell before it breaks. The shaman watches for the brown head to emerge in the swells behind the surf line, and in a moment it does, with a wriggling fish in its jaws.

Negook considers the driftwood that litters the beach and the long journey each pale silver log has made, from its youth as a sapling to its fate as an uprooted tree. He sees the floods and upheavals that wash trees whole from some distant river into the sea, where they tumble until scoured free of bark and limbs, before drifting ashore on this long curve of beach beneath icy mountains. He looks at all of this and wonders if "enough" and "gold" are words that go together.

Without another word to Hannah, he walks away into the forest, winding his way through the field of tree stumps left by the miners, then up a slight rise and into an uncombed tangle of salmonberry. The whoops and calls of the loquacious ravens follow. There is a brief rustle in the thicket, and the shaman is gone, leaving Hannah with the empty coffee cup and an odd sentiment that she has been dreaming. From the shelf beside the cabin door, the pink glimmer of a seashell winks at her from its nest within the pearly grip of a mussel.

Negook does not go far before stopping beneath a tree, where he sits to wonder at the huge stupidity of whites who dig at the ground instead of hunting seals or goats. They wade in the water like children and dig at sand that yields nothing when they could be digging for *k'oox*, the wild rice that grows at the base of the dark lilies. This is actually a woman's job, but that could be why white men are so crazy: They never have enough women around.

The ravens sit above Negook, watching him think. As he considers the odd ways of the whites, a squadron of dark-eyed juncos flits by in ragged maneuvers, moving from alder to alder, pecking at small meals. Negook is so old he remembers the oldest living grandmother among all of the People as a young girl. Now she is an ancient who no longer speaks, but just sits, year after year, humming to herself. Among the People it is not unusual to live a long, long time, through more salmon seasons and winters than there is a number for. Negook is the oldest by far.

He knows that white people believe wholeheartedly that they are only allowed to live just so long, measured in years; to do less is somehow a failure or to do more is somehow a sin. The Tlingit understand that a life cannot be measured in numbers of years, because some people die quickly, and some, like himself, stay a long, long time. Yet to each is given a whole life. Unlike the whites, with their sentiment for record keeping and birthdays and putting things in drawers, Negook does not measure his life.

Negook has heard also about reincarnation, the odd notion being related to him by a prospector who wandered, babbling and digging, along the shores south of here just last year. Reincarnation seemed like a good idea, but the thought of all the lost animals—the slaughtered whales, the millions of fish the whites took every year in their nets and traps, or the herds of mountain goats that had disappeared around settlements like Juneau and Skagway—coming back as white people made Negook nervous. He just did not see how this could be a general elevation or improvement of the world's spirit.

"Ai-ya," he says out loud. That might be what is happening, because there are certainly fewer animals and more white people every year. *Ai-ya, ai-ya.*

Negook struggles to rise and sighs. His feet hurt to walk, and his ass hurts to sit. He knows he must die soon and fervently hopes his soul does not have to come back as a white man. But first he has to deal with the troubles at hand.

"There was a damn blanket-ass in this camp, and you didn't signal us?" Hans is livid. A blue vein pulses in his neck beneath his skin. He is outraged that an Indian, just wandering loose, has come into camp where his jars of gold—and his wife—lay about unguarded. Back in Minnesota the damned Indians know enough to stay on their reservations. The fault must be Hannah's, and he rails.

Today the men returned early from the diggings. For several days the take has been inconsequential, and now Michael's back has been strained by furious, nonstop shoveling in pursuit of another vein. The Irishman is on the boat, in his bunk, being nursed by Harky and Dutch, and Hans worries that the reduction in manpower means even less gold if they do find another vein. He kicks at the table, sending it skittering across the floor.

Hannah assures him that there is no reason to worry, the visitor was a harmless old man. But she is overruled: The old man was likely a scout.

"They'll be back," insists Hans. "They'll steal us blind."

"They won't," she insists. "They know we are here, but ignore us. The old man just came to tell us . . ."

But flustered by Hans's anger, she does not remember exactly what the old man said, except his suggestion that they leave. "He thought we should not stay here. He seems to think Lituya Bay is a dangerous place."

Hans assumes an air of amazement, hands on hips, face caricatured in astonishment. "What did your sweet old man have to tell us? That now that we've done all the work we should just leave so he and his friends can come take everything? That may be fine with you, Mrs. Nelson," he spits, "but no damned Indians are going to get my gold."

Hannah draws back her shoulders, angry at being so abused. All of her stored-up anguish—her misery in Skagway, the discomfort of being a woman alone in the wilderness, and the drift of Hans's passion from their marriage to the hunt for gold—boils over, and she stabs at Hans's weakness. "What gold is that then, Mr. Nelson? Just what riches have you found that have made all this worthwhile?" She waves a hand around her at the crude furnishings of the shack.

Hans turns on his heel and storms from the cabin. Hannah is two steps behind him with more to say. The slamming door strikes her full in the face.

Overhead a raven screams, drops from its tree, and flees.

———————

The next morning Hannah's lip is cut and swollen. She stays in the cabin when Harky and Dutch row ashore. Hans has been solicitous since the argument and keeps looking back over his shoulder as the three men shoulder their packs and hike away. At noon Michael comes on deck, hollering for Hannah to row out in the skiff. His back feels better, he says, and he would like to go to work. She yells back, cupping her hands to her swollen mouth like a megaphone; he should continue to rest, she says. But he insists.

She can think of no way to put him off and tries to avert her face as he climbs down into the skiff from *Tara Keane*'s deck. Settling with a thump onto the thwart in front of her, he says, "Sorry to trouble you, Mrs. Nelson, but I've got to get moving. When my back's out like this, after a while lying about gets to be worse than moving around."

As he reaches to take the oars from her hands, he starts at the sight of her swollen mouth. The image of his mother holding a bloody rag to her own fist-split lip leaps fully to mind, and the old urge to succor or kill uncoils inside him.

"Hannah?" he says gently.

"It was an accident," she says. Tears begin to burn in her eyes. She feels as if the blow has fractured something, some connection to the world that is neither skin nor bone, but the severance of which has left everything full of sharp angles and dangerous; she feels alone.

"I'll have his hide," growls Michael as he reaches for her.

A spike of irritation at the willingness of men to always offer violence as a solution pierces her blanketing misery for a moment, then fades as he draws her to his chest. "It was an accident," she repeats, muffled by his shoulder.

"Shhh," he says and soothes her hair.

The warmth and weight of his arms around her lets loose her sobs.

Michael does not go to work that day. Instead, he holds her and touches her while she cries.

Hans draws the towel from the bottom of the sluice box and lowers it carefully into a shallow pan. Swishing and squeezing, he washes the contents of the cloth into the dish and begins shaking it lightly from side to side. Dutch watches the cleanup carefully. A few fine grains of gold speckle along the rim. Harky probes at the take with a grimed and calloused finger, gives a grunt of dissatisfaction, and turns away.

This is the fourth site on which the prospectors have erected the sluice box since the height of summer, and none has given satisfaction in return. Each successive site is farther from camp; they must now walk more than an hour each day to reach their work.

They have shoveled, dredged, hammered, and panned for months, oblivious to the ripening of blueberries and the changing phases of the moon. They have labored, shirt-less and sweating, while eagle chicks fought free of the egg, fledged, and began to consider their first dizzying step into space and freedom. Salmon have returned to their natal streams and begun the ritual of procreation, while the moun-taintops turned from white to brown, then green as summer advances. To all of this, the miners are blind, impassioned only by the search for gold.

At mealtimes Hannah and Michael are cautious with each other, courteous and proper, though the intimacy of the cabin quickens their blood. Their fingers touch in pass-ing dishes. Once Michael stands close behind Hannah as she brings a pot to the table and without thinking rests his hand on her waist; throughout the meal she is silent, afraid her voice will quiver with the trembling aroused by his touch. In the presence of the others they are careful to always address each other as "Mr. Severts" and "Mrs. Nelson."

On a day of heavy rain, while a wind from the south cuts rags of cloud from the sky and slings them loosely around the mountains, Michael returns to the cabin alone, to fetch a forgotten tool. The tide is low, and the fine, strong smell of the sea blends with the delicate perfume of the dripping summer forest.

The canvas roof leaks in the wet weather. Pans placed here and there to catch the drips tinkle and plink, playing a sad, musical tune in the key of rain. Hannah sits beside the open door, darning a sock. The light inside the cabin is subdued.

When Michael's shadow falls across her lap, her breath quickens, and she rises. There is a pause as the force of attraction freezes each in the realization they are alone. Michael is acutely aware of Hannah's shape and her softness; she of his full lips and dark lashes above pale blue eyes.

Taking two steps back, she maneuvers to put the table between them, and the moment is broken. When Michael steps forward as if to come around the obstruction, she holds the sock and darning egg to her stomach. "No, Michael."

He holds out his hands, palms raised. "Hannah."

She shakes her head, closes her eyes, and keeps them closed until she hears the splash of his steps retreating through the puddles outside.

Dear Diary,

There is difficulty among our company. The poor return of gold weighs heavily upon Hans, whose temper becomes virulent at times. Meals are often quite strained. Discontent infects Harky and Dutch as well. Mr. Severts remains of remarkable good cheer, but he, too, is sometimes reserved.

The rains continue without cease. Everything is sodden; our clothing molders, as do some of the supplies. I was compelled to throw out half of our stock of potatoes, which had gone black and soft, and an entire sack of flour has clotted and smells so of mildew that I cannot believe it is safe to eat. We have enough dried food to see us through until September and our return to Sitka, but I fear coming to table will be an increasingly bland experience. There is no more sugar or molasses, and the pepper runs low.

Hannah pauses in her writing as the sensation of Michael's hands on her returns, then she touches her fingers to her healing lip. Staring at the half-filled page, she considers what she might say of the pull she feels toward Michael or the tension and confusion that boil within her when she thinks of Hans. But to put words to paper is to risk setting them loose somehow. Feeling duplicitous, she distills the disarray of her feelings into code:

> *There was an accident with the cabin door, she writes. Grave concerns for this marriage.*

Three weeks of cold rain. The creeks swell and can be heard roaring from the mountainsides. Dutch develops a gagging, phlegm-spitting cough that tears at his boney chest. The leather of their boots never dries; their feet grow wrinkled and soft. The ringing, back-and-forth cries of ravens resonate among the trees. Probing and persistent, the ceaseless litany of *kawks*, *klook-klook*s, and pealing bell calls digs at Hans, stirring unnamed fears in his superstitious Viking blood. His grandfather's Old World phrase for a flock of the black birds was *an unkindness* of ravens, and the old man delighted in frightening young Hans with the legend of Odin's pets, Hugin and Munin, who perch on the angry god's shoulders every morning to whisper the news of the world in his ear, particularly the misdeeds of young boys.

Early one morning Hannah hears the shotgun bark

once, then again, as Hans fires a fusillade into the trees. The report of the shotgun wipes out all other sounds, stilling the shrieking of an eagle and the brassy call of a jay. But the outraged cries of the *unkindness* of ravens fade slowly into the trees, profaning the gunman as they go.

Dutch's cough worsens. One day he returns from prospecting the beach west of the diggings with a fantastic story of having seen an odd bear. "Strange-colored animal, sorta shiny all over. Silver, he was. Or maybe gold. Big bugger, too." He persists so hopefully and insistently in the face of Hans's mockery that Hannah worries that his cough has brought a feverish delusion.

Harky does not speak for days. He is a prodigy of labor, burning away unnamed angers by digging without cease, hauling and shoring, carting and cutting. The *thok* of his ax knocking cordwood into stove wood resounds into the night.

Hans mutters darkly, measuring and remeasuring the sparsity of his gold.

Dear Diary,

There was an earthquake in the night. Hans describes it as a "small one," and mocks my fright. The others felt and heard nothing as they slept aboard the boat. There was a rumbling sound beforehand that seemed to come from everywhere and nowhere, then a trembling of the ground that rattled the pots and pans. It was quite the most frightening experience of my life and has left me quite nervous. All day I have been starting at the slightest sound. It gives one a feeling of terrible helplessness to feel that even the earth itself can no longer be trusted.

———

July advances into August, with summer growing weaker and the days becoming shorter; night assumes a larger role in the order of things. Once again, stars appear as points of light overhead, and when the moon is full, the icy white surface of the glacier shines between crenellated, black-shadowed walls. At night, the wind bites with teeth sharpened over the ice field, but during the day, the land basks in a warm breeze.

Hannah sighs with relief. At last the rains have eased, bringing a few days of blue, marshmallow-clouded skies, and for a change the take from the sluice box has been generous. Hans's mood is much improved at the evening meal.

The warm amber light of the lantern falls around the miners as they sit down to heaping plates of bannock and beans, its golden color matched by a glow behind the peaks to the east that hints at a moonrise to come. A fast-moving cloud bank moves in from the west, eating up the sky, throwing a shadow across the stars, and by the time Hannah has scoured and rinsed the dishes, a crescent moon has risen, slid across the sky into the oncoming clouds. Throughout the night, the wind clocks west, south, then west again, gathering its energy.

———

At first light the sky turns the color of a gun. The wind begins to rise, sucking the canvas roof into loose billowing shapes that snap and crack above the roar of heavy surf.

The rain begins as an intermittent mist that steadies into a downpour, as the miners trudge away to their work. Hannah stands in the doorway, watching the stones of the beach go dark and shining and the color of the sea change to match the sky.

Driven by the wind and the pull of the moon, saltwater brims into the bay until it laps into the beach grass along the rim of the fjord. When the tide turns, the outrushing water boils through the channel, slamming head-on into the incoming surf. Alone, Hannah struggles to secure the roof with a lashing of lines and strategically placed cobbles, but the wind fights unfairly, twisting its hold on the canvas, flinging her aside. She wonders that the storm has not driven the men from the diggings and curses the bright light of gold, which so thrills, stupefies, and blinds that anyone would consider its pursuit in such weather.

The rain becomes blinding, rendering the mountains and ocean invisible beyond its dark wall, and when it eases, Hannah sees the furious, windblown bay seething about the cutter. *Tara Keane* bucks against her anchor line, hobbyhorsing and plunging, ducking the angry spray. A small iceberg fallen free from the glacier passes the cutter, sailing absurdly into the face of the wind. It takes Hannah a moment to realize that the bulk of its body, seven-tenths submerged, is being swept so strongly by the falling tide that it overcomes the wind pushing in from the west. Charging like a buffalo straight into the eye of the wind, the ice is at first perplexing to Hannah for its oddity, but puzzlement quickly builds into alarm as another, larger berg appears from the gloom.

Looming larger than the cutter, the second is a massive blue and white juggernaut untroubled by the waves breaking against its base. Hannah stares in frozen panic as it trundles on a course calculated to take it directly and inevitably into the ship. She sprints for the cabin, emerges with the shotgun, raises it to her shoulder and fires. Anyone watching would think her desperately insane: The shotgun has no more effect on the iceberg than it would on a slow-moving train. She fires again, drops the firearm, and clutches at her bruised shoulder before crying out, "Dear God!" and screaming into the wind "Hans! Harky! Help, for the love of God, help!"

The iceberg spins slowly, seeming to stall for a moment. The surf roars and dares it to keep coming; the frozen blue monster rolls and bobs slightly, as if nodding its acceptance of the challenge. *Tara* bucks like a frightened horse, kicking and rising, slamming at her tether.

Hannah scrambles to reload the shotgun, frantic to signal the men. The report—an impotent *pop*—is torn away by the wind. The sound of the ice taking the cutter comes to her as a terrible grating, the crunch of a predator gnawing at a bone.

Stung by the rain, she sinks to the ground, throws her arms around her knees, and wails a death song for the cutter.

ELEVEN

"From hell to breakfast."

This is how Harky describes the shattering of *Tara Keane*'s bones along the shore. "Just broke and scattered from hell to breakfast."

The men stand aghast at the tangle of kindling and cordage awash in the surf. The pounding of the waves has chopped the cutter to pieces, dispersed the splinters along the beach, and begun to cover them with sand. Sodden articles of clothing lie scattered about the shore; a shirt with one arm akimbo, the other flung up in boneless despair; Harky's union suit beaten into the sand and bent at the waist, its legs and arms kiltered at impossible angles. As they watch, the mast comes ashore, its once-slender length broken to pieces and formed into a haphazard bundle by the random knotting of halyards and downhauls.

It is Dutch who moves first, sprinting into the surf to grab at the miscellany of salvage that is all that remains of their supplies: a pot, a shirt, a short piece of line. Harky snags the broken mast by a tail of the halyard and heaves it shore. Hans grabs at a small wooden box of dried apples, but misses. Michael slumps and does nothing, standing in the rain and staring as his dream of a triumphant return to Ireland is broken across his shoulders and drowned.

A raven *hook-hook*'s from the forest; the grass behind Michael rustles with a sibilant slithering of fur. From within a bower of alders, the wrinkles of Negook's old face deepen as he peers at the disaster, sniffing the wind. The sea smells of anger, the rain tastes of rage; Kah-Lituya is walking the land.

We are in a frightful condition. Of food we have little; only what beans, rice, and dried fruit that were stored in the cabin; a few tins of tomatoes and one tin of milk that washed ashore; a metal bucket in which was stored cornmeal and barley (which has now been partially damaged by water); and a half pound of tea. Thank God Mr. Witt encouraged me to bring seeds for a garden, which now bears a few vegetables that will lend to our sustenance. Michael still has a shotgun, and a number of shells since he brought them into the cabin beforehand to protect them from the damp aboard the cutter.

It was providential that I had chosen this day to wash and mend the men's blankets, else all would have been lost. They are now without spare clothing, excepting a few items that came ashore from the wreck. Poor Michael is despondent and bitter, as are we all, with the exception of Harky, who is very brave and jokes about making "gold stew."

We must make preparations for a signal should a ship be sighted. Who can say when that might be? Has there ever been a more wretched party of castaways?

Michael and Harky are pegging together a bunk bed of rough timbers and planks. The small cabin is crowded now, with five people sleeping where once there were two. Dutch and Michael will have the new bunk beds, and Harky will sleep under the table. With no blanket to spare for a curtain, Hannah has had no privacy since the wreck, and the men must do her the courtesy of retiring outside "to check the weather" while she prepares for the night.

Harky aligns a board with a post, gripping it for Michael to peg. Hans toys with a knife and kindling, shaving long, slow curls into a pile at his feet. It has been three days since the iceberg took *Tara Keane* to her death, and no one has made any move to resume mining while they await rescue. A signal fire of logs and brush has been laid on the shore and covered with a scrap of mainsail. They've placed a pint of oil and matches at hand to light it quickly. They have devised a schedule of lookouts, with each person standing vigil for two hours throughout the day and night, in hopes of spotting a passing ship.

Dutch is on watch. He sits on a stump at the side of the cabin, scratching random designs of his name in the sand with a stick. The weather has been decent since the storm, with bands of cloud lying across the tops of the mountains and the sun throwing out long shadows from the trees. Flocks of southbound shorebirds write twisting letters against the horizon, atwitter with the excitement of migration.

Negook's voice takes them all by surprise. "Somebody is pretty mad at you."

Hans leaps to his feet, kindling stick and knife thrust cruciform before him, as if to ward off the primitive apparition in the doorway. Michael and Harky stare. Dutch on his stump is oblivious. Hannah is the first to find her voice.

"Mr. Negook. Please come in." Her own civility amuses her, if no one else.

Negook shuffles into the cabin, ignoring Hans's muttered, "Who the hell?" and places himself before Harky. The shaman and Texan are eye to eye, though the latter remains kneeling, holding a plank in place to receive Michael's peg.

Negook's dark eyes flicker up and down Harky's bulk, taking in the size of his hands, his feet, the width of his chest. Their eyes lock for just a moment, but sufficiently long for Harky to hear all the winds of the world blowing through the darkness of the eyes that regard him.

Negook's hand comes quickly and cleanly from beneath his fur cloak, clutching the dried and severed shinbone of a heron, and points it at Harky. In the swift, fluid motion Hans, Hannah, and Harky all once again see the knife-wielding bedlamite from the lumber ship from Skagway.

The shaman makes a complex passage of the fisted yellow talon over Harky's head, drawing some unknown hieroglyphic pattern, and Michael—the only Catholic among them—sees the silhouette of a Monsignor performing an arcane absolution. When the shinbone swings and points at the Irishman, it becomes a sword, and Michael's heart skips a beat.

The wand disappears back into a fold of fur, and Negook repeats himself. "Somebody is pretty mad at you." He is looking at Harky, but he speaks to the group at large.

Hans starts to sputter, still holding his whittling before him. "See here, we won't be threatened, not by some—" He gropes for the words. "Not by a . . . a . . . drowned rat of an Indian!"

Negook's response to the insult is unexpected. Genuine amusement breaks across his face, a crooked, wide-open smile that exposes teeth yellowed and broken by centuries of gnawing. "You been diggin' at the ground a lot. And the ground moved. Now the ice attacks you, and you got no more food. No more boat, huh?" Negook looks in turn at each of their faces, still grinning, waiting for them to catch on.

"Come on to my village. Tlingit people going to take you back to *Goots-ka-yu kwan*, your own people."

After a long debate in the longhouse, Negook had convinced the people of the Lituya-kwan to take the whites away in their great canoes, take them back to Sitka or Juneau as a way of appeasing the Bear God. Most of the young men had argued for killing the whites by putting them into the crevasses of the glacier, the blue ice caves in which the bear lives, until the shaman reminded them what had recently happened to the village of Angoon.

A Tlingit shaman working for the white man's money on a whaling ship had been killed by the premature detonation of an exploding harpoon. By Tlingit law the whaling company was required to indemnify the man's family by paying the "blanket price," a few stacks of blankets as tall as the man. The whaling company refused, and when the villagers of Angoon took the whale boat and a couple of company men into keeping as a way of demanding payment, the company had sent a greatly exaggerated message to a U.S. Navy warship anchored in Sitka that said a general uprising was under way and the slaughter of every white man in the north was imminent.

By the time the Navy responded to the whalers' plea, the council of Tlingit elders had already decided to pursue litigation "white man style." The company's men had been sent on their way after a banquet and dancing to show that their detainment had only been a matter of custom and nothing personal.

Duly informed that the company managers were safe, the captain had nonetheless decided to administer summary justice in true white man style and ordered his cannons turned on the village, setting it on fire and utterly destroying it. Hundreds of men, women, and children lost everything—shelter, clothing, weapons, food, and tools—at the very beginning of *T'ak*, the longest part of winter. The suffering was terrible and the people learned a valuable lesson in the savage and arbitrary law of the *Guski-qwan*, those cloud-faced people with no blood in their hearts.

Caught between the hammer of the white man's cannons and the anvil of Kah-Lituya's rage, the villagers accepted the words of Negook. The Dogfish Clan will supply a canoe and ten men to paddle; the miners will be evacuated immediately.

Hannah asks, "You mean you will take us back to civilization? In the large canoe that was hunting here in the bay?"

Negook nods. Hans looks suspicious.

"How much?"

It takes the shaman a moment to realize the blond cloud-face is asking about price, not how much time it will take to paddle them away or how much weight the canoe can carry.

White men, he thinks to himself, *everything is business.* This is something that was not discussed in the longhouse. The only thing of importance is getting the whites away, getting them to go in the canoe.

To make it easy for them to agree, Negook looks around the cabin, considering a price. They don't have much, just some clothes, a few dishes, but they will need those things, and Negook does not want to leave them with nothing. Winter will come, and they will need supplies back in Sitka.

He considers asking for the stove—useless, hungry thing; a man can't even sit around and poke at the fire with a stick, watching the visions in the flames—but the whites will know they cannot take it anyway, it is too heavy; they take business seriously and might get insulted if he asks for such worthless payment. And if he asks for the shotgun or the pistol that bulges under the giant's shirt, they will be afraid he intends to shoot them. No, the only diplomatic thing to do in this delicate situation is ask for something they treasure, but which has no real value to their survival through the winter.

"Gold. Trade us gold and we will take you to your people."

The howling and barking that ensues shocks Negook. Hans pounds on the table, Michael takes a threatening step forward, doubling his fists. Even Hannah's mouth tightens into a straight line. Only Harky seems unaffected. Negook conjures a talisman of raven feathers bound with plaited grass and beads from beneath his cloak and holds it before him, hoping the charm is strong enough to protect him from these violent lunatics.

Dutch abandons his lookout at the sound of the commotion, steps in the door, and asks "What's this? What is it?"

His shoulders jerk when he spots Negook. His head bobbles on his neck as if it were attached by a spring, and he warbles. "Who's this?"

"This here's the bastard wants to steal our money, that's who it is," shouts Hans. Michael nods in agreement.

Dutch jumps back, gawking cross-eyed at the bundle of feathers in the shaman's fist, then looks puzzled, mouth agape, as he tries to figure how the fetish might take the place of a gun or knife.

Harky makes a rumbling sound, and his chest starts to quiver. Hannah at first thinks the sound is a precursor to an angry eruption, then realizes the Texan is laughing.

"Horseshit," says Harky. "Horseshit!" and shakes his head.

Harky rises to his feet and takes a step toward Negook. Hannah fears for the shaman's neck, but the Indian relaxes, nods toward the Texan, and replies in kind, "Horseshit." What a fine, useful word.

"How much gold?" asks Harky.

The shaman imitates a gesture he has seen white people use: He lifts his shoulders up and drops them, shrugging.

Harky picks up a spoon from the table and holds it out. "This much?"

Negook pushes out his lower lip and ponders the spoon. Negook raises his hand, holding the fingers spread wide.

"Five spoons of gold?" Harky says. "Five?" In pretext, his voice is sad and full of consternation at the same time. He sighs and shakes his head, laying the spoon back on the table.

"It's a big spoon. Two is plenty." Harky learned to bargain on the streets of Juarez, where dickering is a good-natured sport. The Tlingit, too, are avid traders and dealers, and may spend days haggling over a carving or paddle. Negook plays the game better than most, but today he just wants it finished. He holds up three fingers.

Harky holds out his hand and says, "Done."

————————

At dawn the sky is blue, fading to mauve in the west, and as Negook leads the prospectors into the wilderness, the colors of the forest reach out in tousled grays and greens. They walk in single file, pushing into serried tangles of blueberry shrubs and devil's club along a subtle path that rises and twists across broken and gullied ground. They move through a continuous mantle of sun-dappled emeralds and shadowed browns, following the trail's windings among Mamelon hills, along steep, crumbling bluffs. After the first hour, none of the miners has any sense of direction and each guesses differently at the alignment and location of the mountains, the sun, and the sea. By noon sweat runs in their eyes and Negook must pause every so often as the whites gasp for breath. The shaman's bare feet are black and cracked as macadam, and as he walks, his toes splay cloven and grasping over stones. He never stumbles, never pants, and never speaks, as he leads the party through the winding, cathedral maze of the forest.

The devil's club raises its claws to the miners as they push along behind Negook down the faint, tangled trail. Negook slides through the barbed and stabbing undergrowth with hardly a rustle while the abundantly thorned stalks and broad, palmate leaves of the plant brush at the whites' faces and stab at their shins with its needle-sharp spines. Dutch cries, "Damnation!" when a naive handhold inflicts a painful punishment on his palm. "How much farther is this damned place?"

Negook shakes his head at the ways of the white men, wasting themselves on words that mean nothing and questions with no answer, when already they run short of wind and still have far to go.

The blue black rustle of a raven's wing flickers high overhead, indistinct in the canopy of greens. When a smooth, ebony feather flutters down and places itself at Hannah's feet, she picks it up and pins it into her hair. The gesture draws a glance of rebuke from Hans and a long, black-eyed stare from Negook.

After a march of long hours through trees pillowed and quilted in moss, the party breaks out into a meadow.

Negook lets loose a sudden raucous call, which is answered by a human cry from down river. Hannah smells smoke, freshly cut wood, and the sea; in the distance is the low, mumbling thunder of ocean waves.

"Lituya-kwan," says Negook, pointing to a pale column of smoke rising above the brush. "The village."

The settlement is a cluster of plank-built longhouses assembled in orderly fashion along the rim of a sandy, surf-pounded cove. The face of each house is screened with a broad panel of cedar planks carved into the stylized forms of killer whales, bears, eagles, and salmon. A tall pole topped with a stylized raven stands guard over a number of canoes aligned at the edge of the beach, two of which are mammoth. Large enough, estimates Hannah, for each to easily hold forty or fifty people. The prows of both are decorated with staring, red-painted eyes that give the impression of giant sea creatures, which, having come ashore through the angry waves, now rest in vigilant repose on the sand.

Men and women clad in cedar bark cloaks and clothing cut from trade blankets filter out of the longhouses, surrounding the new arrivals. Negook addresses the assembly in a language that is harsh and glottal to Hannah's ears. Some of the villagers speak to the miners in *Siwash*, the farrago language distilled from a dozen Indian tongues and mixed with English and French to form the dialect of commerce used along the coastal trade routes between Oregon and Alaska. Hannah understands few of the words, but as Negook explains that the shipwrecked miners are ready to be evacuated, his gestures are clear.

A squarely built man with an imperial bearing points to the sea and waves a finger at the churning waters. He wears a woven grass hat in the shape of a cone and a leather vest open to the waist. The muscles of his chest are hard and smooth as plates of armor, bunching and swelling as he makes a paddling motion, saying, *"Ta dar da nook. Sa-cum. Sagun kleh ar."*

Another paddler, this one with the lean, dark features of an otter, a labret piercing his lower lip, and a pattern of smallpox scars across his cheeks, leaps forward shouting, *"Ya yuck-e-ya. Andai! Andai!"* Planting himself in front of Hans and Harky, he yells again, *"Andai!"*

Hans and Hannah step back from the open hostility. Harky holds his ground. All look to Negook for translation.

"Ta dar da nook," he says. "The wind is southwest, it makes the sea too heavy. Tomorrow, *Sa-cum*, or maybe two days more, it will be better. But this man . . ." He points with his

chin at the dark, weasel-faced man. "This man says you must go now. Today."

Harky looks out at the sea hurling itself headlong onto the shore. His eyes squinch, his face knotting. "Tomorrow maybe. Looks rough for a canoe today."

Hannah feels the sting of fine, windblown sand against her cheeks and nods in agreement. The canoe will be open, cold, and the furious state of the sea evokes the terrifying power of the surf that pounded the *Tara Keane* to pieces. Dutch, too, eyes the surf warily and agrees with Harky. "Sockum sounds good to me. What do you think, Michael? You're a sailing man like me, what you wanna do?"

Michael has been sullen since the loss of his ship, darkly quiet and unsmiling, speaking only to Hannah if he speaks at all, and addressing her carefully as "Mrs. Nelson." Hannah's heart aches for his loss—it was everything he had—but he is removed and self-contained. Now he glances from the canoes to the sea and around at the villagers. He shrugs, makes a slight spitting sound between his tongue and lips, and looks away. A small boy imitates his dismissive gesture, spitting repeatedly as if trying to clear a shred of something foul from his lips, then laughs aloud. The otter man again shouts, *"Andai!"* and waves the miners toward the canoes.

Negook bends, pulls a weed from the ground, rolls it rapidly back and forth between his palms, and turns in a circle, muttering. With a motion like a man releasing a captive bird, he tosses the tattered plant aloft and stands aright, palms upward, watching the shreds of leaf flutter between the wind and the earth.

"Tomorrow," he says. "Tomorrow there will be no wind."

Then he shouts in his own language this verdict to his people. Turning to the miners, he repeats himself. "No wind tomorrow. You go back to your people, go to Sitka, go to Juneau. Go away."

A place is made for the whites to sleep in the longhouse of the Dogfish Clan, where they are surrounded by laughing, walnut-colored children. The children reach out to rub at the miners' skin, tugging at their beards and squealing with delight. Old people marvel at Harky's size; girls and young women glance sideways at Michael; teenage boys assume fierce, glaring postures. Motionless warriors sit back in the shadows and bide their time. Hannah is handed a baby, and the chucking sounds she makes at the small, astonished black eyes brings a smile to the face of its mother.

The miners, so recently threatened by privation, wander the village, staring at a cornucopia of plenty. Food baskets filled to overflowing line the walls of the houses. There are blueberries, nagoon berries, thimble berries, and strawberries. Some are dried, hard as raisins; others are heaped like fresh jewels, glowing with freshness and the sweetness of the sun. The rafters of the house are hung with bushels of wild vegetables and roots of numerous varieties.

When the miners walk around the village, there is more harvest to be seen. There are huge moose hides stretched between trees, dense, rich pelts of otters and wolves drying on wooden stretchers, a smokehouse bulging with the purple black meat of seals. In an open space behind the longhouses a half-dozen white goat hides lie pegged to the ground.

Upstream from the village the river accelerates into a downward curve, just at the lip of a falls, congregating itself into a flow with the shining texture and color of green glass before breaking into a thousand pulsing streams of white. At the foot of the falls lies a swirling pool, thick with salmon layered into its depths like cordwood. The fish surge and spawn in the current. Along the banks of the river a dozen wooden racks sag under the weight of countless muscular silver bodies, which have been split and hung over low, smoky fires to dry. It is a display of such natural wealth and plenty that the whites stand speechless, wondering at the ignorance of their own poverty.

Michael fingers a strip of the ruby-colored meat, looking ponderous as his eyes roam these riches. But it is Harky who speaks first, and his words surprise Hannah. "We ain't going back, are we?"

Severts smiles slightly, gives a single shake of his head. "No reason now, is there?"

It takes Dutch and the Nelsons a moment to decipher what Harky and Michael have decided: There is no shortage of food, no reason to fear; the land will provide all that they need to continue mining.

"There's still a chance," Michael says, placing his hands on his hips. "We ought at least recover our losses."

Hans shakes his head. "I don't know. It's a lot of work to feed five mouths. How can we run the operation and feed ourselves hunting and fishing?" Waving a hand at the fish racks and meat houses, he repeats himself. "It's too much work, all this cutting and drying. No time for mining, if you still want to eat."

"This is all for winter, Nelson," Michael explains. "They're putting food away. We only have to get it on the table for now, nothing more." He looks from Hans to Hannah and back to Hans. "I'll do the hunting and bring in the fish. Mrs. Nelson can gather the greens and berries. With a few things from the garden and tightening our belts, we'll be all right."

Hans looks at the ground, considering the proposal, then shakes his head. "I don't know."

Dutch looks around at the villagers at work preparing for winter. "I ain't too sure, Michael. I think maybe we ought to get away while these Indians is willing to take us."

Severts's face grows dark, and his lips draw tight across his face. Hannah has the same odd, unsettling sense she had when Dutch's lie of having prospected Lituya was first exposed: That there is someone unknown, of great fury and brooding violence, looking out through Michael's eyes. When he speaks, his voice is like broken glass. "Well, that's damn-all fine for the lot of you. We split the take and go our merry ways, huh?" One fist clenches white on his waist; his eyes narrow, and he hunches his shoulders, settling the shotgun slung across on his back. "Well, I've lost my ship, and a single share won't cover my losses. And that isn't good enough."

Michael turns his back on the Nelsons. Hans's face mottles at the implied threat. Taking a pace forward, he says, "Now see here, Severts," and stops, uncertain what he wants to say.

Hannah sees Michael's chest swell as he takes a deep breath and forces his shoulders to relax. When he turns to face them again, his face is composed with studied ease.

"Sorry, Hans. I didn't mean to go off so hard. But really, what difference does it make if we leave now or next month?" Making a broad sweeping motion with his hand, as if presenting them with the bounty of the fish racks, he promises, "We'll make out all right."

When he continues, his words are soft, yet urgent and convincing. "One thing's for certain. We won't hit pay dirt back in Sitka or Juneau. As long as we're at work here, there's always a chance, hey?"

Dutch wipes a hand across his mouth, bites at his lower lip for a moment, then whines, "I dunno. This weather's getting worse all the time. Few more weeks, it might be pretty tough getting the Indians to paddle us to Sitka."

Dutch's wheedling tone settles Hans's opinion, and he curls his lip. "You got us into this mess, Dutch. Now you want to cut and run." He shakes his head, condemning Dutch as a coward.

Dutch's hands tremble, and Hannah realizes he is caught between fears: the fear of facing the autumn ocean in a canoe and the fear of being thought poorly of by others. His shoulders slump, and one eye looks at the sky. "I just don't know. It'll be winter 'fore you know it, that's all."

Hans looks pointedly at the sunny sky and the river brimming with salmon, the green foliage and grasses nodding heavy with seed.

"Winter, Dutch? Winter? It's full summer!"

Hannah remembers the ambush of winter in Skagway, the cold fist of snow and wind that fell out of a clear, warm sky and hammered at the tarp under which she huddled. She considers speaking in Dutch's favor, but she cannot bring herself to contradict her husband in front of the others.

Michael looks from Hans to Harky, who has remained silent throughout the exchange. "Agreed then, Harky? Hans?

We stay and work the claim, get the Indians to paddle us into Sitka in a month or so?"

Both nod in assent.

Dutch is overruled, and Hannah's opinion remains unsolicited. Misgiving nibbles at her thoughts, nudging her in the ribs. She holds her tongue.

———————

Negook does *not* hold his tongue as he stamps at the dirt floor of his hovel. A bundle of herbs and feathers plaited about a leather thong hanging from the rafters jerks and sways as he howls, "Horseshit! Horseshit!"

The lines furrowing the shaman's windswept brown face knot into patterns of anger and disbelief as his voice rises. "You dig at your mother's bones! You dig and dig until the ground shakes and the ice kills your boat! You must go! Go!"

"Mr. Negook, please, let me explain." The men are wandering the village, bartering for food, and Hannah tries to be reasoned and calm, since it falls to her to placate the irate shaman. "Mr. Negook, we simply must stay a few more weeks. We must work doubly hard now to recover our losses."

Wattles of loose skin along Negook's neck tremble. He shakes his head. "You will have great losses if you keep digging at the ground!" He is so angry his eyes bug until the huge, dark pupils seem to strike out at the woman. These idiots. Kah-Lituya will kill everyone! Perhaps he should let the young men put the *Guski-qwan* into the ice caves, feed them to the great bear. But then the smoking boat will come and shoot its cannons into the longhouses of the Lituya-kwan, and winter will take them all to their graves.

"Why you are staying here? Why don't you go back to your own people?"

"Sir, we have risked everything to come here. Our success has been limited, and our expenses high. And now Mr. Severts has lost his vessel. We simply must recover more gold before we can return to civilization."

"More gold! More gold!" Negook hacks a gob of phlegm onto the ground at his feet. "You must have more gold to buy things in your stores! You get clothes, fancy things. You buy food that comes in metal cans. Your man got to have more gold to buy another boat, but white men already got a lot of boats!" The shaman pounds at empty air with a clenched fist and stamps a calloused foot in the dirt. "Ayah!"

Their logic diverges as each tries to show the other the blunder of their opinions. Hannah argues calmly, as a dispassionate woman reasons with an uncontrollable child. Negook browbeats a fool, an imbecile who does not know how hot the coals are when she sits on a fire.

A clamorous barking of dogs breaks out in the village, and there is a long howl, which Hannah cannot distinguish as animal or human, followed by muffled shouting. In a moment the ragged blanket across Negook's doorway is thrust aside and a battered Dutch stumbles inside, pushed through the opening by Harky, who follows with his pistol in his hand. Blood streams from a cut across Dutch's forehead, flowing in a bright mask down his face. His eyes are wide with shock.

Hannah jerks upright and covers her mouth, trapping a gasp beneath her hand. The wall of the hut rattles with a banging of sticks and thrown stones. Outside, Hans's voice shouts for Michael. Both men burst breathless through the door.

Hans's hair is disheveled, and his coat is askew. "What in the hell, Dutch? What did you do to rile them?" Michael grips the shotgun to his shoulder, fingers the trigger, and levels the barrel at the door.

Dutch shakes his head. Mouth agape, lips wet and trembling, he looks as if he is about to start crying. Clutching at the wound on his scalp, he flinches, pulls his hand away, and gawks at the blood on his fingers.

Negook shouts through the wall in harsh, barking syllables. A yowling caterwaul of voices responds. *"Klute utardy tseek! Tseek-noon! Tseek-noon!"*

The shaman turns and stares at the bloodied Dutchman. Hannah tries to press a handkerchief to Dutch's wound, but he ducks away, whining, "Christ, all I done was ask a feller about a bear."

"What bear?" asks Hans, his voice shaking with suspicion and anger born of fear.

The shaman answers for the wounded man. *"Klute-utardy tseek.* The bear has come down from the glacier."

Dutch probes at the laceration with a tentative finger and curses. "Damn that fella. I seen that bear skin in his house there, and thought I'd get him to sell it to me for my bed."

A rock *thunks* against the roof; everyone but Negook flinches. Michael asks, "What's that, Negook? That bear you're talking about?"

The shaman's lips turn down like an overturned bowl, and matted gray locks of hair jangle about his face as he mutters, *"Tseek-noon.* The people are angry about *tseek-noon,* the bear coming. Because you keep digging, *tseek-noon* came down from the mountains and showed himself to you." It is not safe to mention the Bear God Kah-Lituya's name out loud or explain to these people how the silver bear comes as his messenger.

Michael looks at the others, the puzzled look on his face asking if any of them understands.

"What the hell did you do, Dutch? What's this about bears?"

Dutch shakes his head and takes the handkerchief Hannah offers, wipes it across his face, and whimpers at the blood.

"Jesus, all we was doing was talking back and forth, him in his heathen siwash, and me trying to talk American so's he'd understand. I told him about that odd creature I seen, that gold color bear on the beach. Just being friendly, you know, telling a couple of stories. And mother-a-god, he got all agitated and hit me with a paddle."

Harky nods in agreement. "That's right. Dutch and that Indian were just dickering over a bear hide, then Dutch starts in with that wild story. Next thing you know, the Indian's knocked Dutch over the head and is trying to club him. He'd of killed him if I hadn't showed my pistol." The hulking Texan shakes his head in wonderment, either at Dutch's endless folly, the warrior's unprovoked violence, or both.

Negook stares at Dutch without expression, then sighs and nods to himself. Mumbling, he digs into a dark corner piled with oddments of animal parts and skins and emerges with a bag knotted about the throat with a cord. Kneeling, he groans, opens the bag, and upends the contents into the dirt. Teeth, vertebrae, shells, and colored stones rattle onto a pile. There is a coin stamped with the Russian eagle, a spent bullet, and a splintered bone. Seeds mixed with birds' beaks and pearly bits of abalone shell filter from the bottom of the bag. Negook shakes it empty, then probes at the mixture with a finger.

Moaning and keening, he stirs the pile, picking out bits and pieces, rattling them like dice in his hand before spitting gently on the selected parts and pouring them out in a curving line across the ground. The prospectors stand frozen, disbelieving, but nonetheless waiting for the primitive divination to render a forecast or sentence.

Negook nudges the spent bullet from the line of fetishes and inspects it before sitting back on his heels, purses his lips, and blows a long sigh. When he speaks, he whispers, "The bear will give you what you want."

The shaman's eyes shine like wet coal as he peers up at the miners, who cluster like quail. Turning his back on them, he shuffles away, motioning for them to come.

"Where we going?" asks Dutch, anxious at the thought of paddle-wielding warriors beyond the sheltering walls. "Where you taking us?"

Negook replies, "I'm going to show you gold. Lots and lots of gold."

And, as if he can see the quizzical looks exchanged behind his back as he pulls aside the rag door, he says, "That is the best way to punish you."

TWELVE

A steady breeze stirs the feathers knitted into Negook's matted hair into elliptical flutters. A finger of black bedrock splits the stream in which he stands into two parts, flowing left and right around its base before joining again into a single run of water. He whispers; the stream answers in low murmurs. The miners dig, shoveling gravel into buckets and pouring the buckets into the Long Tom sluice box the shaman insisted they erect on this spot. Believing, they dig. Disbelieving, they dig harder.

While Harky and Hans shovel, Michael and Dutch divert water from the stream into the sluice. The flow slurries gravel the length of the box, driving it over the wooden riffles with a hissing sound. As the water runs, Michael and Dutch take turns rocking the box, shaking a post nailed upright to one corner. Tools clang on hardpan, water gurgles on stones, gravel rattles and grates down the boards in a rhythm of labor that hypnotizes the men with its consistency of motion.

While they work with mud and cold water, Negook reluctantly instructs Hannah in gathering various foods in the forest. There is the leaf and stalk of *l'ool*, the bright, tall-flowered fireweed, with its crimson and purple blossoms; *K'oox*, the chocolate lily, whose root is like rice; cloudberries—*n'ex'w*—and tart thimbleberries called *ch'eex'*, which can be mixed together, pulped, and thickened by adding *k'eikaxetl'k*, bunchberries with the seeds removed.

None of this will do any good, he knows, but when the spirits of divination had whispered to him what the Bear God has in store for them, his anger toward the whites had abated. Because *T'ak* is coming—*T'ak*, the terrible child-dying time, when even the waterfalls are frozen and no living thing stirs in the land. When winter is at its worst, Kah-Lituya will destroy these people, but first he will raise them up on dreams of gold and drive them mad. And for that Negook pities them. He shows Hannah how to wrap a whole salmon in a broad leaf of skunk cabbage and cover it with coals, steaming the delicate flesh until it flakes in buttery pink layers. "Eat the head and the eggs," he tells her. "Lots of good fat there."

The men shovel and sluice; the shallow trench they dig grows to the depth and size of a grave. Michael stands upright in pain, clutching at the small of his back, then forces himself to bend to his shovel again. Harky whistles a tuneless melody, imitating the buzzing calls of southbound thrushes and kinglets flitting through the trees.

When evening comes, Hans calls out, "Let's clean up!" and pickets his shovel with a stamp of his boot. As he washes the concentrated fines from the riffles by pouring water carefully down the sluice with a can, the others gather round, watching as the slurry is gathered in the nap of the towel, the towel folded and lifted from the bed, then the concentrate carefully divided into waiting pans.

The largest is a shallow dish two feet across. In Harky's giant hands it looks like a butter dish, and he dips it carefully into the running stream, using the kiss of the current to wash away the soil. Swirling and rocking, he distills the contents, boiling off the silica and sand.

The sun dips behind a thin band of cloud, losing its intensity, and at that moment he sees it: a solid rim of gold glittering along the edge of the pan. The sun reemerges, illuminating the crescent with the glow of a blacksmith's molten cauldron. Harky cannot breathe, he cannot speak, and the others are afraid to look until he holds out the pan. Heads together, Hans, Michael, and Dutch bend to stare into the amalgam. The glimmer pierces each in turn, stabbing deep into that part of every man that is a thief, firing the greed in their veins.

"Jesus," says Hans.

"I told you," says Dutch. "Didn't I tell you?"

Michael just stares, acutely aware of the sound of his own breathing, the chuckling of the stream, the play of the breeze on his face.

Dear Diary,

The advance from rags to riches has been swift. Thanks to the Indian Negook, we have at last achieved our goal of striking "pay dirt." The strike is wonderfully rich, yielding four or five times as much gold as any ground we have previously worked. At the present rate of recovery, we shall all be very well off by the time autumn forces us to retire to Sitka.

The days now grow rapidly shorter as winter approaches, and Hans, Harky, and Dutch work from daylight until dark, while Michael hunts. Hans speaks of working by torchlight, but the others decline to work any harder, as they already return to the cabin at night, exhausted and bleeding from their palms.

The men's days are strictly scheduled: Breakfast before daylight, work until dark, bathe in the pool (which grows chillier these days, but is still the best part of my day; I have my bath after the men have left in the morning), then the evening meal, after which the take is weighed before we retire to our bunks. Dutch crows and struts like a banty rooster each evening as Hans weighs out the take, but it is easy to forgive him his unseemly exultations, for he has been richly vindicated by Negook's strike.

Michael is proving to be a fine huntsman, adept at bringing fresh meat to the table. The flesh of the goats and sea lions is often stringy and tough, but he has fashioned a mallet from a spruce knot with which I beat the meat tender.

Only Harky seems untouched by our fortune, but he is always such a silent man it is difficult to say whether or not he shares the exuberance of the strike.

I must admit that the gold ignites grand dreams in my own mind, dreams of a fine home and nice things, but it stirs a certain fear as well, an uneasiness I cannot define. But until we are done here, it remains for me to pick berries, till the garden, and gather greens from the forest just like any primitive Indian woman (only the Indians are much more adept at these tasks than I).

———

Canvas bags of gold are piled on the table like so many sausages. Outside the cabin, the night air is thick with mist. A cold wind sucks a swirl of bright sparks from the stovepipe and sends the glowing fireflies fleeing and blinking into the forest to extinguish themselves on damp foliage. Michael and Hans figure and refigure estimates of the company's worth in columns and tables penciled on a page cut from Hannah's journal.

The open door of the stove casts a glowing light that dances across the floor and over the faces of the cabin's inhabitants. The jump and swirl of the fire shadows remind Hannah of the flight of birds, the sudden uprush and circling of pigeons in Trafalgar Square, or the dance of swallows in the burnt umber air of London after it has gone thick with coal smoke in late evening.

The shadows retreat as she turns up the lantern, hangs it from a roof beam, and angles a skillet into the light to inspect it for cleanliness.

"Goat meat again, Mrs. Nelson?" asks Dutch. The question makes him feel very homey, almost as if he were inquiring of his own wife what they are having for dinner, and he wishes he had a pipe to smoke or a dog at his feet.

"That and a salad of greens," replies Hannah. "I've taken the last of the kale from the garden. It was going to seed."

Dutch leans back on his stump-chair and crosses his arms. "Be time to dig the potatoes, too, I imagine."

Hans looks up from his figures and sighs. "Meat and greens, meat and spuds, meat and meat. The menu is getting rather bland."

Negook's voice startles the miners as he steps through the door. "Plenty of white man's food in Sitka."

The wind enters with the wizard, eddying angrily about his feet before grabbing the open door and slamming it. Beads of mist cling to the shaman's hair, glittering in the lantern light. His legs are bare, muddy to the knees, and he carries a walking stick carved from the rib of a whale.

His voice is low and mixes with the sound of the wind as he points with the bone at the sacks stacked on the table. "You got plenty now. It is time for you to go. *Andai*. Now."

No one is able to reply. The sudden appearance of the shaman from out of the darkness seems to bring all of the wilderness into the tiny cabin, and they are suddenly, keenly, aware of the space beyond the walls, the immensity of a world filled with unbreachable mountains, fierce churning storms, the rumble of glaciers, and the mourning of wolves.

Hans looks down at the paper worked with figures and clears his throat. He feels ridiculous and small, sitting like a bank clerk with the pencil in his hand as he *ahem*s and says, "Well, we were just discussing this," knowing as he says it that the shaman has been listening outside and will recognize the words as a lie.

Pressing ahead, enslaved by the craving for more gold, Nelson claims, "We've tallied the take. And we need to keep going."

Negook fixes him with a black-eyed stare. Unnerved, Nelson turns the paper toward the shaman, as if offering it for his inspection, and taps it with the pencil.

"Eight thousand. That's what we've got so far."

Negook continues to stare. Hans shuffles, fidgets, taps the paper again.

When Negook speaks, there is barely controlled rage in his voice. "You got lots of damn gold. Now you must go. Storms are coming. Winter is coming. *T'ak* will be a very bad time for you." He slices the whalebone through the air like a sword. "Enough gold. Leave before the Bear comes again."

The door springs open behind him, and a gust of wind billows the canvas roof over their heads. The lantern flares, swinging and throwing wild, harsh shadows across the walls. Negook spins on his heel and steps out into the darkness.

The miners sit silent, speechless, and frozen in their places, watching as the rain blowing in through the open door draws a faint, glistening pattern in the light of the lantern until Michael rises to his feet, walks to the door, and peers out into the night. The rain splinters against his face for a moment before he closes the door, wipes a hand across his eyes. Drops of water turn silver against the black of his hair, and Hannah's breath catches, arrested by the sight of how beautiful he is.

"This bear, Dutch. Where was it you saw this silver bear?"

Dutch sits upright on his stump, looking puzzled by the question. "What? The silver bear? I seen it down to the west there, on that little creek what comes from behind a hill. Why?"

Michael pulls a handkerchief from a hip pocket and rubs his face before answering. "These Indians. They give away gold, but seem uncommonly worried about some silver bear. Seems queer, that's all."

Folding the handkerchief carefully, he squares the edges, patting it flat. "Must be a pretty valuable bear."

When dawn comes, the sky is as clear and blue as a robin's egg. The air carries a crisp sweetness, like the smell of something clean, and the highest ridges along the fjord are laced with fresh snow. Hans, Harky, and Dutch prepare to settle into the gut work of mining, barrowing stones and earth into a sluice. Michael settles an oar into the thole pins of the skiff, passes a loop of line over the shaft, and nestles a pack stuffed with rope, water, and ammunition into the bow along with Hannah's oilskin coat and the shotgun, wrapped in a square of tarpaulin cloth in case of rain.

Hans thinks of nothing but gold these days—how to move more earth, channel more water, recover more ore— and seemed distracted when Hannah asked his permission to join Michael on a hunt deep into the fjord. Now Nelson frowns at the sight of his wife climbing into the skiff with the Irishman, but unable to think of an excuse to rescind his consent, he simply growls, "Be back before dark." The tide is rising, covering a band of seaweed along the rim of the cove.

"We'll ride the flood in," says Michael. "That'll save me rowing. And with Mrs. Nelson along to carry the pack and help with the skinning, I'll be able to get a young goat and still ride the ebb back down the fjord. We'll be home well before sunset."

Hans looks dark and doubtful. Hannah is careful not to look at Michael as she climbs into the skiff, but turns and smiles with a wave at her husband, feeling deceitful.

The tide hurries the skiff along the beach and close along the upthrust walls of the fjord. Icebergs blue as the sky drift and sparkle in the sun and as Michael's strong strokes wend the skiff expertly through the belts of floating ice, Hannah has a sense of being in another world. Seals at rest on low, bobbing icebergs raise their heads to stare as the skiff passes. Once away from camp, Hannah is keenly aware of being alone with the Irishman. He knows this by her silence and by the way she avoids his eye.

An hour later the keel scrapes against a mossy, bouldered beach, and Michael jumps out to steady the hull. Moving to the bow, he hoists the pack to one shoulder, braces the skiff with both hands, and instructs Hannah to step out. When she slips on the slick stones underfoot, he catches her about the waist, lifting her effortlessly to her feet; she blushes at the firm touch of his hands.

They secure the skiff, binding a boulder into a double loop of line for an anchor, then begin climbing toward the cloudless sky. The mountain rises steeply, and Hannah quickly finds herself warm and panting. Michael goes ahead, the shotgun slung down his back, searching out a route that switchbacks along grass-covered ledges, across slopes of loose, rattling shale. High overhead, below the new snow, a small herd of goats forms a cluster of white dots in the alpine. They climb steadily higher, ascending first through alder, then grasses, then into a band of low plants blushing red at the brazen approach of autumn.

Far below, a pencil stroke of coastline unreels to the south. In the north, the spires of the mountains reach up from shadowed valleys, turning rose-colored, then white as the sun rises. To the west the sea is a shimmering expanse of silk.

Hannah and Michael pause in their climbing to watch the thin line of the surf knit itself to the land, the rise and fall of the swell like a loom weaving silently through beds of kelp until some trick of the wind brings the rumble of the waves to them on their perch high above the sea. Another shift of the wind, and they hear the mad, muddy rush of a river tumbling from a cliff at the head of the fjord.

From above, the elements of the world are obvious. Bold faces of stone worked smooth by the glacier stand high above plains of blue ice. Steep valleys carved by eons of rushing water fall away in all directions. Below, the shape of the sea fits neatly into the land, then reaches out, curving sinuously into the horizon, blending sky, stone, ice, and water together into a complete picture of creation.

Hannah is breathless from the climb and envious of the eagles and goats that awaken and rise from their beds to such a vista every day. All around, the immensity of the mountains gives way to the space of the sky, and she lifts up her arms, feeling free.

Michael motions for her to bend low. Pointing at a large shoulder of stone a hundred yards away, he whispers, "The goats are just over there."

Hannah tucks her heavy wool skirt about her knees and crouches, suddenly aware that the beauty of the day is about to give way to killing.

"Stay here," Michael directs her. "I'll go up and come down on them from above." Shading his eyes against the sun to inspect the route of the stalk, he says, "This shotgun has a limited range. I'll have to get close."

Shrugging out of the pack, he drops it to the ground and digs out a handful of shells, gives Hannah a dazzling smile, and crawls away, slithering from shadow to shadow. Watching him go, Hannah understands he is showing off for her, moving silently and smoothly through the broken stones and heather; once he glances back to see if she is watching, and she wonders at the joy men find in killing. Then she remembers Uliah Witt's description of most interplay between men and women as simple biology: man, the provider, woman the nester. She pictures herself standing between Michael, the huntsman, and her husband, who digs at the ground, both compelled by the same urges.

But I have never known a man like him, she thinks, meaning Michael's exuberance, his willingness to joke, sing out loud, and laugh. Hans, she realizes, has never made her laugh. She feels a twinge of guilt, as if the very thought has made her somehow unfaithful. Then she watches as Michael eases forward on hands and knees, and feels that which binds her to Hans to be on the verge of fleeing, of casting itself into this vast and beautiful wilderness.

A twist in the wind ends the hunt before Michael can raise his gun. The cool air over the snow carries his scent like a thin tendril of smoke to the delicate nose of an old nanny grazing close to the ridge. She springs away, scattering stones that clatter and slide down the mountain, her fright sending the herd bounding out of range.

Michael rises to his feet, watching the goats go, then turns toward Hannah and shrugs. He returns with long, bounding strides, springing down the steep hill from foothold to foothold with the balance and grace of a stag. He smiles. "We're all getting a bit tired of goat meat anyhow."

They share a drink from the flannel-covered canteen. The water is sweet and cool. They sit together quietly, watching a soaring eagle pass below them. The sun falls into the layer of clouds and emerges from below to bathe the sea with a color that is between scarlet and gold. Michael sweeps a hand before him and sighs. "All this space . . . ," he says.

She knows what he means, how it reduces you.

Hannah looks at the color of the sea and feels the bite of winter in a breeze drifting down from the snow-covered peaks. "It does make the gold seem less important," she replies.

"Aye," says Michael, coming to his feet and holding out a hand to Hannah, "but it also makes our larder seem rather empty. We better get on. We'll try for a seal on the way back." Their hands linger together as she rises. Hannah feels the planet wobble beneath her and pulls away.

———————

Ice hisses and grumbles at their passing as the tide draws the skiff down-fjord. Aging bergs, the size and shape of wrecked houses, fracture and splinter into smaller bits to the sound of rifle cracks, booms, and echoes. As the sun lowers toward the horizon, points of light begin to sparkle along the ice's fissures and serrated edges.

Michael rows slowly, letting the tide and the breeze work the boat westward. The color of the sun on the water, the feel of the oars in his hands, and the penny-pipe calls of seagulls draw him into a waking dream of his childhood, when he rowed with his father through the chill, gloaming waters of Ireland, and in his mind he rows now among the reefs of the Atlantic instead of between Pacific icebergs.

The birds among the alders and willow thickets ashore have just begun to mourn the approaching loss of daylight, when Michael spots a herd of seals on a low, tabular berg. Shipping the oars, he draws the gun.

"Don't move," he instructs Hannah, raising the weapon to his shoulder. "The wind will drift us down on them."

The skiff creeps inexorably closer, slowly broadsiding itself to the sleeping seals. A mother on lookout raises her head and inspects the strange apparition, stealing quick glances over her shoulder at the pups behind her. Hannah closes her eyes and holds her breath; Michael braces the gun; the ice mumbles and grates against the hull. The sleeping seals, used to the chatter and pop of the ice, hear nothing unusual and slumber on.

The lookout grows nervous, staring wide-eyed and considering alarm, but stays her warning too long. When Michael fires, Hannah jumps at the report and opens her eyes to the panicked splashing of the fleeing herd. A young seal remains behind, its body arching and thrashing. A bright flower of blood blooms intensely red against the blue ice, and as the skiff comes alongside, the wounded seal rights itself, lowers its head, and considers its approaching executioners with eyes huge and round with fear.

The eyes of the seal as it regards the approaching knife in Michael's hand are as tender and soft as anything the Irishman has ever seen. The rowing dream of childhood still lingering, he sees in the dark and frightened orbs an image of himself looking up at his father as his elder loomed over him, damning his son's English blood and preparing to beat him for something minor. A tear of self-pity starts at the corner of Michael's eye. Hannah, believing the tear is for the seal, says to herself, against her own will, *I could love this man—* and knows that the world has suddenly become a very bright and dangerous place.

A stab and a slice, and the seal's young life is ended. Michael strips to the waist before opening the small body. The gut cavity steams and smokes in the cool air. Red to his wrists, he asks Hannah to hold the carcass by the hind flippers while he works. The spotted and glistening hide, layered in fat, peels away in a blanket that smells strongly of fish and the sea.

Hannah stacks the purple meat in neat piles on the hide. Michael folds the lot into the tarpaulin, forming a pack, which he hoists to his shoulder and carries to the skiff. After rinsing his hands in seawater, rubbing at his nails and wrists to clear them of blood, he helps Hannah into the skiff. The smell of warm blood and meat fills the air.

She is elated and frightened, avoids Michael's eye, and studies carefully, without seeing, the ice and mountains around them. As the skiff draws away, a pair of bold ravens swoop in to squabble over the pink and gray entrails.

———————

The keel of the skiff crunches ashore, shattering the litter of mussel shells strewn about the beach below the cabin, just as the reddest part of the evening light floods in from the west. The low-angle light bathes the thick stands of fireweed along the edge of the forest in crimson and emerald, highlighting the copper in Hannah's hair. Her color is high from the day, her face warm and ruddy. She feels flushed with the tension that sings back and forth along invisible nerves strung between her skin and the Irishman's.

There is no response to Michael's *haloo* to the cabin; the miners work late at their digging. Hannah is relieved. She will have time to compose herself before Hans returns.

As they pull together to raise the skiff above the reach of the tide, Michael and Hannah feel as though they're being watched. The door of the silent cabin stands ajar—Hannah is certain it was secured when she left—and the atmosphere is tense with the electric, silent sense of another's presence.

Michael yells *haloo* again, then stands quietly, watching and listening, before unlimbering the shotgun and motioning Hannah to stay back.

Easing forward, he notes first the garden. This morning it was a neat plot of beans and leafy plants laid out in straight rows; now it is a square of plowed wreckage. Stepping slowly and carefully to the cabin, he pushes at the door with the barrel of the gun, then pauses, cocking his head to listen. Hearing nothing, he risks a quick glance inside, then steps back and motions Hannah forward.

"We've been plundered! It looks like a bear."

Inside the cabin is a litter of crushed cans, scattered blankets, and splintered wood. The bear has scratched and bitten at every item, and the interior looks as if a madman has run rampant, axing and smashing everything within reach. Grains of barley and rice litter the dirt floor. The tins that contained them are smashed flat. The small store of flour has been invaded, and white bear tracks mark the scraps of lumber that once were the table and bunks. Clots of ticking bleed from wounds in the thin mattresses; clothing has been pawed into the dirt, and the door itself sprung on its hinges. No single item has been left intact or bit of food unspoiled.

Michael studies the mess, then lowers the shotgun and begins to clean up, salvaging what boards and clothes he can. Hannah joins in, but moves slowly, numbed by the disaster. *Is this punishment?* she wonders. *The price of tempting my marriage?*

Severts untangles the rope weaving of the Nelsons' bed, coiling the line neatly. "I'll fix this tomorrow. There's enough here to rebuild your bed and at least one other bunk." He looks out the door at the gathering darkness. "We best salvage what we can from the garden before it gets too dark. Perhaps it missed a few potatoes or something. Don't want the beast coming back in the night."

Outside in the dark, Michael holds a lantern aloft, and Hannah bends to the ground, probing with a shovel at the claw-tilled earth and vegetation. There are broken bits of carrots and a handful of pea pods, which Hannah drops into a sack. The vandalized garden gives up a small armload of potatoes. Many bear the marks of teeth and claws.

The lantern drops a cone of wavering light around them, isolating them from the rest of the world. Michael watches the firmness of Hannah's slender back and shoulders as she bends to dig at the ground. The soil gives up a rich, fecund smell, and the damp earth clings to her hands. Curls of loose hair hang about her face, and when she brushes one aside, a streak of dirt appears on her cheek.

"I did this with my mother," whispers Michael. "Just like this, stealing potatoes in the dark from the Grady's field. And after . . ." He shifts once on his feet, then again. "She . . ." Just that and nothing more, but there is something anguished and confessional in his words, and Hannah swallows an urge to take his hand.

They work closely together, and when Michael places the lantern on the ground to hold the neck of the sack open for Hannah to drop in her meager booty, the darkness severs them both at the knees. They stand with their faces in shadow, the smell of seal meat and green earth in the air.

Hannah takes a deep breath and tastes the scent of Michael

standing by her side. Shivering and trembling, she feels herself standing above a great vein of gold, and having no other words for the emotion, she names it love.

Fool's gold, she says to herself, wiping the dirt from her hands. *Fool's gold for a married woman.*

The spell is broken by the sound of boots approaching in the dark. Michael raises the lantern, calling out, "Hello?"

"What ho!" cries Dutch and does a jig step as he enters the light. Hans is close behind, his face split in a grin. Harky stops just outside the range of the lantern and becomes a large shadow.

"Big news, Mrs. Nelson. Big news!" laughs Dutch.

Hans pulls a knotted handkerchief from his pocket and undoes it, holding it low to the light of the lantern. Cupped in his hand is a fistful of large nuggets, lumps of gold with the smooth, rounded texture of wax that has been melted and puddled in walnut-sized beads.

"It's solid, Hannah, a streak of gravel that is yellow with gold." He raises his fist as if offering her a closer look. "We're rich. Very rich."

Michael leads a back-slapping Dutch and Harky inside to inspect the damage. Before Hannah can follow, Hans restrains her, saying, "Wait, I've something for you." Her heart skips at the feel of his hand on her arm and stumbles as he releases her to fumble in his pocket.

"I've done a bit of high-grading." He smiles. "But I'm sure the boys won't mind." So saying, he raises his hand. Cupped in his palm lies a tiny, heart-shaped nugget.

"Take it." He grins, mistaking her hesitance for surprise. "It's for you."

Hannah feels frozen, awkward, and it requires an effort to reach out and tweeze the nugget from his hand with a whispered, "Thank you." When he wraps his arms around her, it feels like she is being bound by cables.

"There's more," he says, nuzzling. "Now that we're rich, we can plan for children."

When she stiffens, he pulls back. His smile melts into a puzzled grin. "I thought you would be happy."

"Oh," she says. "Of course I am. It's just that . . ." She stares at the nugget, then makes a gesture that takes in the bear-plowed field, the shattered cabin, the gold, and the darkness. "It's just all so overwhelming."

———

That night she tosses fitfully on the floor, rigid and desperately aware of her place between her husband and Michael, whose presence a few feet away is tangible. The scope of the animal's vandalism had done nothing to dampen Dutch's golden exuberance, but Hans, puzzled, even hurt, by his wife's lack of enthusiasm, had simply shrugged after inspecting the damage and said, "We can buy more. In a few weeks we'll be able to buy dozens of everything."

Hannah dozes, starting at every sound outside the cabin, and when she sleeps, dreams of opening herself to someone or something strong with warm breath.

THIRTEEN

Hannah sizzles the dark flesh of the seal in a skillet before the first crack of dawn, taming its gamey flavor with a handful of diced potatoes and salt. Hans and Dutch are raring to go, lacing up their boots as they gobble their meal. Harky takes his time, saving his energy for shoveling.

The remains of breakfast are still warm when Hannah scrapes them from the skillet into an empty lard bucket and covers it with a cloth for the miners' noon meal. Outside, it is that moment of dawn when darkness first grows pale and objects take shape in the gloom. Michael is sorting out saws and hammers, nails and wire, marshalling his forces to drive the wrecked chaos of the cabin into order. Hans and Dutch head for the diggings, walking side by side with springing strides, shovels over their shoulders. Harky follows slowly.

Hannah, keeping her back to Michael as he works at the bent hinges of the door, arranges the few kitchen items salvaged from the bear's depredations into a small row on the only shelf left intact, scrubbing overly long at the breakfast skillet, folding and refolding a dish towel over the back of a chair to dry. As the light comes, she sees that her hands are dirty with soil. Seal blood darkens the edges of her nails. She sniffs at her fingers; there is a lingering trace of seal fat, rank with the odor of fish, and the light smell of dried sweat from yesterday's climb. Her skin itches. Her hair feels like a mixture of oil and straw.

Sorting out a towel and fresh blouse, she pushes them into a bag with a chip of soap and makes ready to leave. Michael must step aside to make room for her at the door, and they move around each other, excusing themselves in the too-polite tones of a couple who have recently argued. Michael watches her go down the path toward the bathing pool and shouts, "Be careful, Mrs. Nelson. That bear may be lingering about."

Along the trail Hannah listens carefully for the crackling of branches or thud of large feet, but hears only the *yawk* of a raven calling out from its station in the top of a tree. The colors of the grass and foliage beside the trail have turned from a litany of summer greens to the pastel tans and browns of autumn. The mossy shadows beneath the trees are damp with dew. At the pool she slips behind a screen of alders and disrobes, spreading her skirt, petticoat, corset, drawers, and shimmy over accommodating limbs to air.

Wading into the water, she flinches at the chill, raising her hands to her shoulders and taking tentative steps, pausing at ankles, knees, and thighs until finally stepping in to her waist with an inrush of breath. Making sharp, gasping sounds of pleasure, she scoops water onto her shoulders, breasts, and belly.

As she begins to wade toward the shore, the sharp *snap* of a breaking stick shoots a bolt through her heart. There is a rustle of movement among a bank of ferns lining the pool and the brushing sound of a body moving somewhere just out of sight. Hannah holds stock-still, shivering. Her pulse thunders in her ears. Her breath rattles, adrenaline screams through her blood. She waits for the bear to show.

It is no bear but Michael who emerges. Relief, then panic, floods through Hannah, and she crosses her arms over her chest and plunges to a kneeling position in the water, covering herself to the neck. The cold forces a strangled shriek from her throat, and she rises, then drops again.

Michael stands at the fringe of the forest, mute and consumed, shotgun in hand, his chest rising and falling like a bellows, mouth tightened into a single line. Laying the shotgun down carefully, never taking his eyes from the woman before him, he advances to the edge of the pool.

"No, Michael." Hannah holds up one hand.

He pauses, then walks fully clothed and shod into the water.

"Michael, please," she says, backing away.

He advances.

"I mustn't," she says, moving backward onto the bank behind her and rising, lithe as an otter, beads of water freckling the skin across her breasts. Michael keeps coming until he is inches away, then reaches slowly with one hand and touches lightly with the tips of his fingers along her ribs, her belly, her breasts. She does not pull away.

———————

Later, in the grass, exhausted and bruised by the strength of their cravings, she says, "I have a husband."

Michael raises himself to one elbow, unsure whether she speaks in threat or collusion, and gazes at her before replying. "And that split lip he gave you? Is it a good husband who does that to his wife?"

She does not argue—Michael refuses to believe it was an accident, but lies quietly as he curls himself around her. The smell of crushed heather rising from beneath her mingles with his scent against her back.

———————

Later that afternoon Hannah sits with her back to the door, sewing kit open on the table before her, staring without seeing at the crude shelves nailed to the cabin walls and their meager burden of pans and utensils. As she stares, her hands toy with a long piece of thread, wrapping and unwrapping it tightly around one finger. Outside, the buzzing call of a thrush signals the onset of evening. The light of the lantern is soft and orange against the canvas roof.

The metallic clanking of dropped shovels signals the return of the miners, and Hannah rises to her feet as she listens to the sound of boots being knocked against stones to remove mud from the tread. She takes up a spoon and begins to stir a pot that does not need stirring.

Hans is the first to enter, followed by Dutch, who bears a load of firewood in his arms. From outside comes the sound of an ax, as Harky begins a methodical attack on a bolt of wood. The knees of her husband's pants are worn through from kneeling all day in the gold-bearing gravel, and he is whistling. She does not look up as a canvas poke lands on the table with a solid thump. She stirs the kettle slowly, round and round, steam rising into her eyes.

"Hannah! Leave the soup a moment and come see what your husband has brought you!" The cheer in Hans's voice brings panic rising into her throat, and it requires an effort of will to replace the pot lid and lay down the spoon before turning to see what he means.

A litter of gold nuggets washes across the plank table, spilling among her bobbins and needles. An ear-to-ear grin splits Hans's unshaven face. "It's still coming. Every shovel turns up a nugget! We're really on it now." Hans claps his hands together, as Harky enters the cabin with more firewood and kneels to dump it beside the stove. "Ain't that right, Harky? Every beautiful shovelful's a payday now, ain't it?"

Harky favors Hannah with a small, pleased smile and nods. "Pretty good, all right. Michael still out huntin'?"

At the mention of Michael's name Hannah feels a twist under her ribs and turns her back to the men. She retrieves the soup spoon and carefully wipes it clean on her apron before replying. "I haven't seen him. I suppose so. Yes, he is."

Hans sweeps the scatter of nuggets into a heap, flicking aside needles and buttons before transferring the booty back into its poke. "Well, we've done a hungry day's work here, and that soup smells mighty good. I guess he'll forgive us if we go on and eat without him. A man's liable to forgive just

about anything when he comes home to something like this."
He bounces the sack in his hand, measuring its weight and
grinning.

The bowls are spaced four around the table, spoons placed
alongside. As befits the society of the wealthy, Hans and
Dutch sit primly, squares of material cut from an old shirt
stuffed into their collars for napkins. Harky perches, hands
at his side, shifting awkwardly as he waits for Hannah to take
her place. She fiddles, first with the pot, then by feeding more
wood to the fire.

Hans grows impatient with her dallying. The thought of
the gold piled up in his cupboard makes him feel expansive.
"What is keeping you, Hannah? Come to the table."

She pokes at the fire, aligning the new kindling with the
flames. "Hans."

"What?"

The stove door squeaks as she closes it. Her answer is slow
to come.

"Please come outside with me."

"Come outside with you?" Hans looks puzzled, then
piqued. "What for?"

Hannah's hand flexes at her side, gripping and ungripping
at nothing. She holds it against her thigh to still it, without
answering.

At that moment the door rattles open. Severts steps
inside, the twin barrels of the shotgun gleaming blue in the
dim light. In his off hand, a brace of mallard ducks carried
upside down by the feet. The warm, softly feathered bodies
swing loosely in his grip as he turns to push the door closed

with the gun. Holding the birds aloft, he grins. "Tomorrow's dinner, Mrs. Nelson. Two birds with one shot."

Dutch, still playing the laird, yelps, "Bravo, me boy, bravo!" applauding his admiration. "Good shootin'. How'd you do it?"

Michael grins at Hannah, who stands stiffly, staring at the birds. A single drop of blood swelling from the bill of the nearest threatens to fall. The duck's eyes are clenched, and one wing hangs askew. Without taking his eyes from her face, Severts answers.

"Well, you just have to wait. Bide your shot until everything lines up just so. And when the birds are just right . . ." Severts winks at Hannah and clicks his tongue. "Pull the trigger."

Hans, done with waiting, speaks up. "Well, lay them aside and let's set-to on this dinner." He points at Michael's place and drives a spoon into his bowl. "What was it you wanted, Hannah?"

When Hannah replies, "Nothing, Hans, never mind," a small smile flits across Michael's mouth. He smiles again as he sits at the table and raises a spoon to his lips.

––––––––––

Through the days that follow, he comes for her again and again as she picks berries or washes clothes. Dark circles of guilt grow under her eyes from lying all night with her back to her husband, barred from sleep by the untenable impulse to confess. When she tries to speak of her dilemma to Michael, he takes her by the waist, saying, "It's too late to worry about that, girl. It's simply too late." Drawing her to him, he whispers feverishly, "I have to have you. And I will." Neither knows if confession or continuation is her meaning as her reply—"No good can come of it"—is smothered by his lips.

Soon the last of her reserve melts, leaving her awash in a great spasm of pleasure where muscles contract, cry out, and cry out again. A saying of her father's—that a man may as well be hung for a sheep as for a lamb—becomes a taunting dirge that recycles itself over and over again to the rhythmic breathing of the man who sleeps, exhausted from his earthworks, by her side.

Michael is at times tender and gentle, educating her to the many uses of tongues and fingers; at others he growls words she cannot make out over her own cries.

And afterward there are tears, of both heart swell and guilt; it is all so large and so impossible, so rich and so fraught, that while the men see to their mining and hunting, she can only sit quietly, or move mindlessly about the cabin, a swimmer in a maelstrom of things she fears to name.

———

More gold rolls in every day. Hans measures a weighty fistful of nuggets into a canvas sack every night, and the box of sacks becomes heavier and heavier. Everyone laughs when Hannah tries to lift the cumbersome crate and fails.

As she laughs with the men, she is appalled at how easily she has entered into deception, how the blaze between Michael and herself can be damped in the presence of others until it fails to burn through the charade of marital devotion—and how eager she is to feed the fire every day.

Each morning Michael gathers the gun and a pack, bids

the company good day, and walks into the forest. The deceit is completed after the miners gather their own equipment and leave for the gold; following with a bucket or a pan, Hannah stops along the way at a likely patch of berries, then doubles back into a mossy fen.

It is as if she had never known color and suddenly walked into a luminous spectrum; his hands seem to know what her body is thinking, and as they crush the flowers with their bodies, feathery seeds spill into the air from their writhings. Squirrels chatter, and fat, salacious marmots urge them on with ribald shrieks. They sneak away so often, her naked body grows brown as a nut, and she fears Hans will notice and wonder at the coloring of her breasts and back, or the numerous tiny scratches and rubbings left by tree bark and stones. But in the oblivion of his riches, he remains blind to all but the luster of gold.

They grow daring, watching each other's eyes around the glowing fire at night, her awakened body offering a silent invitation in its postures and pauses. She knows from the persistence of Michael's gaze that she is desirable, and she preens for him, standing chin up and erect, brushing her hair back with slender fingers.

In her secret happiness, she believes Dutch when he spins another wild tale of Hawaii, where the women are beautiful and wear hibiscus blossoms and frangipani in their hair. "Left side means a lady's married. Right side's for girls that haven't landed a husband yet." On a whim, she places a small sprig of lavender flowers behind her right ear. Michael's eyes dance, and he can barely control a laugh as Dutch corrects her. Enrapt, they miss the evaporation of Hans's smile.

The next morning over breakfast, Hans tells an involved, seemingly pointless story of harvesting corn as a boy for neighbors in Blue Lake, Minnesota. Peter and "Black Mary" Hansen, as Hans tells it, had everything his own family lacked: Acres of black soil, fat dairy herds, a warm house, and good water. "And money," snorts Hans. "Enough to be called *mister* at the bank!"

"But why'd they call her 'Black Mary'?" asked Dutch. "Was she Negro?"

Hans scoffed. "Nah. Everybody called her that after old man Hansen tarred her."

Harky paused in the middle of spooning pulped and strained berries onto his bannock bread. "Tarred her?"

Hans waggles a cup at Hannah to signal for more coffee. "Yep. Tied her to a tree and shaved her head. Then tarred her."

"Jesus Christ!" yelped Dutch. Hannah imagines the smell of hot tar on flesh and feels nauseous.

"What'd he do that for?" rumbled Harky.

Hans placed the cup on the table and spread both hands flat. "Well, I guess he didn't like the way she was going off with the field hand."

Something inside Hannah quivers at the smirk in her husband's voice. "How was he punished?"

"Punished?" Hans wrinkles his forehead to simulate puzzlement. Michael stiffens in his chair.

"Yes!" demands Hannah. "For what he did to his wife?"

Hans motioned for Dutch to pass the bannock. "Hell, he

wasn't punished," he replied casually. "She was the one. She'd been with another man."

———————

That afternoon Hannah and Michael recline on the beach, embracing to the sound of the tympanic surf. When they walk back to their clothes, panting and brushing the sand from each other's skin, they find pressed into the damp grit alongside their garments the fresh tracks of a bear. And atop Hannah's skirt are three feathers: two black and shining primaries from a raven's wing and a single gray quill from a gull.

October 1 (or thereabout)

Dear Diary,

What remarkable changes come in the course of our lives. I hardly feel myself to be the same woman who married so impulsively just a year ago. Never could I have imagined myself to be in this posi-tion: in this wilderness, becoming rapidly rich beyond my wildest expectations, an adventuress of a sort I cannot believe.

It is apparent that we must leave soon. The snow is halfway down the mountains, but the gold comes so well now that the men only discuss departing in the abstract, as if winter will stay its arrival until we have recovered every last gram. They work like Trojans and eat like bears. It is nothing to consume two entire salmon, perhaps twelve pounds or more of food in a single meal. Fortunately, there have been many fish in the streams, and it has been a simple matter for Michael to catch enough to feed us by using a gaff attached to a

*long pole to snag them from the pools. However, their numbers seem
to be declining recently, and the meat of those remaining is becoming
quite poor in quality. I fear for when even these are gone. Yet when I
attempt to discuss our departure with Hans, he only replies that we
must remain until we have "enough."*

The castaways wake to the glitter of frost. Each leaf and
blade of grass is coated in gleaming crystals. In the rivers,
the strength of the salmon is at an end and the fish lie
gasping in the shallows, spent and dying from the effort of
consummation.

Severts shoulders a canvas sack, the shotgun, and his fish
gaff before bidding the men good-bye, then whispers to Hannah as she gathers wood from the pile behind the cabin that
he longs to be with her.

"My work," she replies in a low voice, shaking her head. "It
is too neglected." But she makes a promise for tomorrow as
he turns to go.

A mile from the cabin Michael pauses beside a shallow
stream and inspects the salmon gathered there. The bodies
of those remaining are marked with bars of red and green.
The tattered edges of their fins and tails fall away in loose
patches. The surviving males have become hook-jawed and
fiercely toothed from an inner alchemy of raging hormones
that contort their bodies into single-minded fighting and
mating machines. The females, too, are ragged and beaten
from the battle of procreation. White fungus eats at their
skins, and the lifeless remains of their brothers and sisters
float in stinking shoals along the banks.

Michael watches carefully, hoping to spot a new arrival still fit for eating. Upstream, a splashing louder and more insistent than the thrashing of dying salmon draws his attention to the narrow throat of a falls. At first he sees nothing except the water tumbling over a collection of large, light-colored stones. When one of the stones appears to move, he wonders, then stares. Standing with its back to him, the round, full body of some animal feigns the shape of a boulder, then raises its head, becoming a bear. Stepping into a shaft of sunlight, the fur along its back glows gold, the color of pure bullion.

The bear grabs at a salmon, plunging its snout into the water and batting with its paws. When the flurry of action is over, a fish as long as Michael's forearm struggles in its jaws. Holding its prize aloft, the animal walks splashing and sloshing from the river.

"Jesus, Joseph, and Mary," Michael whispers. "Dutch wasn't lying."

The creature's hide is yellow in the sun. A crucifix of storm-colored fur marks its shoulders. Black eyes and snout stand out against a blond ruff around its face. It is a beautiful creature, and as it sets itself to tearing at the salmon, its skin ripples with the play of great muscles.

Replete from weeks of gluttony and belly-rolled in fat, the bear is intent only on the finest, oiliest parts of the salmon. Slitting open the belly with one ivory-colored claw, it releases a flood of pearly orange eggs, slurping up the caviar with rapid darts of its tongue. Next it nibbles at the head, tilting its face delicately to one side to bite at the brains. As it gnaws, Michael imagines the sound of cartilage crunching.

The bear moves, repositioning itself to pin the salmon to the ground with one broad paw. Beads of water flicker in the golden light along its bulging belly. Its shoulders are the color of polished bronze.

Droplets of mist from the waterfall tingle against Michael's face, carrying his scent away from the bear. He steps slowly and carefully closer, raising the gun. The white noise of the river covers the sound of his tread.

"Whatever you're worth, you beauty, you're mine."

A squeeze of the trigger splits the light and the mist with gunfire, and Severts feels the weapon kick. A pattern of buckshot slams the bear's side, erupting a burst of shining water from its fur. Leaping cat-quick and hunchbacked into the air, it falls to the ground, snarling and snapping at the pain in its side.

The report of the shotgun seems to extinguish the murmur and chatter of the river; roosting eagles and foraging gulls explode into a thunder of wings and cries. Thrashing furiously, the wounded animal bites at itself and screams, piercing the air with a bayonet shriek of pain. The tortured wailing staggers Michael back, stopping his heart, and from the deepest place of regret he moans, "Oh God, what have I done?"

Desperate to stop the cries, he raises the shotgun and fires the second barrel, missing and blowing clots of moss and dirt from the ground.

At the second shot, the bear flails to its feet and springs for the underbrush. Trees shake and limbs break as it fights through the thicket, running for its life.

Frantic, the empty shotgun naked in his hand, Michael

throws his pack to the ground and tears at the flap for more ammunition. Thumbing shells one at a time into the breech, he fumbles to reload. Trembling, he sits back on his haunches, gripping the gun in both hands, and listens to the diminishing cries.

As he sits frozen on the bank of the river, time passes in an unmeasured gap. The air is heavy with the smell of decaying fish, and the birds do not return. The forest closes in around the damage done by the fleeing bear.

After a while, a raven drops from the sky into the green gulley formed by the trees on either side of the river. The *whoosh-whoosh* of its heavy wings wakes Michael from his stunned reverie, and he rises to his feet, stroking the wooden stock of the shotgun to gather courage. *It's probably dead*, he tells himself. *Dead of its wound*. Then he sets out on the blood trail to recover the meat. And a hide more precious than gold.

———————

For the first part of the morning, drops of blood show dark and drying against the green of the forest, and he follows slowly, pausing often to peer into the brush, fearing an ambush by the pain-maddened bear. As the day grows longer, the blood trail grows fresher, until the drops and streaks began to glisten among the leaves.

In late afternoon, he finds where the bear lay for a moment behind the trunk of a fallen tree. There are crushed ferns, sticky with blood, and a rank smell in the air. Somewhere just ahead a Steller's jay shrieks; his pulse thunders into his ears. He freezes, unable to force himself ahead. *Better wait a bit, let it lose more blood.*

A kettledrum sound rumbles up from the ground, vibrating into a drumroll that begins to shake the log he leans against. The earth dances and jerks beneath his feet, rolling in a succession of small waves until the branches overhead appear to shiver, then whip back and forth as the earthquake builds into a series of sharp, hard jolts that nearly knock Michael down.

The tremor is over before his already-overheating fear of the bear can build into a screaming panic. Gripping a branch of the fallen tree, he stares wildly about, certain an attack of some variety is coming.

A minute passes, then five before his heartbeat begins to calm and reason returns. "An earthquake," he tells himself aloud. "It's over." And as if to convince himself further, "No harm done."

He considers abandoning the hunt, but remembering the exotic shine of the bear's fur, imagines it his, and considers what its sale might bring. *That money's mine,* he says to himself. *No partners to split with this time.* And he starts down the trail of blood again.

———————

The trail leads inland, between steep hills and up draws, climbing toward a ridge that looks down on the glacier. As the land rises, the air becomes colder. The ground grows hard and frozen underfoot.

When Severts breaks free above the tree line, he sees a pale shape ahead. Limping and staggering, the bear drags a foreleg, forcing itself uphill with a faltering three-legged gait at a range too great for the shotgun.

Michael watches as the bear pauses and looks over its

shoulder. Settling its black eyes on him, it lifts its nose into the wind and pushes its nostrils into the creepers of his scent, searching for the identity of its tormentor. Finding nothing, it limps over the ridge, head drooping.

Michael follows, his legs beginning to shake and jitter from the strain of pursuit. He gasps, fighting for breath. The high, thin air snaps with frost, and the cold metal of the gun barrel burns his skin. Trickles of blinding sweat sting his eyes.

From the top, the ridge falls away in a steep crumble that spills down onto the glacier, scattering shards of shale into bottomless blue ravines. Michael wipes the sweat from his eyes and blinks at the sting of a sharp wind pouring up from the valley, then spots the bear thirty yards away, picking its cautious and shuffling way along the interstice of ice and stone.

Lifting the gun, he settles the bead on the slow-moving bear, pulls the stock hard into his shoulder, and takes a deep breath to quiet the trembling in his arms. The metal is cold against his cheek. The weight of the gun feels enormous. When he fires, the recoil nearly knocks him down. Bear and man stagger, propelled apart by the physics of death. The bear drops, slides, and rolls in a clattering avalanche of splintered schist before coming to a halt at the edge of the glacier.

Severts steps over the lip of the ridge onto the loose shale, faltering as the ground gives way beneath him. Sliding and tumbling, he edges downslope, glissading with the loose, shifting stone.

The bear lies angled into the sharp *V* of a crevasse. The ice shimmers with frost and as Michael advances, weapon at the ready, he can see the steam of his own breath. The bear's eyes are half open, glazed and dull. Its lips curl in rictus, exposing the teeth and tongue. In death, the corpse looks small. With the golden light of its life gone, the remains are inert, dirty, yellow, and gray.

Michael stares at the body from a distance, reassuring himself that the bear is dead. Then he removes a skinning knife from his belt and approaches. An overpowering stench of rot and sulfur rises from the carcass, and he gags, covering his mouth and nose with his hand. Stepping back, he pulls a handkerchief from his pocket and breathes through it.

"Shit," he says, stepping back again. "Shit." And walks away.

───────────

When Michael emerges from the forest that afternoon, the earthquake has shaken a beam from the ceiling, and Hannah is working at an arrangement of poles and levers to raise it back into position. The canvas roof has been pulled back, and the stones holding it in place have been cast down. The sun is low on the horizon. A gentle surf eases ashore, tumbling a line of softly golden foam before it.

Michael looks about for any sign of the miners, then pitches in. Saying nothing about the bear, he shrugs when she asks about fish. "They're played out."

Hannah tugs at the canvas to stretch it tight over the beams. "The earthquake spilled the stew I was making. It was the last of the meat. We've nothing left but some berries. Berries and a few carrots."

"They'll be unhappy about that, won't they?" says Michael, meaning the miners.

But the miners do not return. Day fades into night until stars begin to pinpoint the darkness. Inside the cabin, Michael listens for boot steps and runs his hands over Hannah until she pushes him away. "Not here."

The fire burns down, is replenished, and burns down again, but still the men do not return. Hannah begins to fret, pacing the small confines of the cabin, puttering at projects by the light of the lantern, cleaning spotless pans, pushing away the urge to settle on Michael's lap. The night is utterly still, and cold air flowing gently down from the glacier surrounds the cabin, creeping in through gaps between the logs.

"Where are they? Something has gone wrong."

"No," replies Michael. "They've just hit a good streak and can't tear themselves away."

"It is too late for that. Hans might work all night, but Harky and Dutch would not. I hope . . ." Hannah's wish is interrupted by a *haloo* and the sound of steps. The door swings back, and Dutch enters first, followed by a shirtless Harky. The Texan carries Hans on his back, riding piggyback and clinging with one arm about Harky's neck. Hans's other arm is bound to his side by a strip of cloth. In the lantern light, his face is yellow with shock and pain.

"Cave-in," says Harky, lowering Hans to the ground. Nelson takes a wobbly step, then slumps to a bunk.

"That earthquake," says Dutch. "We'd just barrowed out a load of ore, and Mr. Nelson started back inside, when she hit and the roof come down. Lucky me and Harky was still outside, or there wouldn't have been nobody to dig us free."

Hannah kneels beside her husband to inspect the bandaging, then sees it is Harky's shirt, torn into strips. Hans flinches, pulling back when she probes at his side.

"What's broken, Hans? Can you tell what damage is done?"

"Ribs. Something in my shoulder." He winces as he breathes.

"He's lucky," says Dutch from over Hannah's shoulder. "Big slab of rock missed him, but a support beam come down and got him. Took us a god-awful long time to move the rock and get to him."

Harky settles to a bunk, lying back and throwing an arm across his eyes with a sigh. None of them has any knowledge of medical matters beyond sewing up cuts or lancing boils. He knows only that Hans spits no blood, so will probably live. There is nothing more to do.

———————

"It's time to leave," says Hans. After three days of lying abed, he is sitting up again, pale and unshaven, asking for food. In spite of a cold, steady drizzle that moved in on a gusting wind the day after the earthquake, Michael's shotgun has put a young sea lion in the larder, and the strong, gamey smell of it flows from a kettle on the stove. "Food's about gone, and we won't be able to open the shaft again before winter's on us."

Dutch mutters, "Aye," now eager to be done with the wilderness. Michael nods slowly. Hannah is silent. Leaving means . . . what? A return to being Hans's wife? The unthinkable stain of divorce? What of Michael? Her heart begins to ache in time with the steady plink of drops falling into a pan beneath a leak in the canvas roof.

Harky rises without comment, goes outside, and walks down the beach until the cabin disappears in the mist, then settles on a log to stare at the sea. He has not spoken since carrying Hans through the door, and the darkness of melancholia etches itself deep into his eyes. Since binding Hans's injuries, the memory of countless wounds and bindings witnessed during the war have been drifting through his head as unceasingly as the near-freezing rain. The rain itself reminds him of a dreadful rainy day somewhere in Virginia when he had been chosen to participate in a firing squad ordered to execute a deserter. The deserter, a gaunt, gray-headed man with a poorly healed saber wound gaping at the junction of his shoulder and neck, had cried like a baby as he was tied to a caisson wheel with a paper target pinned to his shirt over his heart. Others in the firing squad had mocked the deserter, and Harky had wondered at his own lack of feeling as he pulled the trigger. He came to understand that the worst of the war was not in the killing, but in the extinction of all compassion and kindness in the human heart. Now he knows only that he is tired of the rumble of the glacier and the memory of cannon fire it stirs.

Sighing deeply, he pulls the horse pistol from his waist and hefts its weight in his palm. Peering at the end of the barrel, the black eye bored into blue steel, he places it against his temple, then tries it for fit in his mouth before groaning, shoving the gun back in its holster, and glaring at the sky.

"There is nothing we can do, Michael. It has to end." Hannah speaks in a low voice as they scramble across a face of algae-laced rock exposed by low tide. Dutch is a hundred yards away, intent with a knife and sack, prying at limpets that cling to the stone. Michael carries a basket of sugar kelp. Boiled together, the seaweed and shellfish will make a poor meal, but are a change from roasted sea lion.

Michael kicks at a starfish, flipping it from the rock into the surging water. "Damnation," he mutters. "If my luck was better, that rockfall would've made you a widow."

Hannah gasps and covers her mouth with one ashamed hand, appalled not by the vitriol and violence that burns in her lover's words, but because the same idea has slithered like an eel through the darker caverns of her own thoughts.

Michael's voice cracks with frustration. "I've wanted it since the start, Hannah. I can't . . . I can't stand this." The muscles of his jaw knot as he gnaws at his ire. "If he was gone . . ."

"Still, Michael, you mustn't say such a thing."

Michael stops, thrusts his hands deep into his pockets, and hunches his shoulders before speaking. "I been thinking. As soon as we're out of here, I'm telling him about us. Then you won't have any choice, will you? You'll have to be with me."

Hannah stares, frightened by the idea, then steps back as a wave strikes the rock. In the time it takes for the water to pull back and a second wave to rise, the impulse to believe that such a thing might be possible also rises; she and Michael could run away, go someplace new and start over. A third wave dashes the idea with the specter of exile; she would never see her mother or England again.

The water rushes out, foaming and hissing. Desire and impossibility surge within her. Michael mutters, "As soon as we're back in civilization . . ." and a wave of hopelessness rushes over her; can he not see what it means to be a woman in a world where women like Hans's "Black Mary" can be tarred and tortured for adultery? Or driven to prostitution like John Nightwatch's illicit paramour?

"Are you mad?" she asks, but there is no heat in the words; her voice is weak with uncertainty.

Severts's mouth turns down and tightens. He throws a brooding glance at her and does not answer.

FOURTEEN

Sunrise burns its slow way into the sky as the miners set out on the trail to the Indian village. A strong, cold wind pouring down from the glacier harrows the bay into rows of rushing whitecaps. Hannah pulls the door to the cabin closed and takes a last look at the sea, where the outflowing tide vexes an army of advancing waves.

On her back is a blanket wrapped around her meager store of clothes, a package of seal meat and berries, her Bible, journals, and a bundle of pressed flowers. Dutch and Michael each carry a share of the gold in their packs. Harky carries his own and the Nelsons'. Hans carries nothing and leans on a staff, his face tight with pain. The tools are abandoned, the ax wedged in the chopping block behind the cabin. The skiff has been hauled into the trees. Nothing is said about a return in the spring.

Progress is slow over the faint trail, and Hans requires frequent stops. Though the autumn cycle of frost and storm has thinned the brush, rendering the path more visible than when they followed it, bewildered and directionless, behind Negook, it frequently pales, drifts, and disappears into jumbled windfalls, where they are forced to cast about among fallen trees and thick alder until finding it again.

By noon the sky has turned the color of ashes, and only a pale, colorless light blots through the clouds. Cold sleet begins to fall, stinging their faces and hands. Only Hannah has gloves, and her skirts billow in the wind, pressing themselves against her legs. After months of manual labor, everyone's clothing is ragged and patched, and the soles of their boots have grown thin. They look like a lost tribe of peasants, struggling along with their wounded, and the only sign of the wealth they carry is the weight of the packs that strain their shoulders.

The wind builds until by evening the miners stumble with fatigue and cold through a forest that sways and rattles at their passing. The sleet becomes a dry snow that blows hissing along the ground and curls about their legs in restless streams. At the junction of trail and river above the Tlingit village, Michael double-checks the load of his shotgun, mindful of the antagonism under which they last departed the settlement, then shouts an alert to the inhabitants.

"Hello, the village!" he yells. "We've come to hire a canoe."

The only answer is the mistral sibilance of the wind. There is no chattering of children or barking dogs in reply. The air smells exclusively of snow; no odor of smoke comes to the miners through the belt of alder screening the longhouses from the trail.

Dutch says, "Probably all inside out of the weather," but

his voice lacks belief. The silence from the village is too complete, the quiet too intense. The air resonates with absence.

They huddle together, waiting, then Michael and Dutch shout again, "Hey, hello!" But the wind snatches and flings away their greetings. Harky shrugs and steps forward. Michael and Dutch follow. Hannah helps Hans shuffle along behind.

Dutch cups his hands to his mouth and shouts "Hello!"

"Shut up, Dutch," says Michael. "They're gone." No living thing stirs among the longhouses. The village is deserted, and the cedar eyes of the totems stare down on an empty beach.

The cluster of miners comes apart, with Michael and Harky drifting down to the shore to stand at either end of the naked strand, staring out at the green and white surf. Dutch drops his pack, scuttles crabwise into the nearest longhouse, then emerges wild-eyed and frantic, sprinting toward the next. It, too, is empty, and he makes a strangled, whimpering sound. Hannah takes Hans by the arm, leading him like a child to the sheltered lee of an abandoned house, where they stand mute and stricken, consumed by the finality and completeness of their isolation.

Michael drops to one knee, staring at the empty sea. Dutch wanders in a circle through the village, crying out against his ruthless fate. Harky begins going from longhouse to longhouse, then searches each storehouse and shed, gathering bits of smoked fish, a small sack of something dried and lost, a scrap of bear hide, a bundle of twine.

The clatter of a small, dry bone rattling along the toothed jaw of a bear alerts Hannah and Hans to Negook's presence behind them. The shaman carries the jawbone before him, stroking the teeth slowly with a rib. Dutch rushes over shouting, and Harky comes, too, bearing his small load of treasures.

"What's happened?" asks Dutch. "Where's everybody gone?"

Negook ignores the question, just keeps stroking the broken rhythm from his bones, staring at Michael, who comes slowly from the beach like a man approaching a gallows, until the Irishman is a few feet away. Negook casts the jaw at his feet.

"*Klute-utardy tseek.*"

Michael nudges the jawbone with his foot, touching the yellow canines with the toe of his boot, turning it slightly in the sand. Negook repeats himself. "*Klute-utardy tseek.* You killed the bear. Now the People are all gone."

The others look to Severts, puzzled, and he lifts one shoulder in a shrug.

Hans, impatient with the shaman's gibberish, points with his staff to the beach. "The canoes. They're gone. We need to hire a canoe to get us back to civilization."

Negook's black eyes roll toward Nelson, taking in the sling around his arm and the hunched imbalance of his stance. "You've got a lot of gold. You should buy a boat."

"We need food," says Hannah. "We're out."

"You've got a lot of gold," Negook says, his lips pulling back in a smile. "You should buy some food."

"When will the canoes be back?" asks Dutch.

The shaman turns and shuffles away, bent and stooping as if carrying a heavy load. There is much work to do to placate Kah-Lituya, and he has no more time for fools. At the edge of the forest he pauses. "The canoes," he says. "They will come back when it is safe. Maybe in the spring." He shrugs his shoulders like the white men. "You should all be dead by then. When you are dead and it is safe, they will return."

Middle (or late?) October

Our situation is desperate and growing more so every day. Michael killed a small goat and its mother this week, and we have dried and jerked the meat, but it is hardly enough to maintain our party for long. The roots of the wild celery and dark lily for which the old Indian Negook taught me to forage are readily available, but even a large serving does not seem to fill the belly and leaves one wanting. The meat of wild creatures is lean, and we crave fat. What I would give for a pound of butter or a pudding!

Hans is recovering from his injury and gets around well enough, but seems to have no strength in his arm. We worked to reinforce and sod the roof of the cabin yesterday—Oh Lord, doing so made me feel as if we shall never leave this place—and it was all he could do to lift the end of a beam. Harky suggested commandeering one of the native longhouses, but Hans and Michael argued that we are more likely to see a ship entering Lituya Bay for shelter than anywhere near the exposed coast by the village, and thus more likely to effect a rescue by staying here.

———

Hannah's pen pauses as she weighs the risk of putting her next thought to paper, then shrugs. Who, besides herself, will ever see it? And if at some future date her journal is read by another, will she be alive to care?

I sometimes wonder if our circumstance is punishment for my recent actions. The affections involved are strong, but surely wrong, and I have strayed far. I consult the Good Book for guidance, but find little relief there. And the dietary restrictions of Leviticus and Deuteronomy certainly do not apply to the marooned!

———————

The cabin is drafty and hard to heat, the appetite of the stove prodigious. With only one ax and one saw, feeding the fire all day and laying in a stack of wood for the night is a job for two men. Inadequately clothed in patches and rags, Harky and Dutch take turns supplying the stove, one outside cutting and carrying wood, while the other huddles inside near the fire, trying to get warm. Michael hunts all day and returns each evening chilled and exhausted. More often than not he is empty-handed. Hannah digs for roots and gathers what she can of berries, but the few that remain are often moldy, spoiled by the cycle of freezing and thawing that comes with the alternating rain and snow. Hans sits on lookout for a ship all day, then at night rotates with the others. Fatigue and hunger etch deep lines in their faces. The muscles of their bodies slowly give way to bone.

Harky gathers a last armload before retreating into the cabin, where he stacks the wood in a square rick at the base of the stove, then retreats to a bunk to warm himself beneath a damp blanket. Everything is wet—clothes, coats, bedding, and shoes—and as winter works its grip on the land amid unending rain and snow, the days are growing rapidly shorter. Clear sunshine is rare.

The incessant lapse and fall of the surf eats at Harky. His

eyes grow dull and retreat deep into dark sockets. His shoulders are rigid with tension. He carries about him a silence that is easily mistaken for the quiet of one gnawing a grudge, which only Hannah recognizes as a mute withdrawal. She, too, finds herself reluctant to speak these days.

The miners settle into the evening amid the orange flicker and pop of the fire. The corners of the cabin are dark, the lantern unlit, the supply of lamp oil too precious to waste chasing shadows. Hans coughs outside, watching for rescue. Hannah and Dutch pick at a bucket of roots. Michael watches Hannah, hunger of another sort in his eyes.

To pass the time on his lookout beside the unlit bonfire, Hans falls into his favorite reverie, imagining the admiration of family and friends when he returns to Minnesota with his satchels of bullion. *I'll have some fine boots made when I get to Seattle*, he tells himself, examining the worn leather on his feet. *Something in calf hide, with tooled heels*. As Hans repays his grubstake debt with a fantasy sack of nuggets dropped casually into his brother-in-law's hand, a pale glow heaves slowly above the horizon. Sailing out of the northwest on a course for Cape Spencer, the passenger liner is already abeam of Lituya and less than a mile offshore when its broadside of dim yellow lights pierces Hans's dream.

He stares a moment at the vessel's advance, at the rise and fall of lights on the ocean swell, then scrambles to his feet, groping for the oil and matches. "Help! A Ship!"

The door to the cabin smashes open. Michael bursts outside, freezes at the sight of the passing ship, and is shoved stumbling as Harky bulls him aside. Hans fights the lid from the tin of oil, slinging streamers of fuel as the Texan strips the canvas from the stack of wood. Dutch comes hard behind Harky and runs to the beach, waving his arms and yelling.

Hans kneels, scratching match after match to the beacon fire; the sulfur punks and smolders against damp wood. In the dark he cannot find where the oil has wet the kindling. "Burn, damn you, burn!" He yells to Michael, "The matches are wet! Bring fire from the stove!"

Hannah emerges from the cabin holding the lit lantern above her head. Severts dashes back inside to fetch a faggot from the stove. Hans leaps to his feet, grabbing the lamp from his wife's hand. The wick gutters and flares as he waves it in a frenzied arc.

The signal fire smolders. The distant ship shows its stern to the castaways. Its lights become a dim constellation. Michael fires the shotgun. Dutch waves his arms. Hans casts about for someone to blame.

"God damn it!" roars Harky, slamming a split of firewood to the ground. "God damn you blind piss-suckers!" He hurls another bolt into the darkness, throwing it like a curse after the retreating ship. In the shock of abandonment, Hannah realizes Harky has never used profanity in her presence without immediately apologizing.

The air in the cabin that night is thick with the smell of decay.

———————

"We're walking out of here," says Hans. Since the passing of the ship, he has stared at the mountains, refusing to believe any longer in rescue from the sea.

Severts looks at the upright walls of the fjord and shakes his head. "Can't be done, Hans. Where is there to go?"

Nelson scratches a distorted map of the coast in the mud with a stick, draws an *X,* and says, "Here's Lituya Bay." Then he drags his wand south in the dirt, turns right to go east, and then back to the north, where he draws another pair of crosses. He plants the tip of the stick in the nearest, saying, "The settlement at Haines," then taps the farthest. "Only a few miles from Skagway."

Between Haines and Lituya Bay he scratches a crosshatch of lines. "Glacier Bay and the ice fields lie between us and Haines. We climb up onto the ice fields, circle north across the top of Glacier Bay, and hit the headwaters of the river that drains down to Haines. Can't be more than fifty or sixty miles."

His proposal is met with silence. Harky and Dutch stare at the scratchings. Hannah wiggles her toes, feeling the stones beneath her feet through the worn soles of her boots.

Michael disagrees. "I've climbed the ridges above the glacier when I was hunting and seen the ice. It's impossible to travel there. Too rough, and the crevasses are too deep. Even the goats don't go onto the ice."

Hans nods, then points with his stick at Lituya Bay. "I agree. The glacier where it comes from the mountains is far too dangerous. But I've been thinking about it, and it seems that it must be broken just here, where the glacier comes downhill to the sea. Higher, where it is level, I'm willing to wager it is solid."

Harky looks up and rumbles, "Mountains are too high. Lots colder up there."

"We don't have to go over," says Hans, tapping the ground emphatically with the kindling. "Look, the ice fills the mountain valleys, right? Just think of it as a frozen lake, and you will see that I am right. Lakes are smooth when they freeze, so we don't have to worry about crevasses once we are on top. And it will provide us a level trail between the high peaks. It will be like crossing a prairie in winter, that's all."

With that poorly informed geography and a route hatched in the mud with a stick, a plan is formed; Michael is assigned the task of killing a sea lion; the meat will be jerked and the animal's thick hide used to reinforce the soles of their boots. Blankets must be sacrificed, sewn into coats and mittens. Capes of untanned seal and goat hides will protect them from the cold.

Dutch is reluctant and covers his fright with another of his yarns. "I climbed in the Alp Mountains of Europe when I was younger. It's damned dangerous, I'll tell you. A bad storm catches us up there, and we're done for." Snapping his fingers to demonstrate the suddenness of death. "Done for just like that."

Hans pushes his jaw out and leans forward. "You've never climbed off your own ass, so just keep your poxing lies to yourself. You can walk out with me or stay here and starve. It's your choice."

———

Three days later, as Hannah is helping Michael prepare strips of dark meat sliced from the haunch of a sea lion for drying, he whispers fiercely, "If we get out of here, I'm taking you with me. Tell me you'll come, Hannah."

She hammers at a strip of meat with a mallet, beating it tender, then closes her eyes and gives a sharp nod. When she opens her eyes, she strikes the meat once, then again, without looking at Michael.

The first of November, 1898

Whosoever finds this message shall know that we were five prospectors cast away on this coast in the winter of 1898: Mr. Hans Nelson of Blue Lake, Minnesota, and his wife, Hannah Butler-Nelson of Bristol, England; Michael Severts of Inishboffin, Ireland; and two Americans who we know only as Harky, from Texas, and Dutch, home unknown.

After being marooned and suffering the privations of hunger and cold, a decision has been made, in hope of preserving our lives, to effect our own rescue by walking out over the ice fields to the settlement of Haines, near Skagway.

I ask the discoverer of this note be so kind as to attend to the attached letters and see to their delivery as addressed. Thank you.

May God keep and preserve us,
Hannah Butler-Nelson
Lituya Bay, Alaska Territory

Dear Mother,
If you receive this letter, it will mean that I have perished in the wilderness of Alaska, where I have been prospecting for gold this past year with my husband, Mr. Hans Nelson, of Blue Lake, Minnesota. I write to tell you that my thoughts are of you, my dear mother,

as well as Poppa and my home in England, all of which I miss very much.

We have suffered harsh ordeals here in this wilderness, but I must believe such trials are brought upon us by our own misdeeds. Oh, Mother, I regret so much the unhappiness I caused you and Father when I broke my engagement, and again when I left Lady Hamilton's entourage to elope with Mr. Nelson. Perhaps it will give you some measure of comfort to know that he has been a loving husband, and should we survive, our fortune and happiness will certainly be secured by his hard work and intelligence.

Forgive me and pray for me, Mother.

Your loving daughter,
Hannah Nelson

———

Hannah considers the lie she has told—that Nelson is a model husband, and by implication, that she has been happy with him—and worries what punishment such a falsehood may bring. After all, breaking the disciplines of her life has certainly led to the troubles they have now. Might this falsehood bring more? She weighs the matter carefully, her pen loitering in her hand, then convinces herself that the good intention to ease a mother's loss might offset any judgment, and folds and seals the letter.

Hannah places the note in an empty marmalade jar, then rests the jar atop the letters. There is the letter to her mother, another addressed to Mr. Uliah Witt in Sitka, and a message from Michael to his own mother in Ireland. Hans scoffed at the notion of an epistle to his family in Minnesota. "I'll write 'em from Skagway, just to tell them I am rich!" Dutch sniffs and rubs at his nose. "I don't reckon anyone'll miss me." Harky just shakes his head and says, "I don't write."

———————

On the next windless morning, with the sky clearing at sunrise to a mottled blue and gray, the weight of the gold is again distributed among them. Harky carries half the gold, a load of firewood, and the iron kettle as well. The straps of their packs pull at their shoulders with the heft of ore, meat, ropes, blankets, a scrap of canvas that will serve as a rude shelter, and what extra clothing they own. Hans carries the ax, intending to use it as a mountain staff, and Michael the shotgun as he leads the small party along the hunting trail to the alpine. Underfoot, the moss crackles with frost. Crusts of snow lie in the shadows of the trees.

An *unkindness* of ravens plays in the sky, singing *klook-klook* to each other as they soar, dipping and rolling through the clouds on broad wings like dark angels, watching from the heavens as the marooned miners rise steadily higher.

Once clear of the timber, the castaways pause for breath, and on the mirrored waters of the bay far below, they see clusters of white seabirds. Slow wisps of clouds move across the sky, by turns revealing, then obscuring, the peaks. They climb higher. Everything not in direct sunlight becomes frozen.

By noon they have come to the highest point of the alpine, and the glacier lies tumbled and broken below. Everything above is snow and stone. They move slowly, carefully, their hearts in their mouths, across slanting, frost-slicked ground.

In the light, the ice is bone white; when a cloud sails across the sun, it turns gray. They climb higher, looking out at an unending treatise of blue mountains, and as the uppermost limb of the sun falls below the horizon, Michael rigs a windbreak, and everyone spreads blankets on the bare granite shoulder of the massif.

"Don't be so niggardly with that fire," orders Hans. Harky is sparing with precious splinters and shavings as he kindles a flame to melt a kettle of snow.

Ignoring Hans for a moment, he shakes his shaggy head. "Gotta make it last. No wood up here." His feet ache from the weight of his burden, but the load of firewood he carries must last as long as their journey, or they will be reduced to eating snow and warming their hands on their empty bellies.

"It's only going to take three days, maybe four, to get across," argues Hans. "We've got enough to warm ourselves properly."

The others look out from their precarious perch and see a universe of bare stone that goes on for eternity. The air grows still and cold, and when Michael hurls a stone into the chasm, everyone listens to the endless, rebounding echo of its falling. Harky picks up a stick of firewood the size of a hammer handle, considers it a moment, then lays it aside. Dutch moans and mutters God's name. The fire and their lives seem suddenly no more than brief, weightless sparks.

Heaped beneath inadequate blankets, the miners shiver and tremble in a mind-numbing search for warmth. Overhead, in a night sky that is luminous and hissing with silence, the aurora borealis dances: greens the color of sea moss, reds the exact shade of war. Stars shine like fireflies through the curtains of shifting light.

———————

Rising before daybreak, Hans blows on the ashes of the fire and feeds shavings to the coals until a small flame begins to snap and push against the darkness. Harky must be helped to his feet and groans as he straightens his legs. Michael and Hannah scrape frost into the kettle, while Dutch digs into his pack for a coil of small-diameter rope, cuts it into lengths, then demonstrates how to take several turns around a boot and whip it to a finish at the ankle to improve the friction of slick leather soles against ice. "It's a trick of the Prussians. They ain't the climbers the Swiss are, but come up with a dodge or two anyway."

With daylight comes the disheartening prospect of the country they must travel, and there is a brief, guesswork discussion to plot a route through the knobbed and broken mountains. As they climb, the snow underfoot grows drier and squeaks in the cold. On the slopes of steep ridges, Hans hacks steps with the ax, and the men pass Hannah from hand to hand across the dangerous traverses. Her cheeks feel frozen. Her fingers go numb.

After hours of climbing, they come to a place of such terrible perspective that they crouch down and stare, silenced by the great distances and spaces. The chalice of the mountains is filled to overflowing with a sea of ice; sidestepping peaks fade away into infinity. The air is thin and hopeless, and a vast silence fills the sky.

"Yield," whispers a wind that freezes the tears in their eyes.

Overwhelmed by the impossibilities arrayed before them, they agree.

———————

A north wind sweeps across the spine of the mountains, lifting a stream of fine, hard snow that stings their bare skin and smooths the outline of their tracks. They stagger in retreat, screwing up their mouths as if sand were being flung in their faces; their eyes burn from the white strength of the sun, and the cold saps the vigor from their limbs.

Harky stumbles, lamed by his freezing feet and by the weight of the gold on his back. Hannah's fingers are without feeling. She trembles without cease. In the lee of a cliff, the sudden lack of wind gives the illusion of warmth, though moving air whistles above and behind them. Where the ice has separated from the cliff, a snow-packed *bergschrund* provides a small, secure place for the party to come to a halt and lower their packs for a rest. The slope below is steep, slick with frost, and gives way sharply to a void that hums with the vertigo of empty space.

"Fire," says Harky, unstrapping the wood lashed to his pack. "We've got to warm up."

Michael shakes his head, then mumbles through lips blackened and cracked from the cold, "We should keep moving. Get as far down as we can before dark." He squints at the sun, measuring its arc above the southern horizon with the caliper of two extended fingers. "Two hours, maybe less."

Harky does not pause in his preparations for a fire, untying the splits of wood and setting his heavy pack aside, hooking it on a sharp fang of ice protruding from the edge of the *bergschrund*.

"The ax," says Harky, beckoning to Hans.

Nelson repositions himself, bracing against the rock face with one hand as he moves around Hannah and Dutch to split a bolt into kindling. Harky hands him a wedge of wood and watches as he kneels, places the butt of the wood against the ground and raises the ax, gripping it one-handed and high on the shaft. The first blow is weak; the wood bounces and falls without splitting.

Hans balances the log again, standing it upright on its end, and takes a firm, two-handed grip on the ax. The *thonk* of the blow is solid. The bolt splits cleanly along the line of its grain, leaps into two parts, and falls against Harky's pack.

There is a snapping sound as the fang of ice on which the pack is hung cracks, then a moment without motion or sound before the pack begins sliding. The miners, dulled by the cold, watch as it slips away. The grating hiss of its motion grows as the pack accelerates down the slope, then ends as the pack flings itself over the edge of the abyss, disappearing without a sound into eternity.

The weight of the loss drops crushing and hard onto the cold-addled miners when Dutch thrusts out a hand and cries, unbelieving, "The gold!"

FIFTEEN

In the lee of every object, blowing snow aligns itself into dunes as smooth and perfectly curved as the inside of a seashell. A skin of ice scrubbed slick by the wind covers the bathing pond. The door of the cabin rattles. Inside, the four men and Hannah huddle around the stove, feeding splinters of wood to the fire, listening to the sound of surf pounding at the shore. Hannah stitches mittens of seal hide and canvas. The smooth, spotted furs—poorly tanned by a mixture of urine and ashes—leave a revolting smell on her hands.

Winter has brought seals crowding into the bay to feed and rest on the icebergs. Two days in three the wind rages so wildly that it would be foolhardy to leave the shelter of the cabin, but in the three weeks since they returned from the ice field, Michael has become adept at floating into the herd while lying in the skiff, shotgun braced against the gunwale to supply a steady aim. The flesh and organs of each seal he kills feeds the party for exactly three days. The miners' stomachs bloat and cramp on the diet of pure meat, but there is enough to assuage their hunger. With Harky's willing arms to cut firewood, they have time on their hands.

"Tell us a story, Dutch," says Michael, hungry for diversion. "Another of your tales."

Hans barks, "Bah!" and makes a dismissive slice of his hand through the air. Even in their tedious imprisonment, to solicit another of Dutch's odd fantasies offends his practical, Nordic sense of life. Severts ignores him.

"What'll you do after we get out of here, Dutch?" asks the Irishman, smiling. "Spin us a yarn."

Dutch's lips form an *O*. His wandering eye tracks an invisible mote as he replies, "Owyhee?"

"Hawaii?" asks Michael. "What about Hawaii?"

"Well, they've never seen ice there, have they?" says Dutch, shrugging. "After Lituya Bay, I don't ever want to see no snow or ice again."

"Amen," agrees Hannah.

Encouraged, Dutch elaborates. "Never gets cold there in Hawaii, even at night. And there's fruit on every tree, fruit of all kinds. Things you never seen in the United States, like papayas and pineapples, or them alligator pears."

Dutch sighs and makes a show of smacking his lips. "Maybe I'll take that gold and buy myself a little trading schooner. Just work around them islands, you know. Never get out of sight of a palm tree again for the rest of my life."

Hans grunts, a nasty snorting sound. "You haven't done your arithmetic, Dutch. We were wealthy before we took our little walk, but this ox here," he says, jerking a thumb at

Harky, who sits up at the gesture. "He made sure we won't be leaving here rich.

"Losing the big half of the gold like that, we're back where we started. We're splitting half a pie now, and your little piece won't be buying any schooners."

Harky's eyes slit shut, and his whiskers twitch as he chews at his cheek. The muscles of his shoulders and neck bunch as he swallows against the burning rise of bile.

Hannah carefully places a mitten on the table beside her, works the needle into the spool of thread, and says, "It was an accident, Hans. I don't think anyone can argue that."

Hans tries to stare Hannah down, then growls, "Well, all I'm saying is that it'd be fair if he didn't get the same share of what's left as the rest of us."

"Aye," agrees Severts, "and it was your ax work that knocked the pack loose, Mr. Nelson. Maybe that ought to have some effect on your share. And after all, going into the mountains was your scheme, wasn't it? Just a little stroll on a frozen lake, you said."

Michael eyes each of the prospectors before continuing. "And don't forget, I've lost my boat. Maybe I should be repaid for that before there is any splitting."

Hannah senses the emotions in the cabin rising to a flood stage and stands, straightening her skirts. "Please, Mr. Severts. And you, too, Hans. We've worked hard together and have much yet to face. Affixing blame for the accident will improve neither our fortunes nor our comfort.

"We made a contract and must live up to our agreement. We share equally, win or lose." Saying so, Hannah looks across the stove at Michael and sees a twitch lurking at the corner of her lover's mouth and a narrowing of his eyes, then feels herself coloring as she thinks of her own hypocrisy toward the contract of marriage.

"Well spoken, Mrs. Nelson," says Michael with his best Irish charm. He smiles, but there is a cold flicker—whether warning or invitation Hannah is not sure—behind his pale blue eyes. "And two shares are certainly better than one. As a couple, that is."

"How's that?" asks Dutch. "You mean Mrs. Nelson is to get a share, too?"

Harky looks puzzled. It takes Hannah, too, a moment to understand Michael's meaning. She has never expected to share squarely with the men, and wonders if Michael's apparent intention to include her in the spoils is a genuine desire to treat a woman fairly or a part of his fantasy that she will run away with him and thus enable him to recover a larger share of the gold.

Hans, sniffing a fresh opportunity, sits upright and answers Dutch in a too-bright, matter-of-fact tone that fails to cover his own surprise. "Yes, of course, Mrs. Nelson must receive a full share. After all, she has worked very hard, too, and taken the same risks."

Hannah sees the cards fall. She deserves a full portion, but her husband argues for it not out of fairness but out of self-interest, expecting any share allotted her to become his own. If she argues against it—and she will not, she tells herself, dispute her own interests—she will incur Hans's wrath. She knows if she insists on equality it will strain things with Dutch and Harky, who, though kind and considerate men, cannot quite enfold the idea that a wife should gain equally with her husband. She realizes they will surely resent such a division—an unattractive consequence to suffer when confined within a small, dark cabin. Faced with this damned-if-you-do, damned-if-you-don't prospect, Hannah does what the rules of society demand women do—she remains silent.

"I'll bring more wood," she says, pulling on gloves and wrapping a scarf about her neck. Severts stands, offering to help.

At the woodpile Michael uses the ax to break a frozen bolt of wood free from the stack. The winter sun is so low and weak it is possible to stare directly into it without being blinded, and the demarcation between sea and sky is blurred by blowing snow. Michael holds out his arms for Hannah to stack firewood in the crook of his elbows and says in a low voice, "I have to be with you."

Hannah bends to the wood, avoiding Michael's eyes, and kicks at a frozen stick of kindling. "I cannot, Michael. We never should have started." It has been more than a week since their last shivering assignation.

"I love you, Hannah. I want you to go with me when this is over."

Hannah feels the welling burn of a tear start at the corner of one eye; he is so earnest, and his plea cuts at her heart. The vista of a pale and loveless lifetime with Hans stretches out before her, but deserting him is impossible; she cannot imagine returning to England bearing the stain of divorce.

"No, Michael. It would never work. My father and mother . . . They would never forgive me."

Michael's mouth twists, and his face crumples. He sags as if struck with a club, and for a moment Hannah fears he will cry. But then he straightens, clenching his jaw.

"I see how it is," he says, a vein pulsing at his temple. His lips pull tight, and he slams a booted foot into the woodpile, tumbling the rick to the ground, turning everything he feels into anger, as men do when the need arises to protect themselves from hurt.

When he speaks again, his voice is as sharp as a splinter of glass.

"Too fucking—*fookin'*—good for the likes of me, are you?"

Michael's anger strikes Hannah like a fist to her solar plexus. She hunches, bends at the waist, the breath driven from her body, and her hand springs to her mouth. She wants to take him by the hand, to tell him how wrong this is, to say that she has given him all that she can but that she cannot forsake who she is so easily, or how she fears the inevitable retribution adultery must bring, but he storms away, kicking at the ground like a small boy.

Shocked by the strength of Michael's anger, Hannah remains at the woodpile, stunned beyond any awareness of passing time, shivering at the burn of tears freezing on her cheeks until awakened by the pain of frost eating its way into her toes. Straightening her shoulders, she rubs at her nose and eyes with one mittened hand before gathering an armload of kindling and returning to the cabin. Once inside, she is careful to hide her red, swollen eyes, and busies herself with a simmering pot and spoon.

———————

That night the miners lie hunched under blankets and rags in the dark, listening to the screaming invective of the wind. The odors of the hut—wet wool, smoke, and the fishy smell of seal—cloy in Hannah's nostrils, and she smells the reek of guilt on her own unwashed body. The lantern is out, and the shadows in the uttermost corners of the cabin are made darker by the dim orange stove light that flickers and dances across the floor.

Their stomachs rumble with yearning. There is no spare lamp oil to burn, but Hannah can tell by the hard, uneven pace of breathing around her that no one is sleeping; the air is thick with resentment from all sides. She can feel the dark boil of Harky's brooding in the Texan's stillness beneath his blankets. Dutch tosses and turns, as he tries to swallow the reduction in his share of the gold. Severts lies on his back, arms behind his head, and when a flicker of firelight sweeps across his face, she sees him staring.

Late November 1898

The men are greatly vexed by the strain of living in such close quarters. There is little sense of unity among us in these difficult conditions. I fear my own presence and actions have contributed greatly to the resentments among our party. Mr. Severts avoids small talk and spends as little time in the cabin as possible, often leaving to hunt at first light when weather allows. Harky speaks not at all since Hans's unjust accusations, and his sullen presence seems somehow threatening. Even good-hearted Dutch is difficult. He pouts and eats with his hands!

Our circumstance becomes a valuable lesson in the qualities of civilization. It is the small courtesies that hold us together, and without which I fear the larger framework of civility may disappear entirely. I will speak with Hans regarding a rapprochement with the others at the first opportunity, though in the current mood, it is clear that any attempt to do so would be resented. At present, all I can do to advance our condition is to keep everyone's clothing in repair and continue to do what I can to bring food to the table.

———————

The sun rises late; its light does nothing to dispel the cold. Harky and Dutch linger at splitting firewood. With each blow of the ax, the steam of Harky's breath gouts from the tunnel of his sealskin hood, floating like dragon smoke about his bearded face. The woodchoppers talk in low tones, amid much shaking of heads, and, it seems to Hannah, they fall silent when she comes for an armload of wood.

Inside the cabin, Hans watches as Michael reassembles his gun after taking the extraordinary step of boiling the metal parts in a kettle of water to remove the lubricating oils. Yesterday, the temperature plummeted so low that the grease on the mechanism congealed, the firing pin failed, and he missed a rare shot at a deer.

The fine, hard snow that precedes a blizzard is beginning to hiss from the sky as Michael gathers his tack for the day's hunting. When he says, "Maybe that deer is still out there. Venison would make a nice change from eternal seal meat, now wouldn't it?" the forced and hearty tone of his words surprises the Nelsons, and Hannah's voice stumbles as she hurries to agree. "Yes, it would, Mr. Severts." Cold air floods through the open door, swirling about Hannah's feet and sniffing at her skirts as Severts leaves, saying, "Ta. I'll be back around dark."

Hannah uses the rare moment of privacy in the cabin to relieve herself, and when she steps outside to deliver the contents of the chamber pot to a snowdrift in back of the cabin, she is surprised to see Michael still present, deep in conversation with Harky and Dutch. At the sound of the door, the three men look up and cease talking. There is a line in their postures, a stiff, conspiratorial tilt of their heads, that makes Hannah think the conversation was not meant for her ears, and she acts as if she does not see them.

Michael lifts the shotgun in a good-bye gesture, then slogs away, lowering his face into the tuck of his shoulder to escape the stinging wind. Hannah watches carefully as he burrows into the blizzard, becoming first a silhouette, then a cipher, before disappearing into the gloom. All sign of Michael Severts's passage through the world evaporates completely, except for a line of tracks that blur quickly in the drifting snow.

By noon the blow has grown to a delirious blizzard, full of barbarous fury, and the snow no longer falls, but screams headlong and sideways across the ground.

At two o'clock, the cabin is hip-deep in drifting snow and beginning to leak at the seams. Pellets of ice filter in through the tiniest cracks between the logs.

When three o'clock comes, the soft, shadowless gray light of the storm begins to fade and day ends. Inside the cabin, the breath of the miners is measured out in puffs of vapor. As the temperature creeps lower, they don mittens and hoods.

"Wherever do you suppose Mr. Severts is?" asks Hannah, as darkness closes in.

Hans shrugs. Harky toys with a spoon. "Maybe got turned around. Lost his way."

"Will he survive?" asks Hannah, alarmed.

"If he knows enough to let the snow cover him," says Dutch. "It's warmer under the snow than out fighting the wind."

"Idiot," mutters Hans, his voice muffled by a scarf across his mouth. "Where the hell do you get your ideas?"

Over the course of the evening, the ferocity of the tempest wears thin, and the demented screams of the wind diminish to uninspired howls, then fall to an uneasy mumble. The hurried sibilance of blowing snow gives way to a hush effaced only by the feeble crackling of the stove. Dutch feeds another splinter of wood to the flames. Hannah listens carefully for the crunch of Michael's boots.

As she cooks and serves up a broth made from unsalted bones to give motion to the waiting, her cheeks and fingers sting with frost. After taking her place beside Hans at the table, she closes her eyes, tries to cup the bowl in her hands for the heat, but puts it down as too warm, then prays in silent appeal for God to preserve the warmth and life in her lover's body. The prayer is answered by the squeak of footsteps approaching on snow grown hard in the cold.

When Michael steps through the door, his eyebrows and beard are rimed with frost that sparkles yellow and gold in the firelight. His clothing is stiff with ice, and his motions are awkward as he raises the shotgun to port-arms and eyes the steaming kettle.

"Mr. Severts," says Hannah, relief in her voice. "We've been so worried. Thank God you've returned."

Michael does not reply as he shifts the shotgun to his left hand and uses his teeth to remove the mitten from his right. The open door behind him breathes a flow of stinging cold air into the room, and the steel of the shotgun shines blue black as he raises the weapon, leveling the barrel at the diners.

"Wha . . . ?" says Dutch as the muzzle wavers from him, to Harky, then sways toward Hans. His voice climbs as he begins to rise to his feet. "Michael?"

The twin staring eyes of the double-barreled shotgun shift from Hans and center on Dutch's chest. Dutch's chair overturns as he pushes back from the table, stands upright, and cries, "Michael, don't!"

Severts hesitates, the stock of the gun pulled firm against his shoulder.

"Don't!" repeats Dutch, at a loss for all words except the fervent expression of denial. "Don't!"

Dutch's face screws up as he sees Michael's finger tighten on the trigger. Turning his head to the side, he holds up one hand, palm out, as if death were something to be warded off like a splash of water or sand being flung by a bully.

The rip and blast of the shotgun at close quarters lifts Dutch off his feet and flings him backward from the table. Hannah freezes, vaguely aware that Harky is already rising to his feet and in motion, not away from the gunman in flight nor toward him in attack, but across the table, as if to place himself between the shotgun and herself. The Texan's hand is scrabbling under his coat for his pistol.

Severts swings the gun as smoothly as a trapshooter and fires, catching Harky full in the throat and face with the second round of buckshot, before the giant has closed the distance to shield Hannah. Beside her, she hears Hans suck in his breath and shout, "Ah!" but he remains frozen in his chair.

Harky rolls and drops, instantly blinded by the flow of blood from the wounds to his face, clutching at his torn throat. There is a hollow *thonk* as Michael thumbs open the breech of the shotgun, and Harky hears the spent shells clatter to the floor. As a roaring darkness closes in around him, Harky mutters, "At last . . ."

Severts fumbles with cold-numbed fingers at the pocket of his coat. Hannah stares in horror as his hand emerges with another shell. Hans sits owl-eyed and paralyzed, gripping the edge of the table with both hands, as if trying to prevent himself from being blown away on the sudden storm of violence. Michael thumbs the shell into the breech, gropes again at his pocket, and mutters, "Damn it," as more ammunition eludes his lifeless fingers.

Hannah stumbles to her feet, screams, and flings her bowl of hot soup at Michael with a weak underhand motion that tumbles the hot liquid in a wide, spraying arc across the gun and his chest. At the sting of the broth, he jerks back, looking up sharply from his effort to reload the gun, mouth and eyes wide as if insulted. Hannah's scream breaks through Hans's shocked immobility, and he, too, leaps to his feet and hurls himself at Severts, tackling the Irishman to the ground, knocking the shotgun from his grip.

Bear-hugging the smaller Irishman to his chest, he struggles to his feet, intending to slam his opponent into the wall, but Michael rears back his head and screaming a dark, wailing war cry of some Celtic ancestor berserk on the blood of Picts, slams his forehead hard against the bridge of Hans's nose, then lunges, biting at his cheek.

Hans shrieks, drops Severts and recoils, clawing and slapping. Severts lands on his feet, drops into a crouch, and hammers a tattoo of hooks and jabs into Hans's ribs and belly. Hans, no boxer, backpedals, flailing wildly. Severts throws a flurry of hard-fisted blows. Hans recoils from the painful assault. An uppercut catches him on the point of the jaw, staggering him into a backward fall across the table, which splinters, collapsing under his weight. Blood from his crushed nose and bite-torn face streams hot and red into his eyes; his breath rasps as he sucks air into hammered ribs and lungs.

Severts turns, grapples the shotgun from the floor, and steps back. Warmed by the battle, his fingers quickly find the last round of ammunition in his pocket, and he snaps open the breech, intent on rearming. Stunned and fighting for consciousness, Hans raises both hands to his face and tries to yell, but his voice gurgles out as a burbling moan.

In the moment Michael looks down to insert the shell, Hannah catches up the cast-iron kettle by the bail and swings, a full, desperate, long-armed lunge that spins the weight of her slender body behind the mass of the cauldron, striking

Michael squarely above the ear. The gun drops from his hands. Hannah stumbles, recovers her balance, and drops the stew pot as Michael teeters. Wobbling at the knees, he clutches his head, then fixes a dazed eye on her—"Hannah, no!"—and collapses to the ground.

The sudden end of violence and motion leaves a vacuum in which Hannah hears a keening sound she recognizes as her own voice, crying, "Michael, what have you done?" The smell of gunpowder and blood, and spilled broth fills the cabin. Under it all is an odor more foul: the stench of murder, and bowels that failed at the moment of death.

Hannah chokes, sobs, and leans over to peer at Michael's face. Unconscious, it is not the face of a killer, but an angel, with dark lashes dewed with melted frost and a blush on his cheeks.

Hans groans, climbing to his feet, then leans back against the wall and bends at the waist, putting his head in his hands to fight off a wave of nausea. When the room stops spinning, he stares a moment at the great lump that was Harky, then straightens, wide-eyed, and takes a step toward Dutch, who lies crumpled at an impossible angle into the juncture of wall and floor. In the dim light, the bodies lie loose-jointed and flattened, marionettes cut loose from their strings.

"Jesus," croaks Hans. "He's killed everybody."

Hans shuffles to his wife, who stands crying over the Irishman, repeating a rolling incantation—"Why, Michael? Why?"—and looks down at him. Severts lies on his back, his lips slightly parted and moving soundlessly. The orbs of his eyes flutter in erratic circles beneath their lids.

Hans is still a moment, glaring at Hannah. His look

grows narrow and dangerous. The swelling of his broken nose is beginning to spread and darken into the area under his eyes.

"Hans, are you all right?" asks Hannah. Her husband ignores her for a moment, staring down at the man at his feet. When he looks up, his hair and eyes are wild, and the lower half of his face is streaked with blood. It is a face, brutish with anger, twisted by some hissing, animal part of the soul that frightens Hannah as much as the murder that has shattered the frozen night.

Severts moans, lifts a hand weakly from the floor, then drops it again and tries to roll to his side. The motion catalyzes Hans, and he lashes out with a boot to Michael's ribs. "Murderer! Bastard murderer!"

Kicking and shouting, he strikes again and again at the prone man. Hannah screams at the sound of his boot thudding into Severts's side.

"Hans! Stop it! Stop it!" She grabs at his arm. Hans shoves her, and she stumbles backward, trips on the outstretched leg of Harky's body, and falls to the floor. When she pushes herself to her knees, her hand slips in something warm and sticky. "Oh God, Hans, please, you're killing him!"

"Damn right I'm killing him!" shouts Hans. "Murdering bastard!" Swinging a fist hard, again and again into Michael's face and head.

"Stop! Stop, for the love of God, no more!"

Hannah crawls crabwise across the floor, stumbling, her boots catching in her skirts, and grabs up the gun. Without thinking, she rises and swings the barrel down hard against Hans's shoulder, and he howls and falls to his knees.

Stepping back, Hannah raises the gun and points it into the astonished face of her husband. "Hans, no. Get back."

"What in hell?" Hans bellows, as he tries to rise, then clutches at his shoulder as a shock of pain knifes him back to one knee. "What the hell are you doing?"

"I can't let you kill him. Get back." She makes a thrusting motion with the gun barrel that pushes Hans a step back.

The sudden violence and murder, the blood, and the sickening sounds of brutality spin Hannah's mind into a whirl of horror. How has it come to this, that she, who has never raised a hand against another human, or even whipped a dog or used a quirt on a horse, stands now surrounded by the dead, her hands slick and stinking with the fluids of murder, holding a gun on her own husband in defense of her lover? Twice in a moment she has seen murder done, and twice in a moment she has struck with fury and metal against a man with whom she has shared her body. Something splits and cracks within her, as the final reality of how far she has come from all that had been her genteel life spikes itself sharp and deep into her heart. The sensation of a growing web of fractures spreads, breaking away like the fragile shell of an egg, until there is only one desire, one thought, one word remaining:

"Stop.

"Hans, stop. We must stop this."

Hans is incredulous. "Stop? Damn it, Hannah. The man's a coldblooded murderer. He killed Harky. He killed Dutch. And I'm going to kill him!"

"No, you are not!" She glances at Severts, who lies curled and still at her feet. His face is swollen, black from the fury of Hans's blows, and his mouth is a crimson pulp of blood.

Hannah feels a knot cinch itself into her stomach at the sight of his destroyed, beautiful face. "You cannot kill a helpless man."

Hans sits back on his haunches, leans against his good arm, and a calculating look fixes itself in his eyes.

"If we kill him . . ." Hannah gropes for words to explain what her desperate bones know. "If we kill a helpless man, we will be no better than him. We will be murderers, too. We must stop."

"Stop? Hannah, that man"—Hans points at Michael's still body—"just killed in cold blood. What else will we do? Shall I call a policeman?"

Hannah cannot respond. There is no answer in her mouth. There is no one to call, no way to change or affect what has happened. There is only this, the horror of all-come-undone, in the last place on Earth, in a land that feels the farthest any human can be from solace or safety. There must be a way to correct *something*, to bend things in such a way that will give them hope in this hell.

"No, the killing is done. We'll tie him up."

"Tie him up? Then what?" asks Hans.

Again Hannah's mind gropes for a solution, but there is nothing. There is only the smell of Harky and Dutch, whose bodies lie cooling as the blood-warmth of their lives soaks into the cold ground. There is the killer at her feet and the would-be killer she is looking at over the barrel of a gun. There is no order, only chaos. Another piece of the shell flakes away . . .

"I won't let you kill him. If you kill him . . ." She cannot think what to say. "If you kill him, I will see you charged with murder for killing a helpless man." And as she says it, she knows it is true. She will fall back on the law, on the strength of that world that still exists out there somewhere that prevents this sort of madness, where men cannot kill without consequence.

"I will see you charged, Hans. If you kill him, you will have to kill me, too. Will you do that? Will you kill me, too?"

Hans lowers his face to glare at her from under his bruised brow, his eyes growing wary and unsure, as he senses her determination.

"We must hold him until we are rescued and can give him up to the authorities. We don't know why he has done this." She swallows and moves the gun barrel an inch to indicate the dead. "Mr. Severts will be properly tried. Properly, not murdered by you."

Her voice trembles as the illusion of a way out rises before her. "We are not killers. We are not savages." She can feel the ache of tears building in her throat. "We will keep Mr. Severts prisoner until he can be dealt with by the law."

Hans's mouth turns down, and he growls, "Mr. Severts, is it? Mr. Severts?"

Leaping to his feet, Hans bellows, "He called you Hannah! You called him Michael!" Hans charges across the room so swiftly it scares Hannah back against the wall. She screams in fear as he begins kicking again at Michael.

"No, Hans! Stop it!" Pointing the gun at the ceiling, she pulls the trigger. The explosion stops Hans in midblow as bits of roof moss and canvas shower down from overhead.

"I cannot let you kill him!" she screams. "We will not be murderers, too!"

"Damn you, woman! I'm not killing him for being a murderer! I'm killing him for making me a cuckold!" He lunges as if to renew his attack.

Hannah thrusts the shotgun out before her. "No!"

"Will you shoot me, Hannah? Shoot me to save your murdering Irishman?" Hans spits.

Hannah's finger tightens on the trigger, even as she shakes her head in emphatic denial. "No. You're wrong." The lie springs easily to her lips, seeded by a wish to believe that chaos and horror can be corrected and ordered, a wish so fervent that she believes wholeheartedly as she is saying it that she has never committed adultery, that she could not possibly have given herself to a man, no matter how charming or beautiful, who is capable of murder. Wanting, she believes, and believing, she is sufficiently convincing to allay some part of her husband's knowing outrage.

The simplicity of her denial combines with a husband's desire to believe, and a stalemate is reached. The shotgun comes down. The cold creeps into their bones. Hannah closes the door—open all this time—and kneels at Michael's side, peering into his face, trying to discern how a man who cried at killing a seal could send two men to their graves.

SIXTEEN

When Michael awakens, he finds himself embroidered to the frame of a bunk with cords about his wrists and ankles. Spread-eagled on his back, he thrashes, pulling weakly at the ropes, but subsides as stabbing pains pierce his arms and ribs. Through blow-puffed eyes he sees that the cabin is dark. Listening, he hears silence. Tugging against the bindings, he feels the cold of a neglected fire stiffening his fingers and limbs.

Outside, twin blazes rise up from ricks of burning hemlock spaced along the edge of the forest. Hannah huddles close to one fire, Hans the other. They stand with their backs to each other, tending their personal flames. The unwrapped bodies of their murdered companions lie on the ground beside the pyres, the light of the bonfires throwing an orange glow across the snow and high into the trees. Together Hans and Hannah dragged Harky's massive weight to the gravesite on a tarp, while Dutch suffered the awkward indignity of being pulled by the arms. Dark streaks of blood mark the passage of the dead across the snow.

As the ground warms, the Nelsons take turns with a shovel and pick, pushing aside the angry red embers to cut at the slowly thawing soil. Silhouetted by the flames, they hack an inch at a time into the earth, burning, shoveling, then burning again. Gradually, the dancing firelight reveals rude graves that gape dark and bottomless in the night. Progress is slow. Hans's shoulder is stiff and painful. Hannah is numb with shock.

Overhead, the sky clears and the stars take up their positions as first Dutch, then Harky are interred in the charred ground. Before rolling the dead into their graves, Hans relieves Harky of the pistol and Dutch of his boots, which are less worn than his own. The pathos of Dutch's naked feet brings a pain to Hannah's chest, and she cries, rasping in hoarse, angry sobs, aghast at the practicality of the robbery. From beyond the capering edge of the firelight, a pair of glowing eyes watch.

———

The next morning a pale light kindles behind the peaks. The sky is clear blue, the color of ice, and a stream of air so cold and dense it has become a solid substance spills into the fjord. Between the smoldering graves, a line of small human footprints pass, gnarled and splay-toed in the snow. The tooth of a bear has been placed atop each fire-darkened mound. Inside, Severts is sullen and turns his face from Hannah's questions.

"Why, Michael? What reason can there be for this murder?"

Michael jerks at his bonds, a frown on his bruised and

swollen face. He glares at Hans, who holds a rag to the bite mark on his cheek and returns the scowl.

"Doesn't matter why, does it?" growls Hans. "He's murdered them, and we ought to shoot the bastard."

"There will be no more killing," says Hannah. The shotgun rests across her lap. Beneath her gray eyes are dark circles. Scribbled lines of fatigue plow her forehead and radiate from the corners of her mouth. "Mr. Severts is our prisoner until he can be given over to the authorities." She shifts the shotgun, feeling the cold metal of its barrel and the warmth of the walnut stock in her hands, and neither man can tell if the unconscious gesture is meant for himself or his enemy.

Michael hawks and coughs before breaking his silence. "I save your lives, and this is how I'm repaid." He jerks one arm, pulling the rope tight. His voice is hoarse from disuse.

Hannah and Hans exchange looks. Hers is surprised, his suspicious. Severts thrashes a moment against his restraints, then is still.

Hans lowers the rag from his face and looks at the bloodstain before holding it toward Michael. "Saved our lives? By doing murder? And chewing at me like a dog? There's a neat trick."

Severts fists the slack of the ropes in his hands and tests the knots before spitting in Hans's direction. "They were planning to kill you. They tried to get me in with them."

"What?" says Hannah, startled. She knew Dutch and Harky were upset, but it is impossible to believe they could have been plotting murder.

"Aye. They said we'd split the gold three ways instead of

five, with a bit extra for the loss of my boat. I told them to go to hell."

Hans rumbles in his throat. "That's a damn lie."

"God's truth. That's why I had to kill them. They were planning to murder you. And after I refused to join them, they would have had to kill me, too. There was no choice. I had to shoot them."

Hannah remembers the surprised look on Michael's face as she flung the soup, and an inch of doubt worms into her stomach. Harky had once saved Hans's life, but he had been dark and sullen lately. And gentle Dutch, always so eager for approval—surely he could not have been capable of coldblooded killing just for gold. Could he?

"I do not believe you," Hannah says.

"It's true, Mrs. Nelson. Yesterday, when I was leaving. Out there by the woodpile, they said they were going to do it last night while you slept.

"You're trying an innocent man here. It was self-defense, killing them like that." Michael continues. "I saved your lives and my own. We'd be the ones freezing in the ground if I hadn't done what I done."

Hannah's mind whirls, spinning through the facts she knows and the intuition she had, her memory of Dutch, Michael, and Harky standing at the woodpile, stiff with the attitude of conspiracy; Michael, crying for the seal; his tenderness with her and his passion in the fields.

Michael sees the doubt in her eyes and holds up his hands. "Let me go, Mrs. Nelson. There's no need to make me a prisoner. After we're rescued, we'll go to the law, let them decide that what I done was necessary." Lowering his voice, he adds, "I'm no murderer. I think you know that."

Hans bangs to his feet and throws the bloody rag at the prisoner. "Self-defense, was it? Killed them two for us, did you?" He advances on Michael with doubled fists. "You're a lying murderer, Severts. You would have killed me, too, if I'd let you."

Hannah lifts the shotgun from her lap and points it at the floor—"Hans, stop"—and discovers the physical, unrefined authority of a gun, for her voice is firm, and her husband halts with one fist raised to his shoulder.

"He's lying, Hannah. He's trying to save his neck, that's all."

"No, Mrs. Nelson. It's true, I swear. We'd be dead, I tell you."

Hannah wavers, struck between husband and lover, desperately wanting to believe Michael, because then he can be released and the first long step back to some order in their wrecked lives can be made. Her head shakes. "I don't know."

Hans makes a noise like a bull deep in his chest, an ugly snort that is half laugh, muffled and distorted through the swelling of his broken nose. "True? Well, the only true thing is that Harky and Dutch are dead, sure enough." He turns to Hannah with a sly look. "Why do you think the bastard was trying to reload the gun?"

December 1898

Terrible plight. Food perilously low as Hans has little success with hunting. Bitter cold. Nights much worse. Wood scarce near cabin. Snow covers everything. Hans and I guard against Michael's escape

by turns, day and night. Leaves no time for necessities. Very exhaust-
ing. Dear God, how have we come to this? I do not feel I can trust
anyone. Even you.

Nauseous every morning.

————————

Hannah strokes the green leather cover of her journal with a mittened hand and closes the book, too fatigued to be ashamed of how sloppy her handwriting has become. Besides, there is nothing to say, or at least nothing she wants to put into words. And the ink blots and skips in the cold. Her head aches from hunger, and she notices how thin her wrist looks where it emerges from the mitten. Hans hunts every hour of daylight, but is rarely successful. Yesterday he returned with a single ptarmigan, reduced by the large-bore shotgun to a fist-sized bundle of shattered white feathers and stringy meat. Stewed whole—head, feet, and organs—the bird fed each of the three survivors only a cup of weak broth apiece. This morning they had sucked at the slender bones.

Without snowshoes, travel through the forest is too difficult, limiting Hans's hunting range to a strand of wind-beaten beach beside the sea. He cannot duplicate Michael's success with drifting the skiff down on the seals. *Sylkie*, the Irishman calls them, and he has known their habits since he was a boy. Hans grows impatient, moves too soon, and panics the herd before the shotgun can do its work. Then he returns to the cabin sullen and shivering, the skin of his face turning red with frost, peeling away in strips and patches.

The cold is a mortal enemy, and without sufficient food they chill easily. When the wind is strong, Hans cannot stand the exposure for even the minimal hours of daylight at hand, and instead relieves Hannah from guarding Severts. They take turns digging at driftwood buried under the snowdrifts along the beach, skidding and poling the logs to the cabin, where they are laboriously hacked and sawn into pieces to feed the ravenously hungry stove, which eats continuously. So weakened, it is more than they can do to meet its demands, and every day the stockpile of wood dwindles.

"It's a two-man job to keep us alive," says Hans through lips cracked with cold. "Sitting nursemaid to this murderer is sure to starve us or freeze us. And it's a race to see which is first."

————————

"Let me go, Hannah."

Hannah jerks upright from her doze, clutching at Harky's pistol in her lap. "What?"

"Let me go. You know this isn't right."

Her skull feels as if it is stuffed with cotton wool, and the pulse of her thin, exhausted blood beats behind her eyes. She answers Michael with a sharp shake of her head, but pain fills the void left by lack of sleep, and nausea rolls her stomach into an empty knot.

Michael is silent for a moment, lying with his head tilted back, eyes closed, mouth agape. Hannah is slipping away, chin to her chest, before he speaks again. "Either let me go, or I will tell him about us."

Pulling herself back to consciousness, she considers this. Her eye sockets are sinking into shadows, and her eyes are bloodshot. When she blinks, it feels like they are filled with sand. "No you won't. It would gain you nothing."

"I've nothing to lose, have I?"

"You won't do it."

Michael shrugs, then gasps as the motion cramps the unused muscles of his neck and shoulders. "Nothing to lose." Sighing, almost wistful. "Nothing at all."

"He'd kill me. And you." His voice is flat, just stating a fact. "You think he won't?"

Hannah shakes her head, eyes closed, willing Michael to shut up.

"He'd have all the gold then, too. Wouldn't he?"

Michael closes his eyes, turns his face to the wall, and is silent for a long moment before saying, "The shotgun has two barrels, Hannah. Remember that."

"Hannah," whispers Michael. "I'm cold."

Michael's voice wrenches Hannah from a reverie by the fire, starting her upright in her chair. Resentment flashes through her blood. Adrift, she had been for a moment free of worry. Awakened, she is returned to the immediate hell of the hovel. The fire warms only a thin band of air near the ceiling; her feet are cold.

"The ropes are too tight. See how my hands are swelling." Michael raises his head to look at Hannah, holding up one hand. The flesh is puffy, the color of wax. He is trembling, unable to reach down and pull up the filthy blanket that has slipped to his waist. "And I've got to care for myself."

"I'm sorry, Michael. You will have to wait for Hans to return." It has become the routine for Hans to stand guard over Severts with the shotgun while Hannah slacks the ropes so Michael may attend to the chamber pot. Bedbound and unfed, Michael's digestive system has crawled to a near halt, making elimination a laborious and painful process, during which Hannah is relegated outdoors to chop wood.

Michael's head drops back, and he sighs, "Jesus, Hannah, help me." His pleading cuts Hannah like a saw. Helpless and powerless, he reaches out to her with his bound hands. "Please. Just loose enough to let my blood move. He tied me so tight."

Hannah comes to her feet and walks to the edge of the bunk, bends down to inspect Michael's hands. His fingers are locked in a curl like a claw, the skin tight and swollen. The cord bites into the soft flesh of his wrists. He whispers again, "It hurts."

The lack of food has burned Michael's face thin, accentuating his cheekbones, darkening his eyes. In the soft light of the cabin, he has the look of an Italian martyr in a Renaissance painting, beautiful in torment, and Hannah's heart reaches back to the days of their passion.

"Yes, very well." She tries but fails to keep her voice businesslike as she lays down the pistol and reaches for a knot. Bending over, she hesitates, fearing for a moment that an act of human kindness will undo her resolve, and her fingers will fly to free him. Avoiding Michael's eyes, she stiffens herself and slacks the cord around first one hand, then the other. Michael gasps and flinches as the blood begins to burn its way back into his hands.

"Oh, thank you, my angel." His brogue is soft with intimate

gratitude, and Hannah rests her fingers for a moment on his shoulder. His bones announce themselves under her hand, and for a heartbeat he is not a killer, but a child.

"How long has it been?" he asks, and Hannah is not sure whether he means the duration of his confinement or time lapsed since they last lay together. The first is safe ground, and she answers, "Three weeks," then hesitates. "I think."

Michael sighs. "Three weeks. Jesus, Hannah. If only I could move about a bit. My back, it's killing me to lie here on these boards."

"No, Michael. Hans will kill you if he finds you untied."

He groans, tries to roll onto his side, and is brought up spread-eagled and short. "Please. Can you just give me room to lower my arms a bit, then? It's torture, really, it is."

Hannah hesitates. Even in his suffering, Michael is smooth. Over the months she has learned to recognize his charm, but even aware, she remains vulnerable. "I'm sorry, Michael."

"Torture, Hannah. You say you are holding me for the law, but where does law allow torture? Even if you think me a monster—and you know I'm not—you can't believe I deserve to be tortured, can you? Even your English kings gave that up long ago."

Hannah shakes her head. "When Hans returns." Her breath steams in the colder air at the lower level of the bunk.

Michael's eyes flash dark and angry. "That bastard. He enjoys seeing me suffer. You know he won't do it."

Hannah looks away, then stands upright and moves to the stove, bends down to feed another split of wood into its insatiable maw. Michael is right. Hans has shown only cruelty since the killing, brooding and scowling when he has not been describing in detail what he hopes to see done to Severts if they are rescued. Her husband now seems so far from the man who once charmed her on a train, rescued her from Lady Hamilton's employ, and, after having been mugged in Skagway, gave his last coin to a grimy beggar.

The fire licks at the new wood and crackles. Hannah places the skillet on top of the stove. After the cast iron absorbs enough heat from the fire, she will wrap it in a cloth and place it beside Michael as a bed warmer.

His voice is soft again when he speaks. "Remember the smell of the grass, Hannah?" He stares at the ceiling for a moment, then closes his eyes and smiles. "You were so beautiful with the sun on your skin."

Hannah knows precisely the day to which he refers. Centuries ago, when they were heaven-lost and foolish, the crushed heather under their bodies had mingled its soft perfume with the smells of love. There had been bees, drowsy with sun, and a churring escadrille of redpolls playing in the trees at the edge of the meadow. Afterward, Michael had fallen asleep, curled to her back, with one arm around her stomach. She had pillowed her head on the biceps of his other arm and memorized each intricate detail of moss and grass before her eyes while he dozed.

God help me, Hannah says to herself as she holds her hands to the stove. *I am so lonely.*

"Will you promise not to take advantage if I ease the ropes?"

Michael opens his eyes and rolls his head to the side. "Do you really think I would ever hurt you?"

Hannah feels her throat tighten and a squeezing sensation inside her chest. Closing her eyes, she nods, then shakes her head. "Just enough to ease your arms, then, Michael. That's all."

Michael lies perfectly still as Hannah slacks each knot in turn, then sighs and crosses his arms on his chest as she backs away. Rolling onto his side, he groans, "God bless you," and falls silent.

———————

When Hans returns, he is empty-handed. "Tide's low," he says. The approach of a full moon has pulled the sea far down the strand, uncovering a string of rocks and reefs. "Go see what you can find of those limpets or cockles. I've got to warm up."

Hannah pulls on an extra sweater—it had been Dutch's and almost fits, but smells of mildew and dirt—sorts out a sack and a knife for prying the mollusks from the rocks, and goes out the door with a backward glance at Michael, who watches her go. As she pulls the door closed behind her, she hears him asking for the chamber pot.

The way to the shore is barred with snow packed into hard drifts by the wind. The upper reaches of the beach have been swept clear by breaking waves, leaving the stones slick with a dull patina of frozen spray. Hannah picks her way carefully over the smooth obstacles, sometimes going down onto her hands and knees to cross a large boulder or log. At the edge of the water, a lone gull watches with intent yellow eyes as she pokes among the rocks for the coolie-hat shell of a limpet or the rough, leatherlike armor of a chiton. Just beyond the break of the surging swells, a sea lion, huffing and snorting, keeps pace with Hannah's wanders, and she craves the heavy taste of its meat.

Hannah picks and knifes at various bits of fare, gathering the meager sea booty into her sack. She tries a limpet raw, scooping the animal out of its cone with the point of her knife and sliding the morsel tentatively into her mouth. The taste is good—salty and flavored by the sea—but the meat is chewy, like buckskin. She eats another, quicker this time, then another. A small worm of guilt at not sharing with Hans and Michael curls out of the next, and she stays the point of her knife, then continues, eating several for every one she slips into the bag.

An hour of exposure is all she can stand. Her mittens, damp from clutching at tide rocks, are beginning to freeze, and the wind cuts through her clothes and bites at her skin. The sack is crusted with salt ice from the drippings of a small handful of mollusks, and she stumbles on cold-numbed feet as she picks her way back to the cabin.

At the door of the hut she halts, knocking her feet together to clear them of snow. Passing in, she pushes back her hood and sees Hans, arms akimbo, standing over Michael, who hangs half in, half out of the bunk, unconscious and bleeding from his scalp.

"Hans! What have you done?"

Nelson takes two quick steps in her direction and thrusts the pistol at her face before shouting, "Stupid woman! Look what you've done! Your pretty boy tried to murder me again! Look!" Snapping open the chamber, he reveals the five metal eyes of the cartridges inside. The shells are old and gleam with the dull color of weathered brass; the primers are encrusted with the verdigris of neglect, and the round immediately under the hammer is indented with the mark of a firing pin.

"He grabbed the pistol when I let him up to piss, but the cartridge misfired. If Harky had taken care of this gun, I would be dead now! And you loosened the ropes, didn't you?" Outraged spittle flies from his mouth, peppering Hannah's face.

"You did this! You almost got me killed!"

Hannah staggers back against the door and sags, closing her eyes against the cartridge, evidence of what she has done; she did this, she almost killed Hans. And if Michael had broken free, would he have killed her, too? She can no longer doubt he is a willing killer; his defense of an assault planned by the murdered partners cannot be true.

———————

Hannah whets the knife to a keen edge on a flat piece of granite before slicing another narrow strip from the hide at her feet. White hair spills from the ribbon of skin onto the floor as she shaves it bald with the blade. This morning, while digging for firewood, she found the goat hide, cast away from an earlier, successful hunt, frozen into a wad under the snow. Now a cauldron boils slowly on the stove, its contents afloat with fingernail-sized shavings sliced from the cuttings of hide. Bits of fat and a few rare scraps of flesh form a thin skim atop the simmering soup. It is the only food in the cabin.

Hannah's head nods as she works, and she struggles to keep her eyes open. The strain of taking turns sitting guard over the prisoner has depleted her like a medieval bleeding. Severts never seems to sleep, but rolls, moaning, from side to side through the night, or lies still, eyes open and shining in the firelight.

"Yes," says Michael from the shadows. "Yes, I would have killed him." His wrists are crossed and lashed above his head, his legs tied at ankles and knees. He writhes continuously, seeking relief from the pain of bone ends rubbed raw against the planks. "I love you that much, Hannah, that I would kill to be with you."

"There are two barrels to the shotgun, Michael. You were trying to load them both."

"No, I wasn't going to shoot you—or Hans—then. I was just dumbed by the cold, didn't know what I was doing. Out all day in that blizzard, worrying it out in my head to shoot Dutch and Harky, afraid they would have killed you by the time I could work up my courage. I was half out of my mind.

"Now I been hog-tied in this bunk for a month. God, it hurts, Hannah, it hurts." His voice approaches a whine. "It's cruel. Him beating on me every time you're away, and me helpless here. He's no good, that man you married.

"Yes, I was going to kill him," he sighs. "I'm that desperate, seeing him hurt the woman I love."

Hannah is silent, bending close to her work and slicing. She shakes her head in disbelief and replies in a low voice. "All this killing. We cannot." Her words falter. Yearning twists into a tight knot inside her, and she knows it is possible to die from simple homesickness, from wanting the order and reason of streets laid out with shops, the sureness of civilization with its flow of food and clean water, its disappearing garbage. In that world someone else would have an answer for all of this; there would be policemen, barristers, and judges, and the truth would be clearly defined. Hans would have no opportunity to torment Michael, Michael would have no hope of escape, and she would never have experienced the impulse to turn a shotgun on the man to whom she is married.

"Let me go, Hannah. Please, let me go. I'll run away, head for the Indian village or up into the mountains." Warming to his fantasy, Michael's voice grows excited. "Come with me. We'll leave the gold here for Hans. It's all he ever cared about. And if you won't go with me, I promise, you'll never see me again. I'll just disappear."

Hannah minces a piece of the raw skin smaller and smaller, pressing the blade down again and again, shaking her head, vaguely aware that all feeling has fled. "No."

A tear starts at her eye. "No."

The blade cuts and cuts again. "No."

Her eyes fix on nothing and her voice is hollow.

The creak and rattle of the door announces Hans's return, and he enters, muffled to the eyes with a ragged shirt wound round his face as a scarf. He stamps his boots and slaps at the legs of his pants to knock away a rime of ice before advancing into the puny warmth of the stove. Breathing heavily through his nose, he shows his palms to the fire, coughs, and looks around the cabin before rubbing his hands briskly together. In midrub he stops, grows motionless, and straightens. His eyes roam, glittering above the mask of his scarf, and he turns in a slow circle, eyeing the interior of the hovel.

On the table each piece of silverware lies perfectly ordered, shining and polished. Each spoon is perfectly aligned with its neighbor in orderly display. Each plate, cup, and bowl is placed perfectly abreast of its companion. The chairs are as correctly spaced as sentries.

On the bunk, each item of clothing remaining to the prospectors is folded and ordered by category, pants with pants, shirts with shirts. Blankets and towels folded into flawless squares mark the perimeter of the arrangement.

By the stove, the stack of firewood has been ordered into perfect symmetry of size and length, in rows that flow from splinters and shavings to finger-sized kindling and wrist-thick splints; not one piece is out of order. On her knees in the corner, Hannah picks at the space between two slabs of the shale floor, probing at the crack, flicking spruce needles and bits of trash into a rag.

When she looks up at Hans, her eyes are flat and distant. They do not change when he asks, "What are you doing?"

She does not reply.

Unnerved by the silence, Hans reaches for the woodpile behind him, groping at a piece of spruce without taking his eyes from his wife.

"Don't touch that!" Her voice is overly loud, fast and frightening.

Hans's hand jerks back as if it has touched the hot stove. "Wha . . . ?"

"Don't touch it. Don't touch anything." Hannah knots the rag in her hand, rubs at the paving stone beside her. "I just want things to be . . ." Her mouth tightens and a muffled whimper bleeds through white lips. "I want things . . . nice . . . just for a while. Just for a while."

SEVENTEEN

A still and windless day. As Hannah makes the long journey to the sparse woodpile, she can feel the inside of her nose burn with cold. The sounds of the forest carry sharp and bright through the unmoving air. When Hans left before daybreak, after double-checking Severts's bonds, the snowy squeak of his footsteps could be heard for a mile. The only words her husband had said before closing the door behind him were, "Jesus, he stinks."

Hannah pillows Michael's head on a rolled blanket and spoons what broth there is into his mouth. His eyes are bright and feverish, and look huge in his skull. Sniffing, she catches a reek of corruption. Hans was right, Michael smells.

She packs the largest kettle with snow and places it on the stove, adding more as the contents melt. After an hour, there is a gallon or so of water. When steam smokes from the cauldron, she says, "I'm going to bathe you, Michael. I will loosen one rope at a time, and if you try anything . . ." She picks up the cast-iron skillet and places it near to hand. "If you make any move against me, I shall use this. Understood?"

Michael's answering smile is strangely beatific, and she wonders for a moment if he is still in his right mind.

Severts is passive, moving only to lift an arm, then a leg, to assist Hannah as she unbinds, unclothes, then refastens him. His nakedness is pale and wrinkled, his pelvis a shrunken hollow above a penis, shriveling from the cold. Unspoken between them is the understanding that should Hans return during the process, he will certainly kill Michael and perhaps Hannah as well. They are silent as she works, listening carefully for footfalls.

Hannah wrings a rag in the water, and its warmth is wonderful on her hands. Michael sighs, rolls his head to the side, and closes his eyes, lost to the Oedipal bliss of being cared for as she bathes first his chest, his stomach, then under his arms. Her throat catches as she feels the bones of his sternum. Where he had once been so finely muscled, his is now the body of a slender boy, a youth without meat on his frame. His knees are knobs on legs atrophied from disuse, his stomach hollow, and his skin strangely slack. She must fight the impulse to take his helplessness and hold it to her breast.

When Hannah rolls Michael onto his side, she gasps. A biblical penance of boils and sores is spread in a painful constellation across his back and buttocks. The infected bedsores ooze a sour yellow fluid, the source of the odor.

"Hannah," Michael whispers. "Don't ever let me have a chance to escape again. I might not be strong enough to resist. I don't want to hurt you."

She cries as she dresses him.

The report of the shotgun hammers a single barking note in the distance. Hope rises. Hannah's mouth waters, her stomach cramping at the thought of fresh meat.

When Hans returns with a garland of breath vapors frozen in his eyebrows and beard, he claims to have missed a shot at a deer. A fleck of dried blood glues a single downy grouse feather to his chin.

The next day their stomachs are empty and echo with craving. The mountains are draped in gray shadows. Nothing moves in the landscape. While Hans guards Michael, Hannah walks to the river, where she digs the decomposed backbones of salmon from the frozen mud, then gnaws and chews at the gristled remnants until they are soft enough to swallow.

After she is gone, Hans waits until Michael is asleep or unconscious, then goes quietly to the box that contains the remnants of the gold. Probing, he removes a small nugget and holds it in his hand, envisioning the food it would buy; a bushel of apples, a dozen pies, a smoked ham. Placing it in his mouth, he rolls and weighs its smoothness on his tongue and pauses. Then swallows.

It must be near Christmas. Impossible to believe in the birth of the Savior in this place. Endless darkness. Daylight, when it comes, is very weak.

Hans set snares of rope along trails and caught a wolf, but the others of the pack consumed it, and all that remained was the head. Terrible nightmares of its frozen, grinning countenance. Satan in the stewpot. Tongue very tasty. Made a crude headcheese of the skull contents.

Gums bleeding. My flow fails to come. I hunger to be held as strongly as I desire food. If there be a Christ, pray he grants us release from this heartbroke bay.

———————

A wind rises, blowing the stars west toward the horizon. Negook lies beneath a pile of furs, his ear pressed to the ground. For weeks he has drowsed, curled into himself like a hibernating marmot, listening to the secrets carried by running water through the veins of the world. Attending carefully, he hears many things, but—and here he takes a breath that is a bit less shallow and his eyes roll forward behind their lids—Kah-Lituya is silent and sleeps without grumbling or raising his massive head.

Perhaps the whites are punishing themselves enough, he thinks to himself. *I never expected that.*

His mind is still and his heartbeat as soft as a sparrow's, while his spirit walks in dark and shining places, pondering the strange goings-on in the white men's hut beneath the drifts.

First they started killing each other, with the dark one going crazy and doing the shooting. Then, instead of shooting him, stabbing him with a knife, or even knocking his head in with a club for his crimes, the big straw-haired man and the woman tied him up to die slowly. In times past, the Tlingit might occasionally sacrifice a slave by putting the wretch under the corner post of a new longhouse to bless the start of construction, but this sort of thing was new.

What really surprised Negook was that the man and the woman were making themselves part of the atonement, too, starving and freezing instead of using their hours to feed and warm themselves, spending their lives taking turns keeping the dark-haired hunter company as he dies. How very strange these cloud-faces are: cruel, wasteful, and yet very brave in odd, unexpected ways.

"The end will come soon." The words echo in the stillness through which the shaman drifts. "Maybe I should go watch."

———————

"We have to get rid of him, Hannah. We are both going to die. We cannot feed ourselves or avoid freezing to death like this. If we both work hard, we may survive. There could be enough food with the clams and tides and all, if we both dig at 'em." Hans prods within the open mouth of the stove with a stick, knocking the embers down to make way for another piece of wood. "Just feeding this shittin' stove is a full-time job, and we can't do it if one of us is always sitting here watching him."

Yesterday Hans wasted the last two shotgun shells on long shots at a sea lion drifting offshore, firing senselessly at an animal that could not have been retrieved through the breaking surf, even if his aim had been good. There is no more ammunition, and the snares have been unproductive. There is only the tide to feed them and what roots or garbage Hannah digs from beneath the snow.

Hannah puckers her mouth and shakes her head. "No. No

more killing." The sounds and smells of Dutch and Harky's dying flash across her mind at regular intervals. Sleep is a time of screams and red specters, and she often wakes shaking with fear, her ears ringing from the roar of dream shotguns. They live like animals, gnawing at hides and stinking, but she hangs her sanity on a scrap of illusion that there is still some hope of decency, of civility somewhere in the world. Hannah knows that taking Michael's life now would be an act of selfishness, to save their own lives rather than an act of right or justice, and that to do so would surely unhinge her, slipping her into a mad, dark place from which she might never return.

"No," she says, surprising herself with the determination in her words. "We will not do it."

———————

That night Hannah warms a pot of water, gathers a blanket, and carries both outside, intent on reducing her body's musky smell. Peeling down her filthy top, she works hurriedly against the cold, scrubbing at her armpits and torso, wincing at the soreness in her nipples. Shivering, she reclothes herself, folds the blanket on the ground for a place to stand, and removes her boots. Stripping out of her undergarments, she shudders at the soiled, greasy feel of the shimmy's cloth before wringing the scrubbing rag in the now-tepid water and rolling her skirt up to her waist. At the sight of the pale, goose-fleshed skin going slack over her diminishing calves and thighs, she sucks in her breath, lifts the bundle of her skirt to her ribs, and runs one hand across her swelling belly.

I presume it to be January. The days seem to be slowly growing longer. I caught a large hedgehog—Hans called it a porkapine—with the ax yesterday while searching for wood. It is the first thing I have ever killed. Surprised to feel nothing in doing so.

Dreadfully tired. Mr. Nelson has frozen a finger, and it was very painful in thawing. Michael often unconscious.

"Please." Michael's voice is gentle and reasoned, as if negotiating with a child. "Hannah, please. I can't take this anymore."

The irregular *thok* of the ax comes from outside the cabin, where Hans cuts listlessly at a frozen log. Hannah sits beside Michael, huddling beneath a blanket, watching the fog of her breath curl in weak, lazy spirals before her face, daydreaming of Dutch's Sandwich Isles. Owyhee, with its fruit, soft breezes, and the scent of flowers in the air. Michael has been pleading all morning to be put out of his misery, and she cannot look at him when she replies, her voice flat. "I cannot allow it, Michael. We must wait. Spring will come, and we will be rescued. Mr. Witt will surely send a boat from Sitka as soon as the weather allows." Severts groans softly.

"It hurts me to see you suffer so, Michael, but we must hang on. It is all that will save us."

The door knocks back, and Hans enters, carrying a small armload of ax-shattered wood. "Damnation, Hannah, be sensible. We won't make it till spring."

Sitting up straight, she lifts her chin. "I cannot see a helpless man killed. We are not animals." She slumps again and sighs, "We have already talked of this too much. It is a matter for the authorities, not us."

Hans shakes his head at the persistence of his wife's fantasy, her obsession with laws and judges. He will not say the words loose in his brain, but he sometimes sees the Irishman as meat—a roast, slices of steak, a stew. "Tide's dropping. I better go before it gets dark."

After Hans gathers the forage sack and leaves, Hannah feeds the stove and sits down again, eager to return to Hawaii. She often imagines herself in a particular corner of a lawn overlooking a stream bordered in wild, fragrant flowers, a green swath of neatly trimmed grass where there are no clouds between her and the sun. Her clothes are clean and neat, and the regular sighing of blue and white surf mixes easily with the rustling sound of the palms. She is just beginning to feel the heat on her face and the texture of the clipped grass beneath her thighs when Michael's voice breaks into her reverie: "Hannah, I love you.

"I love you, and I can't watch you go on like this. Let me up, and I will hang myself. You won't have to do it."

She feels like a piece of old paper—delicate, dry, and brittle, being slowly torn down the middle. The image of herself clubbing Hans to the ground with the skillet as he comes in the door flashes before her, and she imagines the feel of the ropes in her fingers as she frees Michael's bonds. Her blood burns with guilt and shame as she realizes how badly she wants to fulfill the fantasy: Hans gone, herself in Michael's arms—it could work! No one would ever know; they could weave a tale of some sort to . . .

Hannah realizes she is biting the knuckle of her thumb and pulls it from her mouth, then stares at the shape of the angry red tooth marks and moans.

"God's truth, Hannah. Seeing you waste away is worse than the torture of these boards. Let's end this."

A single great, wracking sob rips from her breast, and she clutches her arms about herself. "It was self-defense, Michael. That's what you said."

Severts shakes his head. "No, Hannah. That's not true. I just wanted the gold. I wanted to go back to Ireland a big shot, a success, with enough to take my mother out of reach of my father. And I was so angry with you after we quarreled out by the woodpile before the storm."

"You are just saying that."

"I swear. It's too late for me to try to save myself. I did wrong, and I've got to pay."

"My Lord." Her voice knots, her mind spins and cramps. Was he lying then, or is he lying now? Either way, he is a killer; either way he might be doing it for her; either way, she wants him. Every way it is turned, there is no way out, no way to decide.

"You want me to stand trial, I'll stand trial," says Michael. "I've been thinking about it, and there is no reason we cannot have a trial right here."

Hannah is sure Michael's suffering has unhinged him; he is hallucinating, imagining them to be in Sitka or somehow otherwise back in civilization.

"Really, we can do it, Hannah. There is no need to wait."

"Michael, please. Try to sleep. I will cook something." There is nothing except some porcupine bones to grind and the hide to boil. Hannah imagines she can strain the crude bullion through a rag to remove the quills.

"All we need is a judge and a prosecutor." Michael laughs. "We've already got a prisoner. And of course, it would be a bit more proper to have a witness. Do you think you could send Hans to the Indian village to find that old man?"

"A trial. It requires a jury, lawyers. You must have a defense," Hannah protests. "You must have a fair trial. A fair trial is . . . civilized."

Michael rolls his head from side to side, dismissing her argument, then opens his hands above his head and raises them against the ropes. Since expending the last of the ammunition, Hans has rebound him tighter and tighter as his limbs waste away, arguing that they have no defense against his escape.

"I'll confess. I'll sign a confession. *Nolo contendere*, they call that. No contest, no defense necessary. Please, Hannah. Please."

He begins to cry. Hannah goes to him, kneels, and cradles his head in her hands, while he sobs, crooning soft, meaningless words to him as if he were a child with a fright.

The idea of a trial swells and grows like rising bread. All laws are simply an agreement among the members of a community, she reasons to herself, a consensus of what is best for all. Three is a small number, but they are still a community—fractured and tortured, but a community nonetheless. For that matter, she rationalizes, they might be all the people left in the world, and still no less responsible for seeing justice done.

The night snaps with cold, and the aurora plays overhead. From the darkness of the forest outside the hut comes the scream of something small dying. Over a spoonful of ground bones and skin-fat, Hannah says to Hans, "You must go to the Indian village tomorrow. Bring Negook back with you."

"All those in favor say 'aye.'" Hannah utters the words in a monotone, looking down at the paper before her. Her fingers toy nervously, touching first the pen with which she writes, then the paper, then the meat mallet that serves as her gavel.

> We, the members of this community located at Lituya Bay in the Territory of Alaska, for the purposes of enforcing the law and attending to the welfare of the members of the community, do by this document create the community of Lituya Bay.

From his perch on the edge of his bunk, Michael whispers, "Aye," staring at his hands, which are crossed and tied before him. Nelson sprawls sideways at the table, the back of his hand propped to his mouth with one elbow. He breathes harshly through his nose as if angry, his eyes tracking back and forth between his wife and the prisoner. Negook squats on his haunches in the corner, a shadow caped in furs, head tilted, eyes closed, listening.

"How do you vote, Hans?" murmurs Hannah.

"Damn it, Hannah." When Hans removes his hand from his mouth to speak, his lips are mottled and red. The first stage of scurvy is beginning to loosen his teeth, and the salty taste of blood oozing from his swollen gums is on his tongue. "Damn it, this is insane."

Hannah's gavel bangs once against the table. "How do you vote, Hans?" Her stare is as flat as her voice.

Hans sighs, tilts his head to cover his eyes with his hand, and mutters, "Aye. Aye, damn it."

The gavel bangs again. "So carried."

Negook smiles briefly to himself at the way the woman uses the wooden hammer to coerce the blond man. The Tlingit, too, use a talking stick in their meetings, a finely carved staff that gives the bearer the right to be heard uninterrupted. But the bulk of their unfathomable impulses and formal procedures are simply puzzling.

The pen whispers, scratching Hannah's signature across the paper before she pushes the document to Hans. "Sign it."

After Hans scribbles his name, she places the pen in Severts's fingers, adjusting the instrument to rest comfortably in his lashed wrists, and holds the paper flat to the table. The Irishman's grip is weak. The pen shakes as it forms his name.

Hannah blows on the signatures, then lays the article of incorporation aside. From her journal she razors another sheet of cream-colored paper, slicing slowly along the book's spine. After carefully aligning the paper before her so it lies square and straight to the edge of the table, she dips the pen into a concoction of lamp black and alcohol and begins to write.

The pen catches, dragging at the parchment, and the nib spills a crude blot of the improvised ink. Hannah's chest heaves at the ugliness beneath her hand, and she wavers, mouth gulping at nothing. Laying the pen carefully aside, she removes the defiled paper and begins cutting another sheet from the journal.

"Christ, Hannah. What does it matter?" Hans's voice is bewildered, taut with frustration.

Hannah does not look up as she concentrates on the razor and the precise excision of the paper from its binding. "It must be proper," she says softly. "It must be done right."

A quarter of an hour passes. Fifteen minutes of the pen hissing *scritch-scritch* between softly spoken questions, the answering "Ayes," and long silences. The tense silences are punctuated by the subdued crackling of the stove and the *kloonk-kloonk* of ravens calling through the forest. Michael shivers and hefts a blanket stiff with grime around his thin shoulders. Hans crosses and uncrosses his legs, jiggles one foot, and rubs his chin. The shaman is as still as a stump. At the end of the quarter hour the single sheet of paper says:

A RECORD OF THE ELECTION OF OFFICIALS IN THE COMMUNITY OF LITUYA BAY, TERRITORY OF ALASKA

Winter of 1899

All votes taken by outcry

In the election of a judge, running unopposed, Hannah Butler-Nelson.

Affirmative 3, in opposition 0.

Hannah Butler-Nelson is hereby declared judge for the community of Lituya Bay.

In the election of a prosecutor of the court, running unopposed, Hans Nelson.

Affirmative 3, in opposition 0.

Hans Nelson is hereby declared prosecutor for the court of Lituya Bay.

The results of this election are hereby accepted and approved for the appointment of judge and prosecutor to Lituya Bay, and all powers of enforcement transferred unto the hands of those elected.

———————

"Michael Severts, you are charged with the murder of your partners, Harky and Dutch. How do you plead?"

"Oh, guilty, your honor. Guilty as hell." A small smile teases Severts's lips, but his voice is serious. Hannah precisely and faithfully transcribes his words upon a fresh sheet.

"The prosecution may proceed."

The *whoosh-whoosh* of raven wings beats through the stillness outside. The sound of first one, then another and another of the black birds pulses in until the noise of the dark congregation circling overhead sounds like the rapid panting of a large animal.

Michael stares at the sagging canvas above his head. Hans darts a glance at Negook, whose lusterless black eyes are lost in the shadows, then sucks at his lips, tasting blood. Hannah repeats her instruction.

"The prosecution shall proceed."

Hans steeples his fingers, holding the tips to his mouth for a moment, then buries his hands in his armpits, crossing his arms on his chest. Arching his eyebrows, he sighs heavily through his nose, then asks, "So you confess? You confess to the murders?"

"I do."

"And you'll sign a confession?"

"I will."

"Your honor." There is fatigue in Hans's voice. "Your honor, will the court instruct the stenographer to take down the prisoner's confession?"

Hannah makes a note on the paper before her, sets it aside, then slides an unmarked sheet into place in front of Michael. Holding out the pen, she says, "Please proceed, Mr. Severts."

Michael hunches forward, elbows on his knees, and stares at the floor, hiding his face behind locks of matted hair. After a moment he straightens, wipes at his nose with the fingers of his bound hands, then takes up the pen:

> *I confess to murdering my partners Harky and Dutch. I killed them in cold blood, using a shotgun while they sat down to dinner. It was premeditated murder. I planned to do it, and I done it, and I won't argue it. I was planning to kill everyone so I could have all the gold for myself. I intended to kill Hans Nelson and his wife, Hannah, as well, then make my escape by rowing in the small skiff to Sitka or Skagway, where I would blame the killings on the local Indians and claim to have barely escaped with my life, a story which would be easily believed.*
>
> *I am grievously sorry I did it. They were good men. I confess and ask to be hung for my crime.*

"Mr. Negook, will you sign as a witness to the prisoner's confession?"

Negook takes the proffered pen then is motionless as he considers. Maybe the paper is a *Guski-kwan* trick, a way of infecting him with their craziness. He has seen many papers, knows how the whites use them to do whatever they please, how they give lies power by putting them in writing. He wants to say, "Horseshit," but holds his tongue.

"What is this?" asks Negook, gesturing at the written confession.

Hannah is patient. "This is Mr. Severts's confession of murder. It requires the signature of an impartial witness to be legal."

"This is not the business of the Tlingit people."

"Nonetheless, Mr. Negook. we must have a witness, and there is no other. For a trial to be legal, neither a judge nor a prosecutor can act as a witness. It wouldn't be fair."

"And if it is fair?" asks Negook.

Hans's voice cracks loud and angry. "Then we'll hang him and be done!"

Negook burns Hans with a black-eyed glance, angered by Nelson's breach of manners. Why do these people bother having a talking stick if they do not respect it? And it seems they are asking his permission to kill the dark-haired white. They never once asked permission to dig at the ground, take fish from the rivers, or seals from the ice, but now they are asking permission to kill one of their own.

"Aye," he mutters. "Their strangeness never ends."

Hans glares at Hannah and hisses, "Christ," wiping one hand across the tabletop as if sweeping crumbs to the floor. "What makes you think he can write?"

At that moment a baritone rumble rolls down from the glacier, thundering in the distance like the cannons that burned Angoon. Negook's hand darts forward, flicks twice above the paper, and the lean, sharp form of a bear's tooth or perhaps a killer whale's fin springs to life on the confession. The shaman points the pen at each of the whites in turn—Hans, Hannah, then Michael—while muttering an incantation of forest and water spirits to protect himself from whatever comes next, then says, "This is not the business of the Tlingit people. Kill him if you wish."

Negook's choice of words—the unmitigated "kill him"—shakes Hannah's bones, and her voice is husky as she lays the gavel aside. "Does the defendant have anything to say on his own behalf?"

The smallest denial, a single side-to-side twitch of his head—"No"—then clearing his throat and straightening himself, Michael says, "No, I think not." His voice is level, almost relieved. "There's really nothing more to say, is there?"

EIGHTEEN

Whirlwinds of snow hiss and spin, dervishlike, across the roof of the hut, leap from the eaves, and dance away into the darkness. Ranks of waves charge out of the night to collapse upon the beach in thundering welters. Boulders the size and color of Spanish bulls glitter under opaque coats of ice. The ice grows thicker with every fusillade of spray.

A crack of candlelight appears along the door to the hut. The foot of the rough-hewn door makes a grating sound as it sweeps a perfect quadrant into the wind drift gathered in the lee of the cabin and the line of light enlarges into a trapezoid of gold.

As the door is muscled outward, a long shadow springs across the doorway of light drawn upon the snow. The shadow diverges into two parts and a pair of huddled figures step out. The figures, one much smaller than the other, lean together into the wind, rolling a barrel before them. A third shadow follows, a short coil of rope dangling from its hand.

The rope is frayed and broken, with coarse strands of sisal bristling along its length. The diameter of the line is no greater than the joint of a thumb, and its bearer worries that its strength has been compromised by months of exposure to salt and sun. Michael shrugs. It is all that is left of the cutter's rigging. It must suffice for the job.

The trio wends its way through a field of stumps. Blowing snow moves in layers, swirling about their feet, sniffing rudely under flapping rag tails of coats stiff with grime. At the edge of the field they stop beneath a spruce tree that bows and nods in the tempest.

Michael bends an *S*-shaped bight into the standing part of the line, holding it as he takes round turn after round turn with the running part, then with cold, fumbling fingers tucks back the end to form a loop. His is a sailor's skill with knots; when he tests his work, the hangman's noose slips and tightens easily.

When he speaks, his voice is weak. "I reckon to do this proper, we'd need something higher than that barrel. It would be better if there was more drop. Quicker, you know." His voice trembles. "This way . . ." He swallows the rest.

Hannah struggles to tip the barrel upright beneath the branches. Hans steps back and watches. Rocking the barrel on the bulge of its shape, she grunts with a surge of effort that upends the cask, then pushes back her hood. Her face is fine-boned and drawn. Her eyes—large in her skull, the skin pulled tight by starvation—are the color of the sky, becoming pearl gray as dawn advances.

A raven appears out of the forest, its wing beats like a sword cutting the air. Lifting and dodging, it swoops overhead on a rising gust of wind. The Irishman follows the arc of its passing with his eyes, staring as if he might see through the wall of the storm into a world less frightful than the one he is about to leave.

"Michael?" Hannah's voice is soft. He turns from his contemplation of the raven and hesitates before stepping, rope in hand, over to the barrel beneath the trees. His movements are slow and weak.

Rolling the coils of line with the fingertips of one hand, the noose swinging lightly in the other, he readies a loop for a toss. The first throw rises too sharply, tangling in the branches of the tree for a moment before unwinding to the ground. Michael sighs, coils the line again, and eyes a lower, thinner branch. The second toss is good.

The wind rises, shaking the tree, but the noose seems to hang without moving. Blowing snow stings their upturned faces. Hannah's nose and cheeks are fiercely red. The first waxy white patches of frostbite are beginning to appear on Michael's hands, which grow lumpish with cold as he struggles to knot the end of the line around the tree. The rope is stiff and reluctant in the bitter air. As he shows her how to take up the slack, tears rolling from Hannah's eyes freeze into lusterless pearls.

Severts tests the barrel for balance, pushing against the rim. Turning his back to Hannah, he places his hands behind him; she lashes and ties. Grunting as he tries to climb aboard the barrel, he falls back, too weak and stiff to rise without aid. Hannah steps forward, takes his arm, and looks to Hans. "Please."

Nelson looks away, trying to cover a looming failure of

heart with bluster. "I wanted this done from the start. Now you can just do it yourself."

"It's all right, Mrs. Nelson," says Michael. He tries again. With Hannah's help, he makes it onto the barrel, teetering and kneeling for balance.

"There's something else, Hans," says Michael. And for a moment Hannah is afraid he means to confess their affair. Lowering his head for Hannah to remove his hat, he eyes the noose before saying, "That bear of Dutch's? I killed it. The carcass is in one of the ice caves along the edge of the glacier. It stank something awful, but it might still be edible, being frozen and all. We're past being choosy now, aren't we?"

Hannah fumbles the noose over his head, then pulls the knot tight beside his ear. Standing on tiptoe, she reaches up with his hat, places it on his head, and pulls it down to his ears. "It's so cold," she says, choking. "You must take care."

Michael's eyes are infinitely sad as he attempts a rueful smile. His lips tremble. "Jesus, I'm scared," he whispers. "God help me, I'm so scared."

He struggles to stand. Once aloft, he shivers in tenuous equilibrium, legs bent at the knees, his hands struggling like small animals against their bindings. The barrel tips an inch under his weight and he jerks into a deeper crouch, eyes wide, mouth twisting in panic.

Placing both hands on the rim of the barrel, Hannah cries out, "Good-bye, Michael!" and shoves with all her strength. The snow beneath the barrel crunches as it drops from beneath his boots. Hannah watches in horror as the inadequate limb sags beneath his weight, leaving him to choke and struggle. His toes scrawl an arabesque of death on the icy ground.

"Hans, help me!" screams Hannah, grabbing at Michael's legs. She tries to scream again, but the words knot and clamp in her throat. Her voice fades and dies to a rasping howl. Nelson turns to run, stumbles, and trips on a stump. When he looks back, he sees his wife kneeling before the strangling man, her arms tight about his waist, face buried to his belly, adding her own weight to the rope. Severts's face is turned upward at an unreal angle, his eyes wide and staring, in a tableau of a saint searching heavenward for ascension, a supplicant at his feet.

NINETEEN

Negook sits in the bow of the canoe, a bearskin cloak wrapped around his scrawny frame for what warmth the coarse fur can bring to his bones. He has been shivering for weeks, since watching the bizarre actions of the whites from the shadows of the forest after the tall, yellow-haired one had come and asked him to make his mark on the paper. It has been a long time since anything scared Negook, but watching the cruel acts of these people drove an icicle into his belly that nothing seems to melt.

After watching the hanging—an ugly, utterly undignified thing—he spoke quietly to his ravens, making soft mewing sounds until the birds flew away to fetch the People home. Now the clans rightly refuse to take the *Guski-qwan* into their canoes to return them to their own people; purifying a valuable canoe of that sort of crazy evil might be impossible. But they have agreed to take the white woman's papers to Skagway and tell the other white men to come for the survivors. He is worried that somehow the whites will think of a way to blame the Lituya-kwan for all of the craziness and would prefer to see the whole thing disappear, but that is impossible. No, he has to do this one last thing, but after this, if he ever sees a white person again, he is going to run into the forest as fast as his brittle old bones will carry him.

The buzzing trill of a migrating thrush calls out from the forest, as Hannah hikes her skirts to her knees and wades out to the waiting canoe, the bundle of papers wrapped in a piece of canvas. The meat of the bear is nearly gone (foul, horrible mess) but there is a certain softening of the air, a dulling of the razor-sharp wind that says spring will eventually come, and she knows that somehow she and Hans will survive. She stops, listening to the call-and-response of the rhyming thrushes, and touches a hand to her throat. Her lips work, mouth opening as if to reply, but only silence emerges.

A north wind curls the heaving sea back on itself. The canoe rocks in the shallows. Salt spray torn from the waves glitters in diamond-shaped points. As Hannah comes alongside, she stumbles, and Negook sees her hand dart to cover her belly before grabbing at the gunwale for balance. Sighing to himself at the thought of the small life he sees struggling in her womb, he signals the paddlers. It is time to go.

AUTHOR'S NOTE

Heartbroke Bay is a work of fiction, based on an actual event that took place in Alaska during the fierce winter of 1899, on the outer coast of what would one day become Glacier Bay National Park and Preserve. Nearby Lituya Bay was said to be home to the angry demigod Kah-Lituya, a toadlike spirit whose fierce temper tantrums were credited by the Tlingit Indians with causing the powerful earthquakes that have ripped through the coastal region at regular intervals, creating huge tsunamis that have wiped out entire villages. In 1958, one such earthquake created the largest tsunami ever recorded in history, a mind-bending wave 1,720 feet high.

The real Hans and Hannah Nelson came to Lituya Bay in September of 1899, shortly after an earthquake of similar size ripped through the coast. They were drawn north into the gold rush by a broadsheet of sweet promises published by a group of "investors" calling themselves the Lituya Bay Placer Gold Mining Company, and claiming offices in New York and San Francisco. In truth, the company had no real assets other than title to twelve hundred acres of mining claims north of the bay, and certainly not the neatly laid-out township or modern gold refinery projected by the pie-in-the-sky prospectus.

Promised easy access to "the biggest fortune ever dreamed of," the Nelsons and their partners—Sam Christianson, known as Dutch; Fragnalia Stefano, known as Harky; and Michael S. Severts—expected a benign climate and easy pickings. What they found instead was hardscrabble mining of the most laborious sort, in one of the most remote and hostile environments in the world, where a long day of arduous pick-and-shovel work might yield a meager twelve to fifteen dollars' worth of gold; nothing like the riches promised by the prospectus. Their only amenity was a small, crude cabin built of logs and moss, a squalid shelter little better than the canvas tents in common use during the gold rush.

Nonetheless, the Nelsons and their cohorts set to work, digging so intently at the sands throughout the summer and on into autumn that they missed their chance to catch the last boat leaving the coast before the onset of winter. Not long afterward, the five miners found themselves marooned by fierce weather and settled in as best they could to pass the long months of frigid darkness.

With food low and rationed, some degree of cabin fever was perhaps inevitable, but there is nothing in the record up to this point to indicate that there was any significant discord among the group, nothing to hint that beneath the time-killing banter of storytelling and card games an ember of violence was smoldering. Nothing, that is, until one October evening when Severts suddenly got up from the dinner table, walked outside, came back inside carrying a gun, and started shooting.

Harky was killed instantly. Dutch fell to the floor with a wound in his neck. Contemporary newspaper accounts vary in detail (and often cross the line from journalism into creative fiction), but most agree that Hannah and Hans reacted quickly, attacking Severts as he tried to reload. Hannah threw a dishcloth around his neck and choked him while Hans pummeled him. Somehow during the struggle Severts was wounded in the leg. At the end of the melee, the battered killer was bound hand and foot and roped in a bunk, and the Nelsons were left with a murderous prisoner to guard. After a long period of deprivation, Severts began to suffer from his wounds and begged to die, but the Nelsons—Hannah in particular—were reluctant to take the law into their own hands. It was not until it became evident that they would all succumb to hunger and the elements if they continued that they decided to extract themselves from the situation by holding a trial and handing down a sentence of capital punishment.

I first came across a reference to the tragedy in 1986, in the opening pages of *Glacier Bay: The Land and the Silence*, a seminal work on the park by the writer and photographer Dave Bohn. Glacier Bay had only recently been designated as a national park, after being upgraded from a national monument in 1980, the result of a long and arduous effort to safeguard a wilderness that has since become the crown jewel of the national park system. I was on a sailing trip to the bay, and moving through the stark, peak-lined fjords in a small boat among glittering icebergs brought to life Bohn's brief description of the ordeal the Nelsons faced over the course of that terrible winter. In that context, their decision to hold a trial seemed a reasonable, though somewhat byzantine, solution.

Bohn took the details of his brief account from a story written by the gold rush era's best-known storyteller, Jack London, for *McClure's Magazine* in 1906, five years after the incident. Shortly after my sailing trip ended, I obtained a copy of London's article from the Alaska State Historical Library, read it, and was enthralled. London's version of the event was clearly highly colored, but the story raised numerous questions. What effect would such extreme duress have had on the psyche of a Victorian woman, isolated in a vast wilderness, when violence and a harsh environment conspired to strip away all notions of law and civility? How could anyone fend off the seemingly inevitable psychological decay inherent under such protracted privation, yet still hold to the values inculcated over a lifetime?

Somewhere in the event, I felt sure, was the material for a novel or a screenplay, so I threw myself into research, threading my way through yellowed newspaper clippings and rolls of microfilm, and learned that word of the hanging had first reached the outside world as an aside at the bottom of a short article on the front page of the May 12, 1900, issue of the *Alaskan*. The newspaper headline read "Sloop Lost," and the article described how a month earlier, a sailboat in tow behind the steamship *Excelsior* had been lost when the towline parted. After entering Lituya Bay during the search for the lost vessel, the *Excelsior* reported that a double murder had taken place there the past winter, followed by a "lynching bee," during which the "Lituyans thought proper to take the law into their own hands," and "hence the elevation of the criminal."

More research taught me that Hannah's maiden name was Butler, and that she had come from England to work in service as a Victorian lady's assistant. After meeting Hans in Chicago, she eloped with the strapping young Norwegian and headed for the gold fields of Alaska, where they connected with Harky, Dutch, and Severts. Over the next few years, I also learned how the story had filtered its way out of Alaska into the world of sensationalist journalism, coming to roost in William Randolph Hearst's notoriously yellow *San Francisco Examiner* under a shrill headline that shouted "Woman Hangs a Man and the Law Upholds Her!" The headline was accompanied by a fanciful illustration of a slender young woman decked out in a jaunty little hat and a bustled skirt, dangling a hangman's noose from one delicately gloved hand.

Whether the reader was supposed to be more troubled by the fact that murder had been committed or that a woman could be capable of hanging a man is not clear, but in any case, it was a remarkably bad piece of journalism. The writer not only had embellished his report with details he could have had no way of knowing but also got Hannah's name wrong, referring to her as Edith Whittlesay instead of Hannah Butler. Severts, the killer, somehow became Michael Dinnen. Jack London apparently used the *Examiner* piece as a primary source for his own story because he, too, referred to Edith Whittlesay and Michael Dinnen.

Reaction to London's version of the event was swift, kicking off a grumbling match between various newspapers (primarily the rival *Seattle Post Intelligencer* and *Seattle Times*) regarding the "truth" of London's story, with each calling on its own experts to confirm its stance. But none, apparently, tumbled to the fact that Sam Christianson (Dutch) had not only survived the wound to his neck but had also returned to Juneau and become a beer wagon driver. By the time London's story was published, he had been entertaining the patrons of Juneau's saloons with his own version of the event for several years.

All agreed, however, that Hannah was a "plucky little woman," as stated by the federal judge who ruled that her execution of Severts was a valid judicial proceeding. This opinion was reinforced by an article run by the *Alaskan* after London's story ran in the *Examiner*. "Those who know her best," declared the article, "say she is a kind, patient, never tiring soul, yet brave, heroic and unflinching for all that is right or good."

Such high praise provided me with a good measure of Hannah's character, which helped answer the question of how she had survived the emotional mauling of being witness to a murder amid grinding isolation, and how she withstood the horror of putting a rope around a man's neck to strangle him. But as I plowed through the research and plotted the novel, one more question kept coming back to me. I wondered how—or even if—the Nelsons' marriage had survived. Looking back from our modern era, when relationships often seem to fail for the smallest reason, I could not help but wonder what effect such an ordeal would have on a marriage.

It took nearly a decade to answer the question, and even then it required a stroke of luck. I was visiting the small mining town of Atlin, a community of less than four hundred souls in the northernmost part of British Columbia. As the crow flies, Atlin lies less than seventy miles from Juneau, but it is seventy miles of cloud-raking peaks, glaciers, and broken ice fields, so getting there requires a sixty-mile ferry ride and a long day of driving, much of it on a narrow gravel road, to make an end run around the impassable mountain range. On the last day of my visit, I stumbled across a slender pamphlet of the sort small-town history buffs put together to document their community's past, and inside the pamphlet was a reproduction of a newspaper clipping titled "New Arrivals in Town," dated almost ten years after the hanging. The writer seemed delighted to announce that a Mr. and Mrs. Hans Nelson had recently moved to Atlin to manage the new hardware store.

Lynn D'Urso
Juneau, Alaska

May 12, 1900
The Alaskan

SLOOP LOST.

The Lituya Bay Gold Mining Co's schooner Dora B., in tow of the S.S. Excelsior parted the tow rope in heavy sea off the bay, but being a staunch boat and perfectly seaworthy, Capt. Whitney deemed it prudent to allow her to take her own course which she shaped for the bay. This happened on the evening of Sunday, Apr. 15, and since then nothing has been heard of the schooner; the supposition is, however, that she was driven ashore and broke up. The body of a man supposed to be one of the four on board was found on the beach at Yakutat but no clue was obtained as to his identity.

The Excelsior also reports a lynching bee at Lituya bay. Two men were murdered there last fall and it being impossible to communicate with the authorities at Sitka and fearing to ser the murderer at large in the community, being satisfied of his guilt, the Lituyans thought proper to take the law into their own hands, hence the elevation of the criminal.